THE COMPOSITION OF A CROW

THE COMPOSITION OF A CROW

EMMA MAY

First published in Great Britain in 2025 by
The Book Guild Ltd
Unit E2 Airfield Business Park,
Harrison Road, Market Harborough,
Leicestershire. LE16 7UL
Tel: 0116 2792299
www.bookguild.co.uk
Email: info@bookguild.co.uk

The manufacturer's authorised representative in the EU
for product safety is Authorised Rep Compliance Ltd,
71 Lower Baggot Street, Dublin D02 P593 Ireland (www.arccompliance.com)

This work is entirely fictitious and bears no resemblance to any persons living or dead.

Typeset in 11pt Adobe Garamond Pro

Printed and bound by CPI Group (UK) Ltd, Croydon, CR0 4YY

ISBN 978 1835743 300

British Library Cataloguing in Publication Data.
A catalogue record for this book is available from the British Library.

For sixteen year old me who had her creative fire stomped out in school, thinking she wasn't good enough.

This one's for you. We did it.

PROLOGUE

There's a small, somewhat overlooked myth that resonates with the story that's about to unfold. Buried deep within the tales of heroes, gods and goddesses quarrelling is a small bird that had a very different beginning to the one we commonly know.

Apollo was known as the god of many things. Early on, he was an oracular god. He then went on to become the god of light, plague, music, healing and those are to only name a few. He was often seen with his musical instrument, which he played beautifully, head adorned with a crown of laurel as he gave his people and other gods the gift of music from his lyre. Interestingly, he has links to not only laurel, but also a flower called gladiolus. It grew from the body of a man Apollo accidentally killed with his discus. The flower in more modern times is often known to symbolise resilience and strength.

He soon became one of the most well-known gods due to this. Perhaps most famously, he was known for the plague he sent to Agamemnon's troops on their journey to Troy.

Agamemnon, King of Mycenae, was brother to Menelaus, King of Sparta. Rather ironically, they married sisters. Agamemnon married the beautiful but vengeful Clytemnestra whilst Menelaus married Helen, the face that launched a thousand ships. However, he would learn of this fact after he had wed her. Helen's circumstance around how she was taken to Troy by the prince known as Paris is heavily debated. Some say she fell victim to his abduction whilst others say she fled of her own accord into the arms of the man she truly loved. Marriages in Ancient Greece, after all, were not well known for being love matches but rather political strategies or alliances.

However Helen ended up in what was definitely not her marital home or bed, it set in motion what was one of the longest and most famous wars. Menelaus convinced his brother to set sail with him to retrieve his wife once he learnt of her disappearance. Agamemnon, an ambitious and greedy king, readily agreed and acquired the help of Greek heroes such as Achilles, Odysseus and Ajax.

These great heroes had a darker side to them that few mention when they speak of the late Bronze Age. As all armies would, Agamemnon's men raided towns and villages, taking what they wanted for themselves. They cared little what was left in the wake of their brutality and destruction. Achilles, arguably a favourite of the heroes in myth today, came upon a woman named Chryseis. She was the daughter of a priest of Apollo called Chryses and yet despite that fact was given as a sex slave to Agamemnon himself. She was a fair-skinned girl with long blonde hair and still a virgin before she was thrown into Agamemnon's tent to be used as he pleased.

Agamemnon insulted Chryses when he pleaded to the king for the release of his daughter Chryseis. Chryses, frightened of Agamemnon and unable to confront him further, prayed to Apollo to take revenge on Agamemnon and his men. Apollo, enraged at the insolence of the king, was said to have 'come down like night', his bow and arrows slung over his shoulder.

His arrows first struck mules and dogs before they did the soldiers. They were invisible and carried the plague. Once he wielded his bow with them, the dead fell for nine days straight. Fires were lit all over to burn the bodies. Eventually it came to an end when Chryseis was finally returned to her father and Agamemnon sacrificed one hundred cattle in honour of Apollo. This was at the insistence of Achilles and Calchas, the king's seer. It was only then that Apollo ceased in firing his arrows into the camp.

He was an easily angered god, one who knew how to make his displeasure known. An intimidating, well-loved figure amongst many. It was a puzzling affair to be a loyal follower of his. His anger knew no bounds and could engulf him and others around him at a moment's notice. However, he was one of the most important and influential gods of his time and so, his volatile behaviour was overlooked.

Out of all the tales we hear of the god Apollo, there is one that we resonate with here between these pages. Our story starts with Apollo's infamous ability to love and the numerous tragic love stories he endured. He bore so many incredible titles that some say he was pure perfection. Despite him being written as flawless by many, he fell short in his love life. Many stories and poems depict this but there is one that struck him hard, causing his anger to flow freely and dangerously as he learned of another rejection. Not only that, but a betrayal.

Years ago, Apollo took a lover. A princess called Coronis. She fell pregnant during their affair and Apollo doted on her throughout her pregnancy when he could. Unfortunately, sometime during this, he had to go back to Delphi to fulfil his role as the oracular god. As he prepared to leave his lover, he sadly suspected she would be unfaithful and sent a crow to guard as well as spy on her. Crows back then were a beautiful white colour all over. It was a terrible truth for the crow to discover that Apollo's suspicions were correct, even more so to be responsible for delivering the devastating news. Coronis begged the crow not to reveal her affair with another man, but the crow's loyalty to Apollo was unwavering. Apollo didn't take the revelation well, despite his already underlying feelings that he was right. So, the crow bore the brunt of the god's fury and was scorched black.

From then on, crows have kept their black iridescent feathers and dark beady eyes. They remained servants and messengers to the god Apollo and continue to have the same volatile relationship under his rule. Their loyalty to him never wavers, though, and they are seen as an extension of him and what he stood for as a god.

The stories above may portray behaviours that seem strange for a god that people prayed to for help or guidance. It wasn't uncommon that the gods themselves were as human and emotional as their worshippers. That's what perhaps made their people so committed to them. A man or woman with the ability to see a similarity to themselves in the gods and goddesses they prayed to could often find solace in the fact that they don't have unattainable perfection to aspire to.

People are allowed to be people and that's something that warms the heart of many.

As time goes on, our cultures evolve to the present day. There is often a wonder as to what became of the gods and goddesses who were so prevalent in our lives centuries before. We see snippets of Greek mythology throughout the years; even the Battle of Troy appears in the Bible itself. These stories have never left us and it may be presumptuous to say, but maybe the gods and goddesses haven't either.

So now the only questions that remain are: what if the god of light himself were a man living amongst us today in our current society? What if these small, fascinating stories were thrust into our present world and he walked amongst us as just another man? Well, get comfortable, because this may just be where we find out.

Before we begin, did you know a group of crows is called a murder? Fitting, really.

PART ONE

PART ONE

CHAPTER ONE

Sixteen days, five hours and twenty-four minutes ago, something was wrong. Something was under my skin, crawling up my throat, behind my eyes and grinding its teeth on my soul. Whenever I looked at myself in the mirror, I could see its face pushing up under my bruised skin, asking me *why*. Why I stayed, why I complied, why I was unsalvageable. The fact these questions resurfaced grated on me. I'd heard them so many times over my years in captivity that they were now just an itch to scratch. A constant nagging feeling all over my body that I couldn't soothe. It made my skin feel foreign as it stretched over my bones. I felt less at home in my body than I already was.

I knew I wasn't far gone. Deep under my depression, manipulated mind and aching body, I knew. I had no illusions in my mind about what it was. I knew I'd been folded away into a box I didn't belong in. Like one of those dolls we buy for children that we never can fit back into the packaging, no matter how we bend, twist and shove at them. I can't count the number of times I'd caught my parents with brows furrowed trying to cram my well-loved toys into tiny boxes that never facilitated them. They had this need to keep the boxes to most of my belongings, so that when we moved from place to place, everything was protected in transit. They'd always let me keep my favourite toys tucked into the middle seat beside me with the seatbelt fastened. God, I miss those simpler times when my only worries were when I'd next be able to coerce my parents into letting me have an ice cream. Or the scolding I'd get feeding part of it to my doll slotted under my right arm.

I'd grown since childhood, but there were things I'd yet to experience. I'd never been touched by sneering, horrible kids in my schools, never there long enough to make that much of an impact. I'd gone through life unscathed by hardships, which made me naive and ignorant at times. Sometimes when people told me of betrayals or heartbreak that they'd suffered, I would remark on how they were better equipped for the world now. They knew the signs and the boundaries they needed to set. Although I tried to learn through people's anecdotes, it was never easy to navigate the cruelty of people. It turned out my first encounter with such a threat was the most damning.

That's how I'd ended up here, locked away in a dull, boring, unassuming house with my keeper. I'd never found confusion like it in all my years. The way he'd presented himself to me, all perfectly pleasant without a hint of malice swimming in those captivating eyes. I'd sat in my prison for months with my brow creased, wondering how he'd warped and twisted his body into this giant, terrifying monster towering over me as the first strike marred perfect, unassuming skin. I'd never seen a bruise on my body until then, and it had looked so ugly and foreign to me. He'd hidden me from my reflection for some time after he saw the damage it caused.

Now a victim of so many strikes like that one, I've got better at dealing with my new appearance. I can't remember when I finally got to look to my reflection again, but it was a while after the first burst of violence.

The hand prints that night looked like home. Staring back at me in the mirror, partially covered by dark knots of hair. That's what triggered a response. I was still silently crying as hard as I always did, still in as much pain as I always was, but the acid in my stomach burned as I realised I didn't know what my skin looked like unblemished. I'd forgotten what a face looked like when it was happy. It had been so long, that I didn't know what my life could be without torture or heartache.

Sometimes when it's quiet in my prison, I'll trace patterns of faces in the bruises on my skin. Almost like people make bunnies or any other animal out of clouds in the sky. I can see them now littered over my skin staring up at me, pulsing painfully trying to offer comfort. I'd like to think they were telling me I still had a strength within me, biding its time, waiting to surface. I could end it all and go back into the world I'd left seven years ago. Relearn how to be human. How to be more careful.

There was, to my dismay, not much of a plan I could conjure in my head. My only thought was that I'd have to be a fighter now, not the obedient little creature with matted hair and bleeding lips. I'd built the perfect persona over the years, choosing to comply with demands where I could. Sometimes my rage consumed me, burning up my throat and spitting fire at the shadow looming above. I never did understand how he could find ways to make himself look like darkness even in fully lit rooms. It was always a short-lived moment that I paid for. For my survival, it was quickly understood that I needed to comply.

I'd have one opportunity where he wouldn't be expecting the walls to close in. One chance to rip his throat out so he'd never condescend to me again. I couldn't count the number of times my jaw had clenched at his spiteful, childish tone. I'd learnt to make my bottom lip tremble when I responded that way so it looked like I was scared rather than furious. So far, my belief was that it had worked. I'd been learning small gestures and tricks to throw him off the scent. Trying to sell that I was close to being compliant now. Close to him having achieved his goal of completely breaking me. I knew I was the longest he'd ever had to work on a victim. I could see it in how his plans got more intense, more sinister. It was a small hope that it meant he'd turned his focus on to the torture he inflicted rather than the possibility of me having a plan to take him down. The face under my bruise was still there but the smile grew. I couldn't return it, but the smile eased the crawling I could still feel under my skull.

It wasn't as though I had nothing in my arsenal to formulate a way to hurt him. There was trust there. In the bathroom. In the dark. A few options on how I could sneak something back to the dim room down the hall. Sharp objects that he left cluttering the rooms to establish his dominance. He knew I wouldn't use them. None of them had appealed to me; most made me feel sick. The razors wouldn't be sharp enough. I'd need something more substantial. I knew I wouldn't be able to deflect a counter attack, consequently meaning I'd only have the one move. One powerful, life-ending move. Nothing was good enough. Nothing was looking up at me offering that kind of hope.

The crawling feeling under my skin became more frantic, as though building to an anticlimactic crescendo of a song, as the intention in me washed away.

The tiled floor was sticky from my blood. The placid girl in the mirror didn't mind. At least if she's bleeding she's surviving. It was a small comfort that my muddled mind had created after I realised he never inflicted anything fatal. She's alive, she's broken but not beaten. The blood still ran down my leg from the broken skin on my thigh. It was sadistic but I wiggled my toes, making a small mess around my feet. It gave me strange comfort. I used to like it clean and bright. Now I found solace in darkness and bloodstained skin.

I swiped my forehead with my fingers, picking up the last few drops that have escaped the wound there. My blood was warm compared to the chill of my prison. Maybe that was another reason I loved it so. The pad of my thumb skimmed across my fingertip and all that's left now is pale white. I sigh as I observe how thin and frail my fingers are.

The crawling becomes more agitated again.

Something's wrong.

Maybe that's why I was always cold. No fat, just bones and veins. My skin was almost translucent and tinted blue with all the veins you could see underneath. They slithered up my arms and legs, twisting and turning inside my malnourished limbs. I lifted my arm up and watched as no muscles rippled under the skin.

Of course not.

My arm drops defeatedly as I realise I'm wasting away to nothing. What possible hope do these arms and legs have of defeating the destroyer of my sanity?

My hands landed on the sink as I doubled over in crippling self-doubt.

I can't. I can't, I can't, I can't. I can't *do this.*

He was stronger. Faster. Heavier.

What if I wasn't strong enough? What if I couldn't save myself? He would kill me.

But what life is this anyway?

No. I can't think like that.

He'd win.

The crawling that had moved to my throat made me choke.

"There's no need to be dramatic. Do as you're told, clean yourself up and come back." His voice seeped out into the hallway. The silent "or I'll make you" echoes down the hallway, making me tremble.

I squeezed my eyes shut as I tried to swallow down the boulder in my throat.

Don't think about it, don't breathe funny, just focus on being normal. He can't suspect if he doesn't notice.

Eyes of fire stared back at me. I screwed my mouth up in anguish as I realised the only thing they've ever done was burn salt tracks down my cheeks these past few years. I had no fire. I'd have burned him long ago if I did.

I couldn't remember the last time my emotions had overpowered me like they had that night. No matter the will, I had to push everything back under. My eyes still remained wet, pouring salt over the lower rim. My sockets are so well sunken into my skin now that the tears pool there before spilling over on to my cheeks, dripping from my jaw. I can't let him see me like this but I also can't test his patience. There's always a special kind of horror he has in store for me when I drag anything out, no matter how many pieces of me I have to pick up off the floor before him. It's always the ticking that bothers him, not the tears. Every time he hears the second hand move on the clock, his storm gathers.

Emotional.

That's what he calls me when I'm too slow, or not co-operative. Co-operative means happy, smart, obedient, considerate, polite, respectful.

Emotional means I'm too human for him. I'm a doll, an object, a thing. Definitely not a human. He can lose patience, take his anger out on me with scathing words or choose violence when his storm thunders in to the room, but I can't. I'm the outlet for that and I'm expected to pay his price without complaint. And I did. I'd been conditioned to, after all. By that, I mean I was fully acquainted with how things went if I prolonged my recovery.

The downfall of making a victim take abuse and demanding they be incapable of feeling anything about it, is that it builds and harvests inside the body. My despair had built for six and a half years after I learnt how to bottle it all up. That was my strength. My glimmering light of possibility.

I was *angry.* I was sick of it all. I was sick that when I looked in the mirror, it felt like familiarity. It felt like my normal life.

It also occurred to me as I propped myself up higher over the sink that I'd got nothing and no one left to lose. My parents were no longer here; I had no siblings. I was sure I had no friendships or acquaintances that would spend seven years hoping for me. That's not something I was resentful of. I knew with my careless ways back then that I would doubt I'd understand what a missing person is. What the impact of a disappearance meant for them. I could never expect better of people when I wouldn't even of myself. Not the twenty-year-old full of ambition and careless wonder.

It did however mean I was now faceless, nameless and without a tie to anyone. No one to do this for, no one to ask myself if this is what they'd want me to do. No one to disappoint. It was just me in this tiny, dirty, bloody bathroom with a plan that only served me. Better than that, it didn't affect or harm anyone else except my destructor. That was a loss I could live with.

An upward tilt on the corner of my lips almost makes me gasp and I slap my hand over my mouth in shock.

Please don't say he heard me.

Maybe I wasn't completely lost yet; there was still fire there. All I needed was enough to get it done.

*

It was after I'd hit the floor, watching blood pool underneath his torso that I got to see the light fade from his eyes. The knife finally sunken in to his side, the feel of it cutting through flesh was surreal. Judgement had been passed and justice had been served in one blinding moment.

Sixteen days, five hours and twenty-four minutes ago, I killed him. And it was beautiful.

CHAPTER TWO

Seven Years Prior

The sun is blinding on the first November morning of the year. It's such a stark contrast from the gloom I grapple with inside. It's only been just over a year since both my parents died. The loss doesn't get easier to bear the more time goes on. It's a common phrase I've heard muttered around me but it's proven to be nothing but a meaningless bunch of words. Time feels like the enemy for my healing. I've lost the only family I have and since they were also my only friends, I've lost that too.

God, I hate how reclusive I was.

As my I watch one foot step out in front of the other, I'm taken back all those years to when I was younger. My childhood was difficult to say the least. My mother had some unsavoury habits so my father would move us from place to place every couple of years. I never really learnt how to socialise or insert myself in to already established cliques at school or in my neighbourhoods. Eventually, I learnt to push people away with a cold, yet timid exterior. I was severely lacking in any knowledge of healthy relationships with others, only having my parents' example to learn from. There was so much love in our household but so much uncertainty and many grey areas. I didn't want the bad with the good like they had; I craved perfection and pure unequivocal adoration in my connections to others. I soon discovered people in my proximity couldn't offer that for me. I'd grown up fast but they still had immaturity clouding their judgements. Children were often mean and unforgiving for no valid reason. I caught on to that once I saw it was a pattern in each place we moved to. They couldn't offer me warmth or comfort so I wrote everyone off.

Eventually, I finished school. I passed exams with flying colours as expected. I wasn't arrogant by any means but I was confident I'd do well. What else was I to focus on in my free time except books and homework with no social skills or awareness? I sometimes look back at my stubbornness at such a young age and wonder what might have happened if I'd tried harder to forge friendships with those kids. Then I'd remember them pushing each other over in the playground, sneering and laughing. It was safe to say I steered clear for the right reasons.

Secondary school was much of the same but the torment was more the emotional type. Girls and boys going through puberty with several insecurities surfacing and others pouncing on the opportunity to tear their peers down.

Fortunately, my ability to coast through school with anonymity was a blessing. I was never touched by the cruelty of them and merely showed up, got it done and left without so much as a snigger in my direction. My heart would bleed for the ones who weren't so lucky, and I always regret not being strong enough to stand up and say something. However, when venting to my parents, they'd encourage me to turn a blind eye. It was easier to just be grateful it wasn't me in their shoes and move on. Now I wonder if that not only made me just as bad as them, but even worse.

I'm so lost in my grief-riddled thoughts that I don't catch the man strolling towards me. Instead, I crash into his solid form and the impact sends me backwards towards the ground. I don't descend far before a strong arm snatches me at the waist and pulls me into a beige woollen coat and blue scarf. Underneath those is a firm, warm body. My eyes travel upward and settle on a strong, tanned jaw. My breath hitches and my chest feels tight with nerves. I flick my eyes up to meet his soft blue ones and if my mouth wasn't already agape, it would be from the sheer beauty of the man. I'd never seen someone so perfect before. His lips curve into a gorgeous shy smile before he begins to apologise.

"Uh, my apologies." He chuckles nervously, his grip on my waist tightening slightly. "I don't usually make a habit of knocking over unsuspecting women in the street." A pinkish hue settles on his cheeks, which makes him even more endearing. At twenty years old, I've never considered myself a woman, more a girl, but hearing him call me that fills me with warmth.

"It's my fault, I'm so sorry I—" I struggle to explain myself and the words get lost as I stare up at him.

I shy away from his piercing gaze, which is when I catch sight of my gloved hand settled on his chest. That's when I belatedly realise it's been a minute or so that we've been locked in such an intimate embrace with no desire to break apart. I blink rapidly at the absurdity of it, trying to understand how this could have happened. By any other normal standards, the way we are right now is out of turn. I look back up at him with matching red cheeks and step out of his hold as gracefully as possible.

"Thank you for the save." I smile. "Those are some great reflexes you have there."

It might just be me, but I swear he inches slightly towards me to close the distance I've put between us. He's tall, perhaps six foot or so. He leans forward to meet my eye line with another heart-melting smile.

"You're welcome. It was the least I could do. I caused the fall; it was only right I caught you and put you right again." He scratches the back of his neck awkwardly as he recounts his part in the accident.

"Please don't feel bad," I beg. I hate to be the cause of someone's embarrassment. "It takes two for something like that to happen."

I can feel myself running out of things to say and I'm already overthinking every single word that comes out of my mouth. Not that anything seems to deter him from the conversation. His eyes seem to drink in the sight of me, which makes me blush even more. Whilst his blush looks captivating on his handsome face, mine probably looks completely unseemly. I've not been looking after my appearance much either so I can only imagine the state I must be in.

"I'd be grateful if you'd let me buy you a coffee." His voice is firm and offers no room for argument. I can't help but think that the way his mouth moves around the words is unusually satisfying to watch.

My chest floods with warmth and my stomach flips. He's taking control of the situation and I've never been more relieved to have someone take the reins whilst I'm flapping trying to think of the next steps. My smile widens at his instruction and I follow him in a daze.

This incredible man who I crashed into has not only been bashful with me but is now steering me towards the small coffee shop on the corner. I can't believe a man this gorgeous is willingly wanting to spend more time with me.

As I walk by his side, our hands nearly touching each time they swing by one another as we eat up the pavement to our destination, I feel the weight on my chest lift. The grief seems like a distant memory and hope blooms in the parts of my heart where it's vacated.

"After you." He guides me in through the door he holds open, his free hand settling on the small of my back. Even through my black woollen coat his touch is warm.

He lets me order first and I opt for a hot chocolate. He smirks at my choice and orders himself the same. We make our way to a back corner in front of a fake fireplace. The chair seems too small for his larger frame but he settles into it like it was made for him. From the moment he caught me to sitting in a crowded coffee shop, he embraces it all flawlessly. His movements are smooth and precise in everything he does. It makes me question how he ever managed to carelessly stumble in to me just minutes previously.

"I was hoping you'd order a hot chocolate." He breaks our comfortable silence first. I raise an eyebrow over my mug at that line and he laughs quietly. "No, really I was. It just sounds better when you say let's grab coffee rather than hot chocolate."

I hum in agreement and place my mug on the small table between us.

"I'll let you have that one then. However, don't bash coffee, it's a daily requirement for some of us," I attempt at being coy.

"There's no judgment here." He holds his hands up. "A sweet treat after meeting you just felt like the right thing though."

He watches me carefully as I hide my smile behind the mug I've picked up again. I need to keep my hands busy to ease the jittery nerves coursing through my veins. This is probably the most interest a man has shown in me since the loss of my parents and I've completely forgotten how to act or flirt. My stomach swirls with excitement and anticipation. I'm not sure I can pull off keeping someone like this interested in me.

"You can't go wrong with something sweet," I agree, fighting a grin. I can't show him how giddy I am that he's actually flirting with me.

"That you can't," he muses thoughtfully. "Have I interrupted your day at all?" he worries.

"No!" I insist quickly as the shine in his eyes dulls a little. "I was only heading in to the city for some errands and this hot chocolate with you is a nice diversion."

I only realise after I've said it that I'm almost shamelessly flirting back now. I wince internally at how awful my attempt must have been. I can see the dimple in his cheek as he now smiles behind his mug. I suddenly have an urge to roll my eyes and playfully smack him for his lack of subtlety.

"I'm glad to be of service."

He's less subtle about how his gaze roams over my body now. Not that there's much he can see from my autumnal outfit that consists of boots, jeans and an oversized coat. My stomach flutters with desire all the same. My free hand fists in my scarf to try and keep my mischievous hormones at bay.

I hum pathetically in response as I lose all the composure I was barely hanging on to since I met him. Mercifully, although I watch his eyes focus on my clenched fists and his lips tilt in amusement, he doesn't comment on it. My gratitude for him increases tenfold as we continue small talk with the occasional flirtatious comment for the next hour or so. I don't learn much about him except for his sweet tooth and I like how he doesn't pry for personal information. Everything is at surface level and yet I can feel his presence burying itself deep in the back of my mind.

"Next time, let's go to dinner," he whispers low in my ear, kissing my cheek before he pulls away and leaves me standing just outside the cafe door staring after his tall frame.

I'm lost in a daze, clutching my phone with his number saved in it as I almost skip along the pavement to continue my day. The sun still blinds me but I bask in it now and embrace the new beginnings it's offering me.

Later in the evening, when I'm finally home after a long day navigating the busy Newcastle high street, I see a text from him. It's a date, time and location for when we'll next see each other. He's even included the details on what attire I should wear. I sigh in relief that I don't have to worry about that now.

He's so thoughtful.

When my head hits my pillow a few hours later, I drift off to sleep and dream of his blue eyes and captivating smile.

CHAPTER THREE

Present

Waking up in darkness still brings me comfort. My old routines seem harder to break than I initially thought. The bright lights feel like they're raining pellets on my skin and I can barely breath from the pounding. It's not just the feel of it either, it's the adjustment of my eyes. I've been living in overcast corners and grey-stained windows. Even daylight is hard. It's why I only venture out in the early hours or late in the evening. Mornings suit me better. Somehow those hours between four and six feel safer.

It's no matter to me now, though. This place brings me peace. It's the home of my strength rediscovered, where victory became mine.

I suppose my comfort might not make sense to most, but it does to me. I'm messy, insane even, but I've never felt better. Waking up in my room panicked that I'm back in the past is hard. The relief I feel when the reality comes flooding back is bliss. I love the rush of vengeance through my veins every morning, watching him fade as if it were only seconds ago.

Maintaining a life now is what makes me feel sick. I don't like thinking for myself and having to reinsert myself back into the world. I only follow in the footsteps of before, when he'd needed an errand running and it was more convenient for me to venture out. I didn't like being outside then either. I was so terrified of them all seeing straight through me, uncovering my darkest secrets. I can't explain why. It wasn't Stockholm Syndrome. It was more the terror of being uprooted from a situation without my say. I had little control or deviance from routine in my own life no matter how dreadful. I didn't want another stranger acting on my behalf, taking a choice from me. Now that I've killed him, I wonder if my reluctance to expose my torture was to do with the fact I knew deep in my gut I'd be the one to finish it.

Now I have a bigger truth to hide. Not that I feel shame or regret for his murder on my roster. Most nights I sit in the bathroom and stare at the tub. Perhaps if I'd dragged him in here and bent him over the side when I stabbed him, I could've bathed in his blood. I'm not quite able to feel pleasure yet but a lovely tingle in my belly occurs when I think of that little fantasy. I'd craft rings, chokers and bangles out of his bones if I could. Wear them round these parts like war medals. However, despite how much prison doesn't scare me, he's not worth me spending my remaining years behind bars. He was deserving of the murder though and the honour was all mine. Something I wear proudly over my broken heart. It doesn't fix the cracks he made but it soothes the pain.

As soon as I step outside, the crawling starts again with a familiar but harsh rhythm I know so well. I choke on it clinging to my throat as I return a greeting from a fellow early bird. Rural villages like this one tend to bring out a familiarity in people that they shouldn't possess. The cheerful passer-by doesn't seem to notice how out of depth I look and continues on, his cordial smile never wavering. I let out a breath I'm holding and the chill in the early morning air results in my breath appearing as white swirls before me. I pick my way through the broken slabs that we never got round to replacing on the path leading to the front door. It's not an uncommon sight so it hardly raised an eyebrow from the locals. I frown as I debate whether I should get them fixed now. I wouldn't really know where to start.

I keep to myself as I stroll through the sleepy coast village I now call home, hugging the oversized coat I always borrowed from him to my aching body. It looks as incongruous as ever. I can't help that the wretched thing was bought years ago when I met him. Nor can I help how sickeningly thin I am now after seven years under his care. I wince as I wrap the coat too tight, tiny fists clenched in to the fabric as I try to come to terms with how little there is left of me. Body and soul. Time has yet to be kind to my healing. I can still feel the effects of the last beating as if it hadn't happened weeks ago. My only comfort is counting each day, knowing there aren't many left before muscles unravel and skin heals.

The smaller pathways towards the sea are my choice route. Albeit longer, they have two benefits. The wind is always stronger when I travel towards the coast and I enjoy my hair wrapping over my face to blur my features. Then there was the sea. Something about the sea found my calm and tamed my crawler. It felt needed after my small blunder only a step outside the door earlier.

The crawling eases as I look out at the sunrise.

I know it's too early to shop, so I trek through the long grass hills and look down at the odd dog walker on the beach. I'd mentioned once to him that I liked to watch from afar as small figures danced in light rain and swirling sand from the typical British weather. He hadn't liked that at all. He'd dragged me out to the very spot my feet slip into now, looking out over the bay and drinking it all in.

I stand there for a few minutes, taking deep calming breaths. The heart sinking in my chest seems to lift. The current of the misery swirling inside of me slows, allowing me a small respite. It's a stark contrast from the tingling sensation at the back of my skull. Something is burrowing itself into my hair and tugging slightly. I lift my hand and try to smooth the back of my head to ease the strange feeling. There's nothing there except for the knots in my thick black hair. A shiver runs up my spine and I shake it off quickly, wanting to enjoy my peaceful moment overlooking the morning sea.

The base of my skull just above my neck starts to erupt in pins and needles and my blood turns cold. The wind wrapping around me ceases and even the waves before me seem to slow to almost a complete stop. It's only for a second or so before the world comes back full force and blindsides me into a nightmare.

My scalp roars as I'm dragged back and dumped on to the ground unceremoniously. My body groans as it's yanked through the grass. My skull screams in agony as my attacker does their best to pull my skin from it. Although I have done my best to tame my hair, there are still knots there that their fingers cling to viciously.

The once soft grass blades that tickled my legs seconds earlier now cut my hands and cheeks, whistling in the cold wind. I look up, my free arm following, and try to free myself from the hand in my hair, but all I grab is more blades of grass. I sob as they split the skin of my palm cruelly. I try to clutch on to them to counteract the downhill descent, but I keep getting further away from the sunrise and coastline.

After I throw the last clump of uprooted blades from my hands, the fist pulls me upright sharply. I try to scream from the pain but only a small squeak leaves my mouth. My eyes are streaming. I'm not crying, but my eyes weep from the pain despite my protests.

"What do you see?" The words slice through me. Nothing more than a sentence weaving through the wind and burrowing in my ears.

It can't be.

The crawling intensifies.

Four words. Four words shock me to my core and pound in my ears, echoing down the canal and I can't stop them.

Nothing else happens for a while but I'm still too scared to move. I can see the drag mark in the grass before me; my body has made it look like a neat line despite how much I flailed. It's terrifying that even in his violence the evidence of it is neat and tidy. I attempt to find my footing, regain my balance. My foot catches on the uneven ground and I fall back on to my arse. I'd laugh at the clumsiness of it, if his fist hadn't still been in my hair, tugging again as it followed me to the ground.

My hands curl in to the grass. My head is thrown back to the ground. I pant shakily as I flip over on to my front. My arms are too weak to push up on, no adrenaline left in my veins to help. I whimper in torment.

I can hear his dark chuckle before me and I know now I'm not just insane, I'm delusional. I can't believe, after all these weeks of feeling like he's been erased from my life, my brain has decided to conjure him up in this sinister hallucination. It's unbelievably cruel for my mind to fail me now after I freed it.

I'm unsure why this has come about and can't seem to understand what caused me to get all the way over here from where I'd stood moments ago. Had I stumbled and fallen down here? I look back over to the drag mark; by my angle on the ground it looks narrow, exactly how it would look if I'd slid down head first.

Just like my delusion I'm in right now.

Only I'm not delusional. My thoughts stop as I look down at a small mass of hair no less than a foot in front of me. That's my hair. I can tell by the oily black colour that it's mine. I've been here before; this wasn't the first clump of my hair I'd seen over the years.

But how is it here?

My lower lip trembles. My teeth sink into it harshly as I will myself not to let the fear consume me again. Not when I've vowed that fear will never become me again. My eyes are already wet so I allow the new tears to wash over the existing salty streaks on my cheeks. What's a few more when you've discovered that your ex has come back from the dead?

So, I do what any insane person would do. I throw my body on to my back and land on my elbows so I can prop myself up to see the source of the chuckle. Because no matter how crazy I may be, *there's no way in hell it's him.*

If anyone knows just how impossible that is, it's me.

The boots are familiar, though, the jeans, the dark fleece and matching T-shirt are as well. The crawling in my guts becomes unbearable as it scurries around in agitation under my skin. My blood pumps violently in my fingers.

My lips part as I stare up at my dead lover. Only he looks wrong. He looks wrong because this isn't right. He's not supposed to be here, looking as though he's here to take my soul for what I'd done. What he'd *made* me do.

He doesn't move towards me, though, just feigns disinterest in my throbbing body on the ground and turns to look out at the shore. Just like he did all those months before. My hands clench again as I pull myself up off the ground. There is logic in standing, although I'll admit it isn't flawless. If I stand, maybe he'll be gone. Maybe being on the ground is the issue.

As I rise on shaking legs, I realise I was illogical with my plan. He's still standing there, looking out beyond the horizon in silent ignorance.

For whatever reason, I stumble forwards and slot my feet into the footprints I'd left long ago when we were here last. It was an uncontrollable urge I couldn't protest to. His eyes lower to me briefly; his head never turns, though. I'm not worth the effort. They settle back on to the rising sun.

As he stares out to sea, I take in his appearance. Immaculate as always. The sharp, entrancing beauty was still as breathtaking as it was the first day I met him. His stubble is neatly trimmed and chocolate waves settled over his cheekbones effortlessly.

Bastard.

The peach glow from the morning light makes his blue eyes glitter and the ferociousness in them shines through as though the devil himself is igniting his soul. I should've known better. The blue irises couldn't scream red more if they tried. Even back then when he hadn't fully settled into his demons, the eyes had told me to run.

I swallow down my regrets. Dwelling on them could do me more harm than good. He senses this and turns to me sharply. My breath catches as I realise this isn't who I know. This is something else.

His skin is hollowed in all the places a corpse's should be. Skin paler than I've seen it, almost grey. His hand reaches out to my neck slowly and I see the blood and hair under his fingernails, curling in the gusts of wind charging at us from the east. My whole body launches away from him and I scramble over uneven ground to back away from the presence in front of me.

It's as I finally find my feet that he leaves me. I sweep my hair unceremoniously out of my face and just like that he's not there anymore. I don't waste time looking for him to double-check I'm alone. I just swivel on my feet and march back over the hills towards home. Shopping will have to wait.

I barrel down the hill at speed. I've decided to take the most treacherous path back to the roadside so I don't relive anything I did with him. His method would be perfect and neat, following the footpaths to a letter. Well, *fuck the footpaths.* Everything about what I do now, I realise, has to be different.

I stumble into a woman, a small handful of years younger than me. I've seen her several times before when I ran errands. She was always so polite and friendly to me. I'd found solace in her small talk in the past and didn't mind that she just liked to talk at me as we shopped. I'm not sure why she'd attached herself to me but it was thrilling having safe company for a change.

Eleanor is her name. I carry on past her and stutter out an apology quickly, prepared to continue my self-destructive path, when I notice something.

She's frowning. Eleanor doesn't frown. Not even when the woman at the shops screamed at her for having more than ten items at the self-checkout. For some reason that was an unimaginable thing to do. Eleanor has just ignored her and occasionally laughed at the ridiculousness of it all. Eleanor sees the good in the world and people that no one else can. Eleanor was a sign of hope of what I could be.

I shake my head to dispel my stupid assumptions about her. I've barely spoken to her in the past few years. I can't pretend to think I know anything about her. Small talk is all surface level anyway.

As I hurry home and see my front door come into view, I recall how she frowned. It was almost as though…

No. I'm seeing things. Just like I thought I'd seen him on the hillside today. I'm not right in the head. Why would I be after seven years of him? I'm lucky to be free and functioning now. Sanity may be a luxury I never have again but I need to try. I want my mind back.

I sit down in the living room, in his chair. Like it's my throne.

The crawling starts again. Behind my eyes, it burns with warning but I can't understand it this time. I don't know what it wants.

I fold in half and take deep breaths. That's when the voice starts echoing in my ears. It's not his voice though. I think it's mine.

Something is wrong with Eleanor.

CHAPTER FOUR

One year prior

He's decided that today we'll both go to the supermarket together. I bite back the whimper of despair as he informs me of this and I realise the alone time I was craving so much has been ripped away from me. The smirk he offers as I bow my head in sadness tells me that those were his exact intentions. He loves to give me small offerings of hope, and then, just when it's started to spread through my chest with warmth, he rips it away. The hole it leaves in my heart burns painfully as we wrap ourselves in our coats.

He stops my shaking hand from unhooking my own coat and instead he gives me a warm woollen one. I almost think it's the one I first met him in until I look down and see the fabric is jet black in colour, not beige. It's long and bulky as it swaddles itself around my small frame. I catch sight of my reflection in the narrow mirror that's hidden behind the coats. I look like death but the coat offers a symbol of affection from him. Any onlookers would think it's a woman wearing her lover's coat to feel close to him.

It's not.

I inhale deeply to ready myself for stepping out with him. The thought of all the pain and effort it will take to look like his adoring other half makes me want to retch. Instead, the scent of him drifts through my nostrils and my stomach clenches. He still smells like the home I never knew I needed. I try to refocus but I struggle to put one foot in front of the other as I'm hit with his scent. I haven't smelt it without the tangy bitterness of my blood mixed with it for so long. His hand steadies me as I step out of the house. It still baffles me that he can touch me like that and I don't flinch. My lower lip wobbles when I feel myself lean back into the protection and care I wish it offered me.

I don't know why I keep doing this.

The coat and his hand on my back offers me warmth from the chill in the winter air as we venture further into the coastal village. The cold is especially brutal here due to living so close to the sea. I burrow myself deeper into his coat, my nose firmly tucked under the collar as we push on. His hand flexes in approval and he pulls me in to his side as a reward. I sigh as his body offers me shelter from the winds coming in from the east.

I wonder what we must look like to the busybodies bustling around the streets stealing curious glances at us as they pass by. It must be nice to not have any worries around you that your only way to find anything of interest is to stare at others and try to conjure up a ridiculous story about the locals.

"Let's not give them something to talk about, little crow," he mutters as his fingers hook under my chin so I meet his firm gaze.

Not wanting to do anything to disturb his calm, I smile up at him. My lips twitch at the deceit but I'm confident no one will be able to see from a distance. His thumb strokes my jaw softly before it stops and instead tugs at my lower lip.

He saw that.

"You could do better." His voice is soft but the delivery is cutting. I can feel the promise of pain pulse in his fingertips as they rest on my skin.

"I could," I agree quietly, my eyes challenging.

"Don't start," he warns, his jaw clenched.

I'll pay for that later.

It occurs to me as we start to enter the busier parts of our village that I could kick up a fuss here. I could really start to shout and scream for help. However, it's not something I'd ever do. I've learnt over the years how little we all care for one another. Of course, people look and stare at you in public, but no one is looking to be a saviour or a hero. I'm trapped with him by my own stupidity and desperation to feel loved, but I'm also unable to escape because of *them*. Everyone around me is selfish and ignorant. I hate them all. They're the bystanders that I used to be in my childhood, only they've never learnt or strived to be better. It's when I think of their failures as I watch them peering at us as we pass by that I know I hate them more than I hate him.

So I'll stay in his hold, not in theirs.

Warm air blasts us both as we slip through the automatic doors of the supermarket. I instinctively step out of his hold to grab a trolley, trying to force distance between us now I have warmth of my own rather than provided by him. His long legs eat up the floor quickly and silently behind me, but I know he's there before his front presses against my back as my hands rest of the handle. Hot breath swirls around my ear.

"I *said* don't. Start." He nips my lobe playfully but I feel the sting of his teeth as what it's meant to be. A warning.

We peruse the aisles as any normal couple would. Only I notice how he controls what goes into the trolley to purchase. It doesn't stop me picking small things from shelves that I haven't eaten in years. We don't cook much. He doesn't like to and he likes it even less if I offer. We only pick a few things for our cupboards from here. The cooked meals we occasionally indulge in are delivered to him a few streets away and he then brings it home. It's so much effort that, more often than not, my meals are biscuits, crisps or cold soups. The canned soups are my preference as with them at least they sometimes offer nutrients. The rest just sit heavy in my stomach, making my rotten insides feel even worse.

I pluck some dried fruit packets from the shelf, hoping he'll see them and allow me the small luxury. I turn to look at him, eyes wide and pleading. I haven't behaved exceptionally well today but I hope he can have a lapse in judgment to grant me this. He looks away from the product in his hand to meet my gaze. His lips tilt with affection as he sees me silently begging him to put my item in our trolley. It seems that seeing me yearning for his approval sparks some happiness within. He glides over, discarding his item on the shelf and settles his hand over mine holding the bag of raisins.

"Something you'd like, beautiful?" he murmurs quietly, but loud enough for his term of endearment to be heard by anyone nearby.

"Please," I say as I lean into him.

Please allow me this.

My heart swells as he slips the bag out of my hand and places it neatly in the trolley. He then turns around, engulfs me in his arms as he reaches around me to grab more of a selection. My eyes water as I watch him line them all up alongside the raisins. He pulls my head towards him and kisses my forehead as I stand there speechless.

"You know I'd do anything for you." I feel his lips move around the words against my skin. They linger on my forehead for a moment longer after he pulls away.

He wanders off on his own after that and leaves me to wander aimlessly around with the trolley. His absence should set me on edge. I know there's something he's doing that he wants my eyes away from, but I'm so overcome with gratitude for what he's just done that I can't feel anything but that. My tiny body and mind can't handle too much at once.

"Excuse me?" A gentle, feminine voice interrupts my alone time.

I turn around to see a woman with red hair and green eyes smiling at me. I immediately start to recoil from the unwanted and unprovoked attention on me, stepping back and looking around for someone else she must be talking to. When I discover it's just us two standing there in the aisle, I turn back to face her with my forehead creased in confusion.

"Sorry, I don't mean to disturb but I just see you here a lot," she offers kindly.

I've been so used to being able to slip through the cracks and remain invisible to so many that her revelation shocks me. The feeling of being noticed let alone having someone admit the fact to me is difficult to take in. The whole aisle tilts as she continues to actually *look* at me.

"Hi," I mutter, twisting my hands together to distract myself from the awkwardness. My trolley is long forgotten in front of me.

"I just wanted to say hi and hopefully we can wave to one another when we're next here at the same time." She smiles.

"Um, okay." It doesn't escape me it's an odd request but agreeing will cut the conversation shorter.

She looks quickly over her shoulder as if she's looking for someone else.

"Forgive me, my name is Eleanor. I have to rush off but I hope to see you again sometime." Her hand squeezes my arm gently before she disappears.

The touch feels foreign and unwelcome but it's done so swiftly that I barely have a chance to react. I stare at my sleeve where her hand was and something burns deep within me. She's touched his coat. The coat I'm wearing that he put on me. She doesn't know that, of course, but I feel sick that another woman's touch lingers there.

That's how he finds me only a few seconds later. He smooths out the creases on my forehead with his thumb and each caress lifts my mood infinitely. I'm back in the routine I know, with the only person who's cared for me since my parents' death. Despite the bruises on my body and heart, I can't deny he's as much my safe place as he is my monster.

I didn't realise how hard my heart was pounding until it slows into a more peaceful rhythm as we finish our errand

and head home. My arm still tingles from where that woman touched it. The material on the sleeve now scratches at my skin, eating away at my flesh. There's this niggling feeling that something about the interaction is wrong, but I don't want to dwell on it further. Currently I'm in a bubble of me and him, returning to four walls that keep me hidden away from the world and I want to enjoy it. I have this dread burrowed deep inside my chest that I shouldn't want to know why Eleanor isn't sitting right with me.

Once we're home, I let him take his coat off of me. He seems to see the invisible blemish it's left on my bare arm and presses his lips to it. I instantly feel better. The coat is discarded on the floor rather than on its assigned peg. It's an odd move from him but I don't worry myself over it. Later, I'll have to worry over when the right time is to tidy it away so he doesn't lose his temper at my negligence, but I can't let that anxiety seep in until after he's peeled his eyes off me.

"Now, why don't you show me how grateful you are for me?" he whispers against my neck. I twitch slightly in surprise he's managed to come up upon me without my notice. Thankfully, he doesn't comment on it.

I'm only too happy to oblige as we ascend the stairs. I love him so much when he's like this. Between the sheets we're the passionate lovers we used to be at the very start. His eyes aren't as fearsome when they settle on my bare skin and his healthier body showcasing rippling muscles and golden skin offers me the warmth I've lost over the years of wasting away to nothing.

"You are so beautiful, my little crow."

The sentiment is welcomed as I cling to his affection, praying it lasts longer than an hour or so this time. I arch up into his touch as he wants and I slot myself against his body as I have done numerous times before. The euphoria of being with him, of worshipping his body as he does mine, never fades. It's always so good and takes me so high that it almost removes the memories of the harder times from my mind.

Later, when he's given me instructions to bring us some of the food we bought, I notice the coat is no longer on the floor. It isn't on the peg either. I can't say I'm too invested but I do wonder when it was moved. It's strange that I've not been asked to move it myself. When I finally reach the kitchen and grab what we need, I notice a dark sleeve hanging out of the rubbish bin outside. Seeing as the house is only in darkness, I can see clearly through the window that the sleeve belongs to the coat I wore earlier. The one soiled with another woman's touch.

He must have disposed of the coat somewhere between the couple of hours we've been together. The relief that floods through me is a shock. It's as though the feeling in the depths of my chest has finally ceased its insistent knock, waiting for me to answer its call. It makes me wonder sometimes how he is able to be so attuned to me, but regardless, I'm satisfied with the outcome. Although I've lost one of his coats, I've gained something more with him.

CHAPTER FIVE

Present

She swivels in the frozen foods aisle, and I'm certain this time she's seen me. However, she just smiles neatly at the woman waiting to delve into the freezer she's in and moves out the way with her pizza, maybe? It looks like one anyway and I can't seem to recall anything else coming in a box shaped like that. I'm not sure why it's relevant what food she's purchasing but I carry on stalking her through the shop anyway.

The strawberry blonde curls frame her perfect face *perfectly.* Her pale skin and doe eyes make her enviable to other women. My heart clenches every time I look at her properly. Now that I can hold my head high I can actually *look* at her. Before, I barely caught glimpses with that mantra in my head.

Eyes down, shoulders hunched.

I run my fingers through my dark locks. I recall how they used to be lighter. Like rays of sunshine that fell effortlessly over my shoulders. It was fitting, when I became his, that everything dulled. My hair was tar, eyes were swamps of despair and my lips had been kissed by death so many times they'd screwed up and split years ago. They never have healed fully.

I see Eleanor as my before whenever I look at her. She is the reason I avoid the mirror. I can't stand seeing how far I've fallen. I wake every morning with spiders crawling out of my eyes and my mouth filled with salt. I know I'm mending but I can't stomach the sight of his marks still on my body or the broken look in my eyes. I used to have perfect skin, full lips and although I was carefree about what people thought of me, I took my time applying make-up and dressing each morning. I never did that for a reason, really. Looking back, I think I made the effort solely for myself. I didn't pay much attention to who would appreciate me looking nice. My parents, from what little I remember of them now, always had the opinion to worry less about others. Maybe that was instilled a bit too much in me, though, looking back on how the events of my capture unfolded.

It's not about me, I remind myself. It's about Eleanor. I can't keep living in my past just because I can see something remotely familiar in how she lives now to how I used to. I think if I were to observe everyone here I'd find a way to relate it back to my 'before'. I huff in amusement at how self-obsessed I am now he's left me. After those seven years I wasn't allowed to think of myself, now I can't seem to stop. There's a resentment there about what I've missed out on, what could have been for me. I'm not sure if it's directed at him or me.

I know I'm being beyond creepy and borderline psychopathic stalking this woman whilst she does her weekly shop but I haven't been able to stop thinking about her. Not that my crawler will let me. I wake up gasping for air some nights as it dances on my stomach. It's always the same message as well. I can't function without it circling in my brain. I've had to turn to this obsession with her to ease how intolerable it is.

I don't think it's right this time. Or I'm right. I'm not too sure who does the thinking anymore.

She's harmless enough; I've not been able to pinpoint a single moment where anything has rung alarm bells. I'm an expert in that now, I like to think. I've built a radar within me for danger. She makes me feel uneasy with how perfectly she does everything though. I can't seem to remember if she was as calculated as this when I saw her last. Everything in her trolley is stacked neatly and in categories. Vegetables, protein, canned food, etc. The way every movement she makes looks rehearsed and precise makes me frown. It starts to make me think of him. Although my prison wasn't spotless, he always was and there was a certain need for specific things to be perfect with him. The way he dressed, moved, how we organised the cupboards and how long he liked to look at spilled blood on the floors. I'd only ever clean it up when he would slowly start to ignore it instead of stopping at the sight of the small puddles and smiling.

Eleanor, although perfect and neat, didn't strike me as sadistic. So I overlook her behaviours in organising produce and focus on the task at hand. What's wrong with her?

There are more than ten items in her basket at the self-checkout again. However, this time, there is no disgruntled lady protesting to it. I mean, if her steel determination to carry on about her shopping as she usually does counts as something wrong, I'm again proving to myself I'm going mad. As I watch her pack everything into bags, I liken it to the memory of that day. The situation had almost been enough to tickle at my non-existent sense of humour.

Unless you can call it a crime when she selects 'no bags' but stuffs her shopping in to a couple anyway and avoids the 70p charge, Eleanor seems fine.

I follow her out to the car park and shuffle down the side of two cars near to hers so I can watch what she does next. I duck down so I can watch her through the windows of the Fiesta I'm hiding behind. The bag gets thrown in to the boot carelessly; the spilled contents help me see she's just a normal woman doing a normal thing. There are a few things I recognise, brands of certain foods he liked to have and a few other bits that are much healthier and nutritious than what I've eaten recently. He wouldn't allow it.

My insides yearn for food, but I haven't braved the task of shopping for myself yet. I really need to soon though. My cupboards are sparse.

Eleanor looks up sharply and peers around the small car park. I crouch further behind the car and have to clamp my hand over my mouth when my foot drops into a pothole. I regain my balance just barely and when I look out again, she's still standing there. It's almost like a trance the way she stares out into the dark.

I follow her line of sight and can't see anything. It's odd.

My crawler begins the dance on my stomach again.

She shakes her head and despite the frozen goods in her boot, veers off from her car. It's so sudden I almost get whiplash. Her pace is quick, and she's strutting over to the exit with purpose.

I quickly hurry after her retreating form, having a quick look at the car she's just left unlocked in a pretty well-covered area. The keys are still inside. Now I'm frowning. What the hell is she doing? It's so aggressively odd that I start to contemplate all our previous interactions. She wasn't anything like this when I briefly knew her. It wasn't like her to be distracted easily. She was too focused and giddy about what was going on in her own little world.

Her strawberry blonde locks sway behind her, some lone strands catching on her woollen coat. Of course, she fills it out well, the shoulders don't sag and the arms don't hang past the tips of her fingers like mine. Her legs are wrapped in dark denim as I waddle after her in large baggy joggers rolled up at the ankles. It's humorous how much we contradict one another. I trip over my worn trainers, listening to her heeled boots tap rapidly on the gravel. I'm still struggling with movement and learning how to exercise again. My coordination has taken a huge hit and I struggle trying to focus on not tangling my legs together as I half-walk, half-run after Eleanor. I'm so perplexed at how fast she moves in four-inch heels in the dimly lit streets she marches down.

It's late in the evening, and the pubs aren't on this side of the village. There's a small handful of shops near the larger store but she's heading further into the residential area. I've always been soothed by the fact the large supermarket stands more or less on its lonesome. For how small this place is, its seclusion has been a grace for me. Fewer people around, ergo there are no drunks or skittish people hovering in dark corners. However, in this circumstance, I'm wondering if I've missed something nearby. There's not really much here for her to be doing except driving home, yet she continues on.

She's moving with purpose and it takes me a few attempts to keep up with her. She looks golden underneath the street lights. Every time she passes under their glow, her strawberry hair glistens, her coat flickers with little flames of orange and yellow. Even her skin, albeit quite pale, emits a warmth in the chilly autumn air that stirs a green monster within me. It's a new feeling, one I'm thankful for. Although jealousy is still a negative emotion, it's not half as negative as some others I have befriended. I think that means progress.

I sway under the lamp post she's just walked under and lift up my arm. My fingers peek out from the sleeve. Still deathly pale and almost bone-like in shape. My skin doesn't experience the same effect as hers. The blue tint I still bear clashes horribly with orange. A dismal grey-brown is what the combination makes, not dissimilar from the rotting fence standing tall to my right. I shake my head trying to ignore the self-hatred this is triggering. I push on with my hand back hidden in my sleeves.

It's then that I realise she's on her phone, talking in small harsh whispers. I'm taken aback by how different she sounds. I've only ever known gentle, kind Eleanor who laughs at problems rather than confronts them.

I can't see her face and I don't want to risk that either. Not when I'm literally stalking the woman.

I hear her talking about getting rid of something. It clicks that she's talking about her job. I remember her incessant whining about it once a couple of months ago. The last time I ran an errand I think. She was complaining about wanting to go further with the current project she was working on. I'm not sure where she worked; I wasn't verbal enough to ask. Or I just didn't care. Maybe I'm selfish but I think I had enough on my plate at the time. He'd been exceptionally well behaved in those weeks and the crawling from my gut instinct was screaming at me that this meant something bad was going to happen. I was unbelievably stressed about it, my white knuckles on the trolley encompassing that. Eleanor hadn't noticed as she was more concerned about her problems. I guess I enjoyed the fact she wasn't observant.

From what I did manage to catch in between the voices in my head, it sounded as though she was on about getting rid of something or someone on the project who was her competition. I think it was some*one* actually. I don't recall the specifics of the story but she seemed quite light-hearted about it. I didn't think it ran that deep. I remember her saying it was a matter of biding her time and letting the pieces fall into place. It seemed like a lot of fuss about a situation she was happy to watch unfold.

Now, hearing the distress in her voice made me think maybe that was more. The hands waving wildly as she spoke suggested this was still ongoing and apparently driving her nuts. The whispering is never louder but seems to become more distressed. I checked the clock before I left the house. I estimate I've been out about an hour since it read nine in the evening. So my question, despite being out of a working structure for so long, is why would anyone from work be discussing it this late on a week night?

Her movements stutter and she sighs in relief. Her chin tilts downwards in a submissive move that makes me shudder. It's telling as to who's on the other side of the phone. Someone with authority, perhaps her boss? The movement doesn't seem to mimic that type of relationship though. It radiates off something more sinister and vulnerable. It's almost like an injured animal waiting to see if the hunter strikes or sets them free. So if it's not work, what would it be? Another abuser?

The chin tilt is a staggering pull back in to painful memories but I screw my eyes shut to clear my mind. Memories are dangerous; they feel nostalgic sometimes. I have to convince my warped brain that there's no fondness there. It's harder to stop them the further I get away from the day that changed my life. The day that I finally got to smile at death and became a cold-blooded killer.

Unravelling the knots in my head has been hard. Harder than I imagined. I thought the murder would provide me with blinding clarity but it hasn't. Sometimes I long to be told what to do, where to go, how to *feel* especially. I revel in freedom but I know I'm not managing it well.

Soft murmurs bring me back to Eleanor in front of me. She mewls in appreciation of what seems to be affection offered by the person on the end of the call. The creases in my forehead deepen. This is bizarre, even for my sort of strange.

I melt back into the shadows as she wraps up her call. I can't help but agree with what the voice in my head has been telling me.

Something's wrong with Eleanor.

CHAPTER SIX

Fifty-six days before his death

It's a beautiful day today. It's why I feel the happiest in the last few days of summer as everything fades away into autumn. The sun stops lighting me and my scars up with voracity but the chill of the air hasn't quite settled in yet. The thin coat that I've hung on my frail body is more a statement I'm his than actually serving a purpose. I made sure he saw me don the thing before I hurried out the door to run errands for us. There was no smile from him as there usually was. He's been a darker shade of anger these past few weeks and I feel it in my broken body more than ever.

Still. He's given me the solace of a solo trip to the shops and I don't even mind the burn of my battered limbs as I trip and stumble over the uneven ground. The sensation is welcomed happily. Mainly because, deep down, I know that although the first injuries are from him, this pain I'm feeling right now is all down to me pushing forwards to the shops.

I've set off at my normal time, which means I'm following the same pattern as Eleanor. That part is confirmed when I finally fall through the automatic doors and she's there straight ahead of me. She turns and smiles warmly. I don't return it and quickly busy myself getting a basket. My arms thank me with an even deeper ache as I push my body to carry itself as though we've never known pain.

Eleanor quickly links her arm through mine as she pulls me around the shop with her. I ignore the ache it sends through me and try not to tense my arm in response. She's started to understand my routine and happily follows it with me so I don't feel the gut-wrenching worry of deviating off course. It's an adjustment to her routine she's made for mine and although I haven't told her how much it means to me, I hope she knows.

"I thought we'd never see each other again; you've been gone such a long time!" she exclaims with mock horror on her face.

I can't tell her that the reason she's not seen me is because when we were last together she'd encouraged me to try another brand of soup that offered better nutritional value. She'd placed it in the cart and I hadn't had the stomach to take it back out. Something about the impending embarrassment and attention I'd draw to myself for making a fuss seemed infinitely more dangerous than what would await me at home for this disobedience. She looked so happy with herself as well and I hadn't had a friend in so long. I wanted to cling to her a little longer so I could prove to myself that I was capable of making friends with someone other than him. I'd paid for it greatly when I got home and the last few weeks consisted of my dragging my beaten body around the home as much as I could to do the bare minimum. There was no way I'd be able to heave it to the shops.

"I've been busy," I stated simply after clearing my throat uncomfortably. I want to change the subject but I've never initiated any point of conversation in years. The words and questions on how to do that are lost on me.

"Okay. Well, shit at work hit the fan." She starts to ramble on about her day and I breathe a small sigh of relief that she knew not to dig.

"Hmm," I hum in response as I browse the aisles for food.

When I'm in the middle of chucking some bits in my basket, she tugs at my arm harshly. I suck in a deep breath as pain shoots up and down my arm. The floor tilts a little as the pain increases, but eventually I come to. I look up at her in shock and pull my arm out of her grip, cradling it.

"You're not listening to me!" She pouts.

"Sorry, I… I have a lot on my mind at the moment." The apology is sour in my mouth as I spit it out to her. I don't feel sorry but it's hardwired into me to apologise whenever someone inflicts pain on me. I have to take a moment to remind myself she's not him.

"It's okay." She waves her hand dismissively. "Can you please pay attention whilst we finish the shop? I've been needing to unload this for a while." She throws her hands up and then smiles, which seems like a contradiction but the action matches her fast-paced personality. She can go from one emotion to another pretty quickly so I simply nod at her request and push on beside her for the rest of the aisle.

"So. I've been having issues. There's this one woman at work and she's doing the same job as me. She's done it for longer but has started to get careless with what she's doing.

I've stepped up and cleaned things up for her but she's still able to keep her position and my boss's favour!" Her hands fly up again in frustration.

I flinch a little at how loud she's got. She doesn't seem to understand how far her voice carries when she's speaking at a normal volume. Luckily, at this time there are not too many people to offend. The rush of the afternoon has dwindled off and there's only a handful of people lingering in the aisles. Still, it's enough people to worry me. I don't need the added attention.

As a woman looks up at me with a furrowed brow, I direct my eyes back down to the floor. I adjust the dark cap I'm wearing so it covers more of my face. I can feel the tingling in my cheeks as they paint themselves pink. A dead giveaway to any onlooker that I'm flustered beyond belief.

I turn away from Eleanor, hoping to leave her as well after the scene she's caused but my hopes of an unnoticed getaway are dashed.

"Where are you going? We have to go to the produce aisle next," she asks, genuinely confused at my actions. I look down at my feet in shock.

Where am *I going?*

I shake my head, trying to dispel the clouds of confusion gathering in the corners of my vision. My toes curl up in my trainers in rejection of the thought that I'd tried to break out of the predictability of my shopping habits. I never deviate from the routine I have. I shop the aisles by number one at a time and pick up my food in order as I go. The subconscious action makes me pause for a moment or two. I slowly walk back over to Eleanor with a frown on my face. She looks just as puzzled as I am and my steps falter.

Does she think this is out of blue for me too?

I offer a small shrug as I feel my eyes well up. I'm doing everything wrong and I can't afford to make another mistake like last time. I just need to get through this. There are only four more aisles to shop before I can pay and go home.

Eleanor says nothing as we start walking through the shop again. She side-eyes me a few times. I can't see her do it, but I watch her strides become shorter and her heeled feet click on the floor outside of their normal rhythm. Her upper torso rotates only slightly towards me but it offers enough for me to know she's studying me. I squeeze my eyes shut. I just want this to be over so I can go.

"So… anyway." Eleanor quickly recovers. "Like I said, she's getting all this praise and recognition for what she's doing and I get nothing. It's infuriating to watch when I know how hard I'm working to be better than her and earn some reward for myself." She's spitting fire at this point with how worked up she is over this colleague.

I tune the next few bits out. She has a habit of repeating the same scenario several times over just to process it and I don't have the energy to be the person she dumps her problems on.

"I know it's only a matter of time though. She'll drop the ball eventually right in front of him and I'll pick up the pieces and slide into his good graces," she declares. Her voice is lower and I can hear the way the corners of her mouth turn up as she says the words.

"Okay," I state. It seems simple enough and she's a managed to come to an agreeable enough outcome to the issues herself.

"You know, for someone who doesn't say much you have a way of helping me process all of this." She nudges my shoulder with hers playfully but I can't ignore the pain that pulses through it.

"Thank you," I mumble.

We managed to complete the rest of our shopping in harmony. I fill my basket with what I need and she does the same. She doesn't push any other types of products on to me, which I'm relieved about. I still don't know if I'd have the guts to stand up for myself and say no to her. She's not scary as such, it's more that I don't know how she'd react if I said no. I don't have a good track record with things like that.

I lift my arm carrying my shopping as a semi-wave to Eleanor as I wobble outside and start the journey home. The bags are heavy, seeing as neither I nor he have run this errand for weeks now. I have to keep stopping and putting them down to catch my breath and rub my delicate fingers. They're purple where the handles have dug into my palms as I carried them. Every time I pick them back up, the bite in my skin is worse and even though it's windy, my eyes stream more than they normally would in this weather all the way home.

When I walk back through the door he's waiting for me in the kitchen. His large hands rest on the worktop beneath the cupboards I need to fill. He's deliberately situated himself in the way so I can't continue my chores until I've acknowledged him.

"Let's see," he snaps as he snatches the bag out of my left hand.

It takes everything in me to stand there with the remaining two bags in my right hand as I wait for him to ask me for them. He takes each item out slowly, inspecting it to ensure it's correct. He lines everything up on the worktop, exactly the way it needs to be put in the cupboard. I silently say a thank you to my past self for packing the shopping methodically like I normally do when he's with me. It felt right to do it at the time and now I know why.

Everything is to his standards, fortunately for me. I breathe a sigh of relief as quietly as possible when he unloads the final item from the last bag and places it on the worktop. His nod as he does so means he's appeased. For now, at least.

"Do you see how much distrust I now have for you?" he asks, demanding an answer.

"Yes, I do," I answer quietly.

His large hands grab my face between them and my eyes meet his. They look so hurt, even in the dim lighting.

"You really hurt me when you came home those weeks ago. And you hurt me more when you made me do this to you." He has the nerve to sound sorry as he gestures to my swollen body and dark bruises.

"I'm sorry," I say; I don't mean it but I have to apologise to keep the peace.

"You don't look it. You look like you're still the same little manipulator you were all those years ago when I first found you." He observes me as if he senses that, although I've moulded my face to look remorseful, inside I feel nothing at all.

"I *am* sorry. I'm tired and everywhere hurts," I explain, trying to lean into the regret he showed earlier at the state of my body.

"Okay, little crow. Go to bed." He nods, rubbing his thumb over my chin as he does.

I back out of the kitchen, my mind reeling as I watch him put away the shopping. This is a rarity for him to perform chores that are mine. It's definitely not something he'd do for me after I'd upset him.

Still, I wait until I've stepped out in to the hallway before I run up the stairs and fling myself under the covers on our bed. They smell fresh. He must have washed them after the disagreement we had in here last night. I can't even remember what it was about as I sink further into a bed he's remade for us. The comforting fact that he seems satisfied with me for now eases me as much as it can into a restless sleep. I'll have to wait until he joins me later before I can truly settle into the reassurance that I won't receive another injury tonight.

CHAPTER SEVEN

Present

S plashing some water on my face, I try to calm myself.
There was a woman. In the shop. It was as if she was
staring into my soul. The eyes almost dark holes
against her pale, wrinkled skin. I don't understand. Had
I drawn attention to myself? Had I been too conspicuous
picking up that bottle of mayonnaise? Did she know I was
following Eleanor?

I don't *understand*. I just don't know what I'm supposed
to do anymore. I don't look normal, act normal. I have to
get my shit together.

Fuck.

I can't really blame the locals for detecting I was a far cry
from their normal crowd. He'd chosen the smallest village he
could find to burrow us away in. Somehow I'd dismissed the
whole village gossip aspect of the plan. Small towns talked.
Newcomers were rare. Not that I'm *new*, but I've not been
seen regularly around these parts. That is the juiciest piece

of gossip for me to offer up to the retired busybodies that are too often found in shops or walking down the street. A strange newcomer with dark scraggly hair, beady grey eyes and horrendous baggy clothes.

I stare in to the sink trying to figure out what I can do next. Nothing. A big fat nothing apart from try not to sweat buckets next time someone looks my way. I can't fight the dark feelings that chill my blood about Eleanor. I still have to figure out what is happening there. With the similarities I see in her, I wonder if this is my opportunity for a redo. Not with me, but maybe it's my responsibility to identify those who share the same trauma, or are going to. Could I potentially be capable of helping someone like me? It might be worthy of a deformed type of therapy for me. God knows I don't warrant the normal kind now. The secrets and darkness that would spill from my mouth wouldn't be an easy pill to swallow for any professional.

One more splash of cold water on my face and I heave a sigh. There's not much left to do but go to bed.

I scrub my face with a towel and a shadow in my peripheral appears. I halt my movements and shudder. Not again.

Please don't do this to me.

A sob rips from my throat as I peer over the towel to look in the mirror.

Shiny, dead eyes stared at me with betrayal. The blood spatters still stand out against his decomposing skin, falling off the cheekbones I'd once been forced to caress. I heave almost silently at the image behind me, reminding me of my past and choking me with unbearable fear.

This is the first time I'm seeing his face. The first time he's looking at me through the mirror.

I'd escaped. I'd done what I had to do to prevent this monster suffocating me with fear every night. Yet here he is standing in the same bathroom I stood in all those weeks ago. The fact that I know this is most likely all in my head makes it worse. It's such a precious part of me but I can feel it breaking now that this is the second time it's conjured him up for me. As convinced as I might be that this is wrong, I still maintain the eye contact that he demands. My curiosity might kill me if my sight deviates from what's happening right now in this dingy, horrible bathroom.

He just stares. Cutting me with his anger, his resentment. He knows. And I know this torture is just beginning.

"I… I'm sorry," I choke out to him, tears burning a trail down my face.

I hate myself for that apology. I don't know why I do it when I know he's dead. He's not really here, not physically anyway. It's not as though apologies would ever work on him in the past anyway. The word sorry used to make him grit his teeth. I was a filthy little liar and a manipulative bitch when I expressed remorse. That was the only time he saw through my carefully structured facade. I knew he could taste the bile in my throat every time I did it. He'd find the struggle amusing but the delivery infuriating.

He doesn't respond. Doesn't even acknowledge the – I'll admit, flimsy – apology. I'm surprised at his calmness with my admission. He just studies my shaking form in the mirror as I watch him carefully. His patience allows the fear in my stomach to build.

The crawling starts to run wild, scuttling around, mixing a nauseating concoction of fear and anticipation in my belly.

An arm made of marred purple flesh reaches out and I

see it pass by my head in my peripheral. The tears dry up as fear freezes everything going through my mind. The arm is unsteady, fingers angled menacingly as if ready to tear my flesh mercilessly. I don't look at it, just continue staring into his eyes as they harden. His storm is well and truly upon me now.

The hand snaps up to my chin and pinches it between its fingers roughly. If I weren't already holding my breath, I'd be choking on air.

I let the hand guide my face slowly from left to right as he inspects my features. It's a manoeuvre I know all too well. He's checking for innocence. Any patch of skin that's escaped his brutality so he can aim for it next time round. It sickens him if I'm not black, blue, red or yellow all over. He can't stand to see any part of me that's avoided his wrath. It laughs at him.

I can hear the laughter now. It echoes through stale air. His hand clenches harder and I know he hears it too. I'd smile if it weren't so terrifying that, even in his demise, he's powerful enough to step back into the living world and blemish my skin again. I can feel how much more his fingers bite at my skin as his decomposing body shines through in his new appearance. His bones grind on mine easily with how thin both our skins are. Mine is padding out more now, though; he clenches down harder as he feels that as well.

The hand relents, moving downwards, but remains in contact with my damp skin as he finds he can still wrap his fingers round my throat. They settle at the base of my neck, the hand resting lightly on my collarbones. The softer touch sends a buzzing off under the skin he's touching and in my ears.

The crawling in my stomach intensifies.

I let out a breath steadily, trying to keep my chest as still as possible. It's a small relief when I realise I can take several small inhales and exhales without becoming a trigger for him. My eyes water in torment as I'm thrown back into a mindset and behaviour pattern I thought I'd escaped.

Just as I start struggling with silencing my sobs, my head is thrown back as the hand jumps and latches on to my neck with extreme force. Even when he was alive, he'd never had this much strength. It's so harsh and brutal that any sound I could make is cut off instantly and all I can do is silently gasp for air. My hands claw at the sink, trying to find something to help. I don't even know what would help in this circumstance. How do you fight the ghost of your former lover?

There's clattering as every available item I've stacked precisely on the countertop is knocked over in my struggle. Even in my terror I wonder if someone were to look through the small dingy window, would they see me fighting thin air or would they see him too?

I'm suddenly aware that my flailing body is rising. I'm also aware his grip is stronger than ever and I'm not sure why I'm still conscious. Maybe it's because it's not really happening. Maybe this is all in my head.

Then why does it feel so real?

Tears that have been building in my eyes now fall freely. Every time I blink I can still feel his hand trying to dig its way through my throat. I sob in anguish. Everyone is wrong about ghosts. They don't float through you when you pass, they tear you from the inside out. Although he's not broken skin, it's like he's inside my throat.

The crawling leaves me alone, I can feel it cowering from his violence in the pit of my stomach.

Traitor.

As I'm contemplating my last breath, so furious I'll die at the hands of him even though I'd made sure that wouldn't happen, I drop.

Although I land awkwardly, I maintain the position on the floor, unable to move a limb. I know he still towers above me, waiting for me to make a wrong move to pounce again. I feel his disgust radiating. I'm sure I'm hearing things when his signature sneer rings out above. The sound cuts like a knife and the work I've done to come this far shatters. My eyes are streaming now. I don't even blink to release my tears, they just flow freely. My little waterfalls of fear adorning my crestfallen face.

A significant chunk of times passes before the entity concedes, leaving me to heave silently on floor. Any loud, sudden noises could provoke him to come back. Every shudder wracking through my body feels like it's screaming out through the silent house. I've never heard the movements of this house so well until now, but my heaving covers most of the small creaks and bangs of the piping.

It's not real. It's not real. It's not real. It's not real. It's not real. It's not real. It's not real. It's not real. It's not real. It's not real. It's not real. It's not real.

It takes me a moment to realise I've been whispering those words aloud, not in my head. I can't seem to stop straight away. Eventually my mouth starts to slow. In turn, so does my brain.

I uncurl my body from its awkward position slowly, aches and pains finding me here on the floor. I have to bite my tongue to halt the thoughts in my head that I'm back to 'normal'.

This isn't normal, Lora.

I pause in shock.

My name. I've got my name back.

I laugh in shock. It starts with just one small laugh but then I get hysterical. The adrenaline leaving my body, the horrific shock of him still being here and the treasured moment of finding my name again.

The hallways rings with my laughter and I rejoice in how it bounces off the walls of my home.

The peeling walls and crumbling sideboards don't look quite as menacing in the moonlight now. Not when I can feel my happiness flowing out of me and infecting the walls that know my torment better than anyone. I can feel them sigh with me as my laughter dies.

I wipe my eyes with my palms, leaning forwards into them for a moment to calm myself. My hands then find the floor and I push off the ground. I can't stand the untidiness in the aftermath and quickly realign all my soaps and toothbrushes. They're not much, but they're all I have right now.

Once I'm happy with the way the products lines up in size order, labels facing forwards, I head to bed.

Tomorrow will be better now. I'm sure of it.

CHAPTER EIGHT

Six years and eight months prior

Something's wrong. Everything was going so well with him. The last four months have been so blissful. Every little worry and insecurity I've ever had, he's eradicated. I'd never felt so comfortable in my own skin with anyone else until he crashed into me and changed the way I looked at myself. I can't describe how incredible it felt when I slowly unravelled before him, and nothing threatened to ruin what we have. I'm completely unapologetic about myself and my incessant need to blend into the background has lessened considerably. I'm almost giddy with the thought of all the possibilities I've unlocked for myself now that I love myself truly. He's given me that and I will be forever grateful for what he's done for me these past few weeks. I sometimes feel like he's too good to be true, that he can't be real, but then he comes home to me and wraps me up in his arms and my body softens with relief.

At some point along this journey with him, though, something dark started lurking within our relationship. I've been able to brush it off so far as some possible trust issues from the crippling doubt I've lived with through the years of residing in a broken home. I've always suspected that it never left me these past few weeks, it was just simmering underneath the glow of my new-found happiness.

I should've known better.

Today, it feels the closest it's ever been to me. I can sense it's standing behind me and breathing down my neck. It doesn't strike me as something that I've manifested from myself. It's more a dark imposter biding its time, waiting for the opportune moment. Everything in me is telling me I should know what's to come and why it's here but I don't.

If I look back on the time we've spent together and how rapidly it's become a comfortable co-dependency, I can't pick out any moment where this awful feeling began. It's built up, little by little, over the span of our budding romance until I can feel it wrapping around everything we did together. I can sometimes hear a softly spoken warning floating around in my head after we've tumbled into bed and he's settled into a deep slumber beside me. In those moments, although I can't see it, I know as I look up at the ceiling that it's there, inches from my face staring back at me.

It's the early daylight hours now, and it's become the favourite part of my routine to watch the sunrise with a cup of coffee. He's still asleep in my... *our* bed now. It wasn't a planned thing but he kept leaving his belongings here until eventually he was practically moved in anyway. I can't lie that it doesn't feel nice having this house filled with laughter again and it feels effortlessly right to have made the next step. It crept up on me in the best way possible and his excited grin was infectious when he pointed out how we'd basically moved him in without knowing. I think that love happens like that, though; things fall into place subconsciously and so naturally that it's only when you look back that you realise how far you've come together.

Despite the sunshine reflecting the happy memories I'm sifting through as I look out to the garden, the coffee that was warming the palms of my hands has cooled drastically in a matter of seconds. I frown as I look down at the mug; the bright orange ceramic clashes with the murky brown liquid. There's a chill running slowly down my spine. It's not enough for me to shudder, but it's enough to cause some discomfort.

Before the goosebumps start to emerge on my skin, my personal furnace wraps me up in his arms and kisses my cheek. I smile as I continue to take in the sunrise and he quietly watches with me. He hums a soft tune against my neck and his hold tightens around me. Now the presence behind me dissipates, along with the darkness trying to seep into my contentment.

"Did you move the coffee cups?" he murmurs as his eyes sweep over the kitchen.

"Yes, they look better on the shelves above the coffee machine," I reply, my smirk never faltering.

His hands slip off my arms abruptly and I'm taken aback by how quickly the cold settles in my bones. As a reflex, I go to sip my coffee. I pull back at the cold liquid that kisses my lips in greeting. Even the mug itself is no longer a warm orange, it's almost a dark muddy brown. I frown at it for a moment, wondering if I've stepped into an alternate reality.

"They don't." A hard, firm voice cuts through my confusion.

I whirl around, eyes darting for an intruder, but there isn't one. My sight only settles on him, but he's different too. His eyes are a cold steely blue, his skin greying as shadows fall from his sharp features. My head tilts to try and find an angle where my lover doesn't look so demented, but it proves to be futile.

"Wh… what do you mean?" I stutter, too overwhelmed to process what's happening.

"It's rather simple. You made a decision about our home and didn't even ask me." His anger doesn't subside.

"I was only—"

"But you shouldn't." He cuts me off with a lift of his hand. I'm incredulous as my mouth slams shut the moment he does it.

Did I just obey?

The thought is almost laughable. I don't think I've ever done anything I didn't want to in my life. Call it 'only child' syndrome', but I'd never needed to. It was only me asking my parents for things. I had no objections from any siblings and I'd never had people close enough to call friends where I'd needed to be put in situations I didn't like. It feels foreign now to stand there, unable to try to explain myself simply from a lift of a hand and three sharp words.

There's a glint of a promise in his eyes that I don't want him to deliver on and I latch on to that fear of the unknown to lessen the unease curling in my stomach. I don't know why I instinctively turn into a timid little creature in a matter of seconds.

"Why wouldn't you speak to me about this?" His shoulders sag and his voice softens.

I feel a surge of guilt wash over me. The current of it swirling around inside of me is so strong, I have to blink a few times to comprehend what's happening.

"I… I don't know," I stutter, suddenly overcome with confusion as to why I wouldn't.

"I thought living together, we'd do things like this together, that's all." He looks hurt.

"I'm sorry. I want to do these things with you too." I reach for him but he remains a couple of steps away. He doesn't seem to have any intention of moving towards my outstretched hand.

The guilt intensifies as he looks down at the floor, off to the side. Anywhere but where I'm standing. I never thought my actions could offend him so much. Then again, there's a small voice inside my head telling me to give myself a break. This is the first real relationship I've had with someone outside of my parents. I've never been disciplined or conditioned to understand others' feelings. I need guidance and I need him to be that for me if he'll allow it.

"I don't mean to," I struggle to explain. "I don't want to upset you; I'm not consciously doing it."

"I know," he sighs.

My eyes water as he runs a hand over his face in frustration. I don't know how I can make this better or how to ease the anxiety and hurt I'm drowning in. I *need* him. I've been so happy. Happier than before my parents died.

He's still not making eye contact with me, no matter how much I silently plead. I can feel him building walls up around him even though he's right in front of me.

"Maybe we just need to find a way to ensure you don't upset me in the future," he murmurs. The thud of his feet as he moves towards me sound like a death march.

I nod my head eagerly, tears starting to spill from my eyes. I don't know what to say to that so I just press my lips together so as not to say the wrong thing.

When we're lying in bed later that night with my neck wearing his handprint as a necklace, I finally have the time to think about how strange it is that all this came from some coffee cups. I stare up at the ceiling in the dark and try to pick the moment I started to act unlike myself. It all happened with so much confusion that it's hard to recall what made me take the punishment and the violence without protest.

The darkness still hovers above me, only now I can feel its breath on my clammy skin. The fear I have spreading like wildfire through my body worsens with its presence. It might be in my head, but I'm sure I can feel its hand wrapped around my throat just like his was. The most alarming thing about this is that its hand matches perfectly to his. I try to find solace in the fact that the two of them can't be one and the same. He's too much of a calming presence and pillar of support in my life to be inducing the kind of fear this thing has.

But is he not the one leaving bruises on your skin?

The madness is setting in now; my mind has been bending to his will for months and the fruits of his labours are evident. My thoughts are heavily in his favour; they've even got hands of their own choking the life out of the last remaining sane ones I have. I can feel each one fade away as quickly as it surfaces. They don't stay long enough for me to doubt myself as I snuggle into his back and bask in the warmth of his fury.

CHAPTER NINE

Present

This side of town isn't much to most, but it's mine. The cracks in the pavements and the hollow earth where rabbits burrow. The breeze that caresses swollen cheeks in the cooler months. The bite of the thistles that leer over the worn path. These parts of the north I cherish now that I'm here. There's an innocence in nature I envy, but the proximity to it eases my heaving soul. I suppose that's why I brave the paths again today.

Although the darkness inside me reflects in the skies above, I find solace in the quiet. There are steady rumbles of a storm promising to engulf the shore, but that lingering danger feels comfortable. I'm beginning to think that peace is war to me. Am I not in peril with the things I've done? Am I not menaced by the things I've done to take my freedom?

No passers-by have plagued my morning pondering yet. It's a little unnerving how alone I am this morning compared to one only a week ago. I don't like too much presence on my walks but to have none at all is also unsettling me. The ground is so uneven on the coastal paths that I can't see much further ahead to see who else might be about. I'd take the awkwardness of the 'hellos' over this silence. I like it to be quiet and calm but something about how stagnant it is today is raising the hairs on the back of my neck.

There's another deep grumble that emits from the dark gathering clouds over the sea and my unease lifts. I've always loved thunderstorms. For as long as I can remember I've loved watching them from the warmth of my childhood homes, or even getting caught in the heavy downpours unexpectedly. Although rain hasn't fallen yet, I doubt it's far away. I smile out at the sea, picking my way through the overgrown path.

My shoes are muddy as I tread through drenched grass. I smile at the relief that I can be messy. I can be imperfect. Unworthy of him. I know I shouldn't, but I splash around in small puddles like a child, laughing in delight as my coat runs from beige into brown. A true masterpiece. It helps that this coat is one of his, so the sodden material feels like a victory in my recovery arc.

I settle quietly, walking the rest of the distance to the gate at the bottom of the field. My hands run nervously over my coat as a couple approaches. I can see their foreheads crease in confusion but they don't say a word. At least not with their mouths. I pretend I don't see the disdain weep from their eyes.

I wonder if they realise their silent judgements run the most red. I have killed for my freedom and feel lighter than feathers. They aim to belittle others with silent opinions and yet their insecurities will still weigh them down. I know that used to be me, but now, knowing how deeply secrets are buried behind kind eyes and polite smiles, I'll never judge again. That's the most cutting evil I've ever witnessed: underestimating or belittling what one doesn't know.

I suck in a breath as memories of curious onlookers invade my mind. My shaking hands retrieving groceries weren't subtle. Especially the night I followed Eleanor. Those greedy eyes still haunt me. People used to look at me like I was crazy. I am. But still, it's rude to stare at someone you don't understand. They will *never* understand. Let's face it, the only fucked-up thing in this town is me. They've never known a war raging like mine, never had to behead the monster under the bed that they thought wasn't real when they were younger. No, I don't think there is anyone but me suffering like this. Everyone else is a different shade of normal.

I make sure I lock the gate after me even though the couple stand waiting to use it.

Leeches.

I feel a little better as they huff in disbelief at my ignorance. I bask in it.

I decide not to swerve right and wander up the small tracks leading to the cliffs today. Not after seeing him there. I don't know what he wants. He's left me alone since that night in the bathroom. Not that I've dared set foot in it. It was *our bathroom.* So I figure another one is fine to use now. The mirror's been covered as well. I don't remember when I did that but I don't care.

I turn left, slightly back on myself as I head further inland to my destination. It's undoubtedly a longer way round to where I'm going but I don't protest at the aches that still reside in my body as I trudge on, hoping the journey's end reaches me sooner that I predict.

It doesn't.

I'm feeling worse as I near the butcher's. I can't stomach the supermarket after I nearly exposed myself last time. That, and I'm not willing to run into Eleanor any time soon. I only need a handful of small things to freeze to keep me going. I can't stomach normal portions right now, so my logic is half of what is counted as one will last me for two meals. That means half the load to burden myself with on the way back. It shouldn't be too difficult to carry it home with me.

That's a big fat lie.

One moment, I'm shuffling through poultry choices in my head, the next, my feet catch on flat tarmac and I stumble into a nightmare on the main street.

There's a woman swamped in crimson chiffon, black tangles spiralling from her head. The wind carries her stench of despair to me and the taste is heartbreakingly familiar. It's *me*.

I can hear a wavering cry of horror. I'm not sure if it's me or *me* that makes it.

There's a sort of mumbling rhythm to the cries that builds in my core. I'm not sure I can hear much over the ringing in my ears but each hum pounds on my heart. The force of each one almost pushes me backwards but I narrowly register my heels digging into the ground to keep me still. I'm not sure why that particular instinct cuts through. I'm not sure I want to be stuck here, staring at a version of me that shouldn't be here.

The crawling is digging its claws in as it climbs up my throat.

The skies dim, the darkness creeping into my vision as she blurs. The crimson fabric does little to hide the sinister way she's hunched up against the wall of the shop. The red and black is a stark contrast from the flaking white limewash wall. The way the red chiffon slithers over it looks like blood running. The sight makes me shiver.

My hair whips harshly around my trembling body but hers flows eerily as her face remains hidden.

The air sliding down my throat halts in its movement. I can feel the wind swinging my matted mess of hair around my face, but I don't know how. Not when I feel like I'm suffocating. The parallels of my frozen throat and my swirling locks twist uncomfortably in my gut.

Crimson movement softens and the sick way it flows around the hunched body terrifies me. Why is she the calm whilst I'm the panic? Aren't I the liberated one?

I look around for signs of anyone else and see nothing. Not even the usual suspects rushing in front of me with their long orders ready as they hurry into the butcher's and out of the cold. It's just me standing in the road, being assaulted by a vision I didn't ask for. I scramble through my muddled mind trying to understand why. *Why* is this happening to me? *Why* do I deserve this torment now? *Why* am I spiralling out of control when I've only just got it? All I can breathe is acid and all I can choke on is bile. I can almost see the smoke pouring from each nostril as I burn from inside out.

She doesn't move her body, but her head turns towards me. I can't scream or stop as my feet propel me forwards. I'm being pushed and pushed and pushed as my arms flail and my legs kick up loose stones. There's no preventing the distance closing between us. I'm moving so fast I'm terrified I'm going to collide with her completely. What if this figment or entity or whatever it is can do more than just draw me closer to them?

My body is thrown forwards suddenly, right before the crimson chiffon that kisses my eyelashes as it flows against the direction of the wind. It floats around my face, kissing each feature briefly. Some movements linger longer, the chiffon caressing my jaw in one long sweep, or when it slithers over my hair. It doesn't hurt or cause discomfort physically, but my mind takes every kiss, slither and sweep like a knife to my soul.

Sweat rolls off my upper lip and drops to the ground. I'm dripping in it from every part of my body now. It runs cold over my skin but the shock of the chill doesn't slice through the delusion I'm in. My whole body slows as my eyes betray my instructions to close. They rise upwards to the face I know is there. The in-life reflection that I can't bear to see. Small shudders run all over my chest before I even look upon it.

A single breath escapes from my lips. I wish I could breathe fire with the burn inside of me. The only fire I can see is in the wind, licking at my damp skin wherever it can. The contact is like bullets on my skin.

I see a soft jawline first, followed by mottled skin where lips should be. My heart jerks at the recognition. They look like mine. I don't want to keep going and I whimper as I can't help the trail my pupils paint on her skin. The nose is straight but you can tell it's taken several breakages before. A favourite sight for him. The more the face changes, the more satisfying. It shows him how many times he's moulded you to his liking. He could normally recount every event that causes each break. He thought that was impressive, but I remembered every break, bite, cut, kick and shove he gifted me with. I knew what the reason was for each bruise, scab, ache. I could describe in detail what he wore, what colour the sky was, what he used, where it was that he rained down on me. He wasn't impressive at all, he was just the same as me, only smaller because he had to use violence to get what he wanted.

The nose looks slightly different to mine. I can recall each bump and pale mark where the damage was done and I can't see them in the one before me. It's seen trauma for sure, but it's not seen mine. My eyes continue on despite my reluctance.

I crash harshly to the floor just as our eyes meet. My aches scream but it's not from the abuse they're receiving, but the horror of the eyes before me. My mouth is parted with silent questions as I try to process what is standing over me asking for help. Those eyes aren't grey like mine, they're a dark, dull green.

They're not mine. They're Eleanor's.

I stay frozen on the tarmac staring at the creature above me. She just stares expressionless at the body on the floor below her. My veins throb, wrapping under and over my bones in despair.

The crawling has reached my eyes now. I can feel the claws scraping my retinas.

I throw a forearm over my eyes and screw them shut to try to stop the noise drowning everything out. I remove it when I realise I need to see this again. I don't know why, but I know this means something.

When my eyelids retreat back, my vision is gone. Eleanor is gone and the butcher's shop is just a butcher's shop.

I push up off my elbows, heaving my torso up and over so it's bending over my legs and bring my forehead towards the pavement before me to ease my panic. The crawling descends back to settle in my stomach where it belongs. The jump of each throb from my heart eases so I can feel the scraping pain of my defective joints again. I welcome it.

My palms suffer as I push up from the ground sharply. I can't let people see me like this. I can't ruin what I'm trying to build now. Everything about this is telling me I should run back home but I can't do it. I've run from the outdoors once before because of him and I won't do it again now. Not when this is the most blinding clarity I've received in a long time. My suspicions about the potential trauma in Eleanor aren't unfounded. This is the last push I needed. I'm a loaded gun of unstable emotions and killer instincts, and this moment right here is the trigger to set off a chain of events to put them to good use.

When I step towards the rusting 'Open' sign, the voice singing in my head confirms what I know deep down.

Something is wrong with Eleanor.

CHAPTER TEN

Eleven months prior

We've run out of soup again. I stare at the empty shelf, eyes watering, hoping if I stare just a little bit harder, it won't be true. I close my eyes and count to three, but when I open them again, it's still an empty cupboard. More than that, it's a promise that I will starve again today.

But I've been so good this week.

It doesn't matter how well-behaved I've been, the point of the constant confusion around what I've done to deserve any form of punishment is how he strings me along. It keeps him unpredictable, which equates to him being as fearsome as he was the first time I ever saw him shrouded in darkness. I don't see him without the shadows swamping his body anymore. My whole mind is filled with every dark emotion and he guarantees my surroundings are a reflection of that too. Even on days when the sun shines in through the windows, I don't feel the warmth of the rays on my skin or see the light bounce off the walls in the small rooms of the house. I wonder if it's because I'm already half dead, one foot into the abyss of death, so that even the sun can't find me anymore.

My fingers twitch at my sides, eager to rip the cupboard door off its hinges and smash it to pieces all over the kitchen. My frustration grows more rapidly on an empty stomach and a painful body that doesn't know a decent night's sleep. I maintain steady, even breaths as I stand motionless in the kitchen. One sigh or huff of irritation and he'll descend from the room upstairs and break me into even smaller pieces. I can never show a negative emotion towards my situation. With the exception of fear, of course. Sorrow is an occasional luxury he grants me. I can let the tears simmer on my skin under his burning gaze. Sometimes it upsets him to see me upset, other times it seems to be satisfying. Even so, I take every opportunity I can to cry because I need an outlet for the chaos of my emotions. The dam breaks and the tears that have been pooling behind it burst out over the rims of my eyes. It eases the heaviness in my bones.

"Poor little crow. Her food supply has run out," he mocks quietly from his view leant up against the door frame.

"Do you need me to—"

"No. I don't *need* you to do anything," he glowers hatefully.

I should know better than to assume what he needs.

I bite my lip and nod quickly, ashamed of myself for landing myself in hot water with him so quickly into this interaction.

"You never have learnt how to be around me have you?" He sighs sadly. "Why do you make me paint you black and blue like this? Have I not been here all these years to teach you how to be good?"

He *has*, in a way. I admit at the start I was inconsiderate in some moments with him and I had a hard time learning how to be what he needed. Today isn't a good day for me though. My head pulses uncomfortably as I try to fight it, but in the end the guilt seeps through and pours out of my mouth.

"I'm really trying for you," I whisper, my lower lip wobbling.

"Shh, it's okay. You know I don't enjoy it when you cry." His hand strokes my cheek gently and my head tilts towards it without a second thought. "I just want us to be happy. I want the life we promised each other all those years ago when we first met."

I do too. Sometimes.

"I want that too. So badly." My voice breaks on the last word. I can't help it.

It's a sad and dangerous dream that I have, but I want the perfect life. I want happiness and ease being with someone who loves me despite my flaws. I would kill for the dream I had when I first locked my eyes on his gorgeous blue ones. Not only do I want to love and be loved in the right way, but the sick part is that the only person I see when I dream of it is *him*. I don't want it if he's not there with me.

"We'll get there. We're so close. You've just got to put your trust into what I want for you." His lips press against my forehead, sending a comforting warmth through my temples and down my body.

I lean in to him as he straightens, my head now resting on his chest cautiously. I inhale deeply, my nose pressed against his T-shirt, and let the smell of home wash over me. My tears dampen his clothes but he doesn't seem to mind. Still, I pull away before my nose starts to run from all the crying I've done.

"Why don't you head to the shops after you've cleaned yourself up and maybe that will make you feel better?" He squeezes my shoulders gently in reassurance before he leaves me speechless, rooted to spot.

Before he changes his mind, I've run into the bathroom to clean up and pushed out of the front door. I don't need a list. There are only certain things I can buy on my own and I have them memorised after so many years.

*

"Hello!" A sunny voice calls out to me as I'm standing in an aisle frowning at the new packaging on the soups I buy.

"Hm?" I react as I spin round quickly trying to find the person the voice belongs to.

It's the woman from last month, with the lush strawberry-blonde hair and big green eyes. She looks immaculate. All manicured nails, long lashes and porcelain, unblemished skin. Her smile is as striking as it is terrifying. She never slows her steps rushing over towards me. I try to remain standing in the same spot but the handle of the trolley digs into my back as I push back into it trying to move away from her.

She ends up a little too close for comfort but not enough that it makes other people stare. I'm always conscious of that. I don't need the additional eyes on me. One pair is enough.

"Do you remember me?" she urges.

I nod and she laughs in relief. She then launches into a story about her day as she scans the same shelves I'm shopping at for her own basket, which is hooked onto her forearm. Her gold jewellery glints at me, demanding my attention. There's a sweet smell in the air that's too sickly for me but I imagine it's the most sought-after scent on the perfume market. Everything about her presence oozes a confidence and femininity I've not had even before him. Nausea burns through my stomach at the sight of how pristine she is.

She's nothing like me.

We push through the fairly quiet shop together. Her beige heels fall into a steady rhythm beside my worn trainers. They're the same colour as the walls back home and my heart lurches at the sight. Eleanor carries on as she essentially follows me from aisle to aisle. I can see her gaze flick over the products in my basket. She fails to comment on the absurdity of the canned goods and long-life foods I line up neatly next to each other. For that, some tension leaves my body and I settle into this new 'thing' with a stranger as comfortably as I can.

"You would be so pretty with make-up and the right clothes." She stops me just before the checkout.

He thinks I'm beautiful regardless.

The statement, as well as the defensive thought I have not a second after she's said it, thrusts me into a whirlwind of emotions. My mouth hangs open as I look over in her direction. Never in her eyes, though. I can't look anyone in the eyes.

"And those shoes. Do you pick them out yourself?" she asks, her voice softening. I glance around to see if people are staring. None are, and yet I can feel eyes on me. I look down at my clothes and back at her multiple times, trying to find words or an action that fits the scenario I've found myself in.

"I need to go home," I mutter as I awkwardly sidestep around her narrow frame and scurry over to the self-checkout.

I clumsily scan through all my items. Every noise my shaking fingers make as I struggle to hold onto things feels like a siren sounding out through the store. My eyes water as I try to push through this one little task before I can go back home and fold up by his side. I can't go home empty-handed and I can't let him down, so, as excruciating as my embarrassment is, I need to complete the job.

Eleanor's words spiral around in my head. I know I don't look like I used to. I understand that my tiny new body means my old clothes I've worn for years hang off me awkwardly. Worst of all, I know Eleanor's the one person who's finally noticed I don't look okay and I don't like it. All those months when the assaults first began where I was desperately trying to get someone – *anyone's* – attention. Now that I have it from someone like her, all I can think about is running back home to the monster living in the house by the coast.

How far I've fallen.

Eleanor catches up to me in the car park. Despite my lighter body, I'm so weak from the lack of food that I can't carry myself very quickly over the dimly lit space to outrun her.

"I'm sorry. I don't mean to pry. I'm always talking about stuff like that with other people. I really didn't think it would make you so uncomfortable." Her car keys dangle from her freshly manicured nails as she speaks.

"It's fine," I nod uncomfortably. I give her a tight-lipped smile, which I know looks so weird to other people, but it's all I can muster.

"I don't have many friends that are girls." She says it simply as if it explains everything. It really doesn't for me.

"Okay," I nod again before I duck away from her and head off towards home.

I roll her words around in my head all the way home as I walk down quiet winding paths to my street. I didn't have many friends back before I met him. Every effort to forge friendships with others wasn't well received. I see my younger self in Eleanor. I know I needed someone to take pity on me and form some sort of companionship to appease my lonely heart. Eventually, the wrong person found me and I ended up where I am now. Too afraid to leave and too comfortable to even humour a plan for escape.

Eleanor, although I don't know her, needs me. I'm definitely not the right person for her to pick out in that supermarket, but I am the one who knows how badly this could go. I wouldn't do that to her. I wouldn't do what he's done to me. I'd make sure she was left alone to live her life with me there when she needed a chat when shopping.

As I come face to face with my front door, I come to a decision to humour Eleanor every time I see her. Offer her a very quiet, if not silent, companion. Somewhere, under all the layers of my mind he's fucked up, I can almost feel myself being a better person than I am now. I can't trust myself that this is what needs to be done, but giving myself a small purpose means I can push back at his manipulation. There's something else on the side that I'm doing solely for myself that has nothing to do with serving him.

When I eventually make my way upstairs to him after putting everything away, he's sunken into his armchair, staring ahead at the television like he does most nights. I linger in the doorway, waiting for a sign that he wants me with him.

His long fingers snap and then morph to point at the worn patch of carpet by his side. I jump to it and quickly scurry over to the side of his armchair. My legs tuck underneath me with ease at the recognition of the same routine we've been doing for years. When I'm sitting like this, my head is just as high at the arm of his chair. It's the perfect height for him to run his fingers through my hair as he watches the screen intensely. I, however, don't have the privilege of watching the TV. Instead, I stare at the floor, eyes half closed as his fingers comb out the knots in my hair. He never causes me any pain when he untangles it.

CHAPTER ELEVEN

Present

There are scratches on the wooden bed frame. I've been sitting staring at them as my coffee mug burns an imprint on my palms. My small, neat nails show no signs of trauma. I don't know what or who did it. It's not healthy for me to speculate, but I watch the shape of the indentations and try to picture how these occurred. There's a strong assumption it was him, but I can't confirm or deny. It makes me wonder, though. Was the stale, deteriorating body hovering over me as I slept? Leering over the side of the bed? It terrifies me to wonder but I can't seem to stop.

My arms are littered with the same marks. Some cutting deep but others only surface level. All the emotions I've left behind flood back. The fear of upsetting him, the terror of showing him how much it hurts, the struggle of how I continue to function as he desires, despite injury.

I clutch the mug harder, hoping the burn wakes me up from this limbo I'm in.

I've never been one to embrace the concept behind the paranormal. However, I know that normally ghosts remain when there's unfinished business. I'm willing to argue he has none that justifies him. I murdered him because he made me. I remember thinking that as I stabbed him.

This is what you made. This is what you created. These are the consequences of your actions.

I can't feel more strongly about how perfectly wrapped up his story is. He abused, manipulated, marred and destroyed women until one had enough. Heinous crimes deserve heinous ends. I can't understand why I'm the one being haunted when this is meant to be my paradise now. I know I deserve my freedom. I just *know* this isn't for him to tarnish.

Yet he does it anyway. I should have known with his wicked mind and sharp tongue he'd find me even from the beyond. Something keeps knocking on the back of my brain, urging my common sense to kick in and leave this place. It's not as though the thought hasn't crossed my mind.

The house is in my name. He was smart, unfortunately, which meant he was a nameless shadow that followed me. Completely untraceable. I remember in my early days under his thumb that his anonymity scared me the most. He'd appeared so abruptly in front of me, posing as the saviour I desperately felt I needed at a difficult time in my life. I was so misled, stupid and immature. Something he knew how to take advantage of. I feel so much pain and horror even now at how unquestionable he made himself. I didn't even worry for a name or an occupation. Not until I was already underwater.

The awful magnolia patterned wallpaper is peeling at the corners in most rooms. All the decor is a sickening murky beige. Everything we own in furniture is solid dark oak. Everything *I* own, even. I've had money to my name for years but not a penny in my palm.

There's not one thing in the house that hasn't been perfectly placed and picked out by me. However, by extension, this was him channelling it through me. I bought only what he wanted, stuck to decor that was common and inconspicuous. It was a huge difference from my colourful cluttered way of living before.

If I'd had my way, the walls would be black and the carpets red so I don't have to look at the stains I've made. The ones I'd scrubbed at tirelessly with nothing but a grotty sponge to hand and the salt water pouring from my eyes and on to the ground.

There's one room that I don't mind the blood in though. The room where I killed him. That patch of blood slows my racing mind. It reminds me he's not really in my room splintering wooden bed frames or grabbing me in the mirror at night. He's been sent to the depths, never to surface in body and flesh again.

I know I should fix the never-ending structure issues and clean properly, try to fix up the place, but I never feel up to it. I just like sitting in his chair, head held as high as his and staring at his demise on the floor. It's faded a little now but it still looks as brilliantly dark and red to me. I can almost see it boil, blood bubbling in the carpet with my manic laughter and victory cry.

When my knife pierced his skin, I expected blue. A cold-blooded snake like him should've bled oceans from his wounds. But his blood was thicker than I imagined. Darker, stickier, dirtier. As I look on at the greying stain inches from my toes, I can finally settle. I love that little mark of death; I'd even love it if it still smelt of his rotting flesh.

The crawler in my belly starts to stretch my organs apart as it wakes from its sleep. It's been suspiciously quiet in the night. Something I find discouraging as this is what makes me feel like my mind is sharp and my gut is right. I wait for the familiar pinch of claws as it starts its climb but the stretching is over before it starts. I almost feel its yawn as it settles back into its long slumber.

My thoughts spiral. The anxiety of everything being fine despite his fingernails carving my skin in the night puts me on edge. Something should be wrong; the pit of my stomach should have that wrong feeling in it. My crawler should be peering up under my bruises, asking me the questions I need to answer.

My coffee has long gone cold as it spills over the rim of my mug, splashing onto my leggings and oversized T-shirt.

When did my hands start shaking like that?

Why are my insides so silent?

Where is the sour tongue I choke on in anguish?

So many questions, so much panic, but it's not festering in my insides like I need it to. Almost like I'm only here in this moment on a surface level.

My coffee mug bounces off my toes and even the slight pinch of that doesn't feel right. It's not the pain I love, not the one that visits to kiss promises all over my broken parts and whisper that this means I'm still alive. Still surviving, still wanting to fight one more day. Not that I'll ever see my reluctant obedience as fighting. Not even if someone rationalised it to me. I know I've been dragged through hell. It was my choice to endure for seven years, my choice to let his hands plunge through my eye sockets and remould my brain to his liking. I sat there, legs crossed, dry eyed and allowed it. Maybe even welcomed the fact someone was going to make decisions for me. All of mine had led to situations where I was a terrible person. I think in the face of his terror, that's why I accepted it. This was my karma for my naivety and lack of forethought in my previous life. I hated myself so much in those final days that I thanked him for kidnapping and punishing me.

I know that there is one thing I'm grateful for after these years with him. I learnt my self-worth all over again. Understood what true deception and destruction looked like. Whilst I had been young and foolish, he'd been wise and cunning beyond his years. The knowledge, the control he had was like I'd never seen before. The way everything was delivered with precision, every word from his mouth was intentional. Every movement filled with quiet strength. Even a loving caress on the nights where he decided to 'treat' me to his affections oozed with the threat that those hands could just as easily wrap round my throat.

Ironically, his affections were what I hated most. They filled me with confusion and heartache. I'd mourned the dream of being saved by him the same day I realised he'd trapped me. Yet he had a cruel way of reaching deep within and pulling what little hope I had in him back to the surface. I think in those moments I truly felt weak. Those were the moments I knew I was lost.

It takes me a moment to realise my mind has wandered. The panic has eased with my reflection of the past and I'm thankful I have such a past that can pull me from reality so easily. I decide to swallow down the lump in my throat and not question the detachment of my emotions to my crawler.

My mind is so fragile from such intense emotions these past few years that I can't afford to be subject to another.

I sigh, heaving myself up off my throne. My aches still groaning with my movements. I wonder if I feel them lasting longer now because I've never lived in such comfort for so many consecutive weeks. Maybe all those injuries I had never did heal like I believed.

The bathroom is only a short walk down the hall. I suck in a breath as I remember this walk all those weeks ago on that fateful, freeing night. It's the first time I'm venturing in here since I saw him last. It's not something I want to face now but I have to start living like I'm not this haunted woman. He's not making me into something else from his castle in the underworld.

The mirror is still covered in a beige cloth. I huff at that stupid colour. I will never have anything beige in my life again. I go to yank it off but my shoulder screams in pain as I realise it's not budging. It's impossibly hard to pull it off the mirror. Not even the mirror shakes on the wall as I go crazy with my yanking. I ignore the pain it inflicts. That can heal later; I have a point to prove now and I'm not having anything in my way.

It's as I lean back to put my full weight into pulling it off that a hand threads through my hair, cupping the back of my skull perfectly. The size of the palm and the length of the fingers make my head feel tiny in its grip. Almost like a little china doll with how gentle the touch is. Each tip of a finger sends bolts of lightning through my skull. The tingles fizz down my neck and around my eyes.

I keep my breathing steady, trying to embrace the sensation rather than running from it. Perhaps my fear is the reason he keeps coming back. I just know it's him; no one else bothers me like he does in this room.

With my hair tangled in his palm, it's lifted the strands that cover my neck. It's purposeful, as suspected, as I feel his hot breath on my neck. I can sense his mouth move over the skin, lips a hair's width away. It's the building of tension that he loves so much. Nothing is right if it's sudden; there's more shock and horror in suspense. His fingers flex as he rearranges his grip and then he's tilting my head back slowly as I shake, unable to prevent the tremors in my body.

My crawler is creeping up my body, weaving in between my ribs towards my throat. I feel no relief in its return.

Then his tongue is on my clammy skin, my T-shirt ripped from my body so I'm left in just a small bralette. The contact isn't sensual, it's harsh and hard as he digs into my skin with his tongue, dragging it from the back of my neck to the collarbone. The occasional scrape of his teeth over my skin-clad bones makes me jerk slightly, but my head is pulled back harshly now as his hand retreats from my skull and grabs the fistful of hair in his palm.

The movements soften and so does the grip on my hair as small kisses pepper over the sodden skin. I know it's because there's a bruise there; he's showering the same skin he used to abuse with his affection now, but it's not welcome. It doesn't feel right. It's not a good enough apology. I don't think anything would make me feel like he was sorry enough for what he's done.

I'm starting to screw my mouth up in anger, readying myself to fight back, but he takes my strength from me cruelly. His hand returns to press flush against my head, long fingernails piercing my scalp; a small sound escapes through my teeth at the sting of it.

My eyes fly open as my head propels forwards at speed. I barely have time to notice the cloth from the mirror is gone and I can see his dark eyes glint just before my head smashes in to the mirror. The cracking of the glass works its way slowly from my bleeding forehead outwards. I breathe quickly, psyching myself up to peel my head off the mirror, but the air in my lungs leaves me as I realise his grip is still there, still strong.

It's a quick moment of realisation before he drags me off the mirror again. I can hear small shards of glass fall into the sink below, some even to the floor. Blood runs from my wound into my right eye. I blink trying to expel it but my world turns red instead. The next blink, I'm hurtling towards the mirror again, only this time I see his hand is no longer in my hair. The same patch of skin hits the mirror with even greater force. I grunt as it further mutilates my broken skin. The force means I bounce off the mirror and fall backwards clumsily. The back of my head hits the edge of the bathtub. I can see the blood staining magnolia thermoforming acrylic as I look up at it from my humiliating position on the ground.

Even though the bathroom is not particularly small, the whole five foot and six inches of me doesn't fit the span of the floor. My legs are bent awkwardly to allow my upper body to rest flat on the floor. I huff, annoyed. It's looking like an awkward manoeuvre to pick myself back up off the tiles.

The light-heartedness of my thoughts wrenches a sob from my throat. I can't pretend to be aloof to what's just happened. Like I've just had a fall due my own stupidness, rolling my eyes as I think about how clumsy it will be to untangle my limbs and dust myself off. My emotions feel the most unhinged they've ever been and I don't know how to control them anymore. I feel like I'm the kind of crazy that admits people into an asylum. I've been convincing myself this is just the realignment period before I emerge a normal human. That I won't be this glassy-eyed, emotional wreck forever. Now I'm not sure if I was lying to myself.

My joints groan is disagreement as I shuffle my body round so I can push myself up off the ground. My back creaks as I slowly straighten and roll my shoulders to alleviate the stiffness. My hand covers the slime left on my neck from his disgusting tongue. I wipe at it as best I can and try not to heave at the fact it remains even though he's far gone.

So, he really was here.

I tiptoe over the shards of glass on the floor, stopping at the door frame. I lean on it cautiously before peering down the hall to the room where he usually retreats to after the beatings. The armchair he sits in, nose turned up, nostrils flaring as he calms his storm. He does this like clockwork. And like clockwork, you can always see the flashes of anger in his eyes as his temper flares. Threats glint in his green irises for every wrong move I make. The most I've made it to is sixteen seconds before he's pounced. That was the time he thought he'd killed me and slid my shattered body on to the metal table in the workshop below the floorboards. I'd been there only a handful of times before, and waking up to every wall covered in clear plastic ignited a new level of blinding white fear in my soul. That was the day I knew I didn't want to die here.

I don't see any sign of him in the hallway or in the dark doorway to the living area. I hobble over to it, dragging my feet. I don't want this to be another encounter if I step into that room. The crawling that is still dancing over my heart seems to think there'll be something waiting for me in that room. Unfortunately, I'm inclined to agree.

The armchair, or my throne as I call it now, is unoccupied. The corner of my mouth twitches. That's one positive I guess. Seeing him in that chair now would certainly break me. Not that I care to admit it, but my mind is porcelain, and there are too many cracks to take another blow.

I lower my body onto the chair and wipe my eye. The blood in it is making it water constantly and I'm now aware that it looks like tears I'm not shedding.

"I see you've had time to think about the consequences of your own actions." A deep voice rumbles from the sofa along the left wall. I know the voice like I know the blemishes on my body. Extremely well.

I don't look at him in response, just grip the arms of my chair tightly and breathe through my nose. My anger is not something I need to bite back with now. Even if I am sure he's just a ghost. He's a sinister presence that can still cause me as much pain in his death as he did in life.

The sofa creaks and I take an educated guess he's leant forwards, elbows on his knees, his perfectly manicured hands interwoven in a sophisticated manner. I don't understand how this man has the ability to have even his actions sound as though he's put himself high above others. A pedestal I thought I'd kicked out from under him. It seems that I failed there too.

I can feel his gaze burn through the curtain of hair I've managed to cover my face under. I despise my glass mind and how easy it was for his fiery eyes to turn it to molten and shape to his desire. Now I cower under his stares, knowing they can see me at my most vulnerable, no matter what I use to hide behind. Deep down I know that's not logical, but it doesn't matter.

He sighs and I can see him remove his glasses and shake his head all too clearly. It's still only an assumption of his reaction as I don't move an inch.

"Do you know what disappointments me most?" he asks and the second creak I hear confirms he has stood from the sofa. "The fact that no matter how many times I remind you, it seems you are intent on believing the opposite, little crow."

I shudder as the nickname resurfaces. I remember the story behind it; funnily enough, it was a story I knew before meeting him. The reference to that story that resonates so deeply, ignites a fierce bitterness within me. I was once golden in colour, from hair to skin, now I am a walking image of death. Black is my heart and dark is my appearance. The paleness of my sun-deprived skin makes the dark clothes and hair stand out more. No doubt I am an eyesore to most.

I still bite my tongue even though I told myself I wouldn't anymore after his demise. It seems he's bringing out the worst in my old habits. It's probably his intention to confine me to the walls he crafted years ago that I've been tearing down with each passing hour.

"You were born into a fire of my creation, little crow, and I made sure your wings were broken that same day. There is no higher calling you can fly to, no sun on this scorched earth you can melt under into non-existence. I created this all for you. The perfect paradise to tuck you into." I can hear the tone of his voice change. The brutality of his words that he tries to hide in soft-spoken sentences. I hate him.

The crawling has climbed up into my mind now, trying to hold together the pieces of it that I've built brand new. It's no use, though, my head is spinning and the truth and the lies are shuffling and spinning round. The dizziness is unbearable.

"Hush now, don't cry." He tries to soothe me but it's a pathetic attempt. "It's just taking longer to break you in, darling. It shouldn't be long now, then this will all be over."

It's when the word 'over' leaves his lips that I jump from the armchair, claws out and aiming for his face.

I don't remember much after that, just that he disappears before me with a farewell smile and devious glint in his eyes. I hit the floor soon after and following so many hits to the head, finally the blackness takes over. I sigh in contentment as I realise this means a dreamless sleep.

Another thought hits before my eyes close that startles me.

I'm not sure anymore if I want to wake up.

CHAPTER TWELVE

Despite my will not to, I awake several times after that night. There's a heavy blanket of a foreboding feeling smothering me, making it hard to breathe through the twilight hours. The moving pictures painted on the inside of my eyelids are gone. No positive thoughts are left to cling to as I dream, so I don't. I'm grateful there aren't any night terrors, but I don't suppose I need to dream of those. Not when I wake up to the same one. Every. Single. Day.

I still feel far from defeat, as strange as that may sound. But then again, I've prided myself on how well I blend into a world of upside downs and spiralling sanity. So maybe it's not so strange that I still move forwards with that small glimmer of hope that I can get through the turmoil his ghost has thrown me into. Thankfully there are other things going on to serve as a much-needed distraction. I've still got that plague of concern overwhelming me when I think of Eleanor. Granted, with everything going on within these four walls, she's not my number-one priority.

However, I've made time to wander through the shops and cobbled streets where I can, trying to aim for the times in the day where I know she's normally there. Luckily, she is similar to me with her patterns. Darkness has to have fallen before she surfaces. Contrary to my best efforts, she's nowhere to be seen these days. I've not yet had the energy to let the impact of that hit me. The moments where I worry about myself frighten me, let alone her. I find it so hard to draw a line between what is selfish and what's normal. Every little narcissistic thought, where I worry more for myself than others, makes me wonder if I'm that terrible, fickle person I was before.

I'd never tried to be self-absorbed but I was fiercely independent and determined to work hard for my goals. Not that I had any idea what they were. I just found something I excelled in and propelled forwards from there. However, I was quick to swerve into something else when it appealed to me, wanting to live whilst I was young and try new things early in my life. The same applied with people. As soon as their morals and behaviours didn't match mine, I would quietly excuse myself. The hateful gossiping and incessant gloating used to launch me backwards away from friends and relationships.

Looking back at that now, it does cause a discomfort in my chest. My heart bleeds because it's now that I realise, as demeaning and terrible as those people were, my unwillingness to bend to their ideals meant I'd been left with no one to care for me. There's a small voice telling me that they wouldn't have cared anyway, but I ignore it. There must have been something wrong with me to have not maintained any lasting bonds with others. I'd always suspected I may have been built wrong, like some important parts didn't come in my box. I couldn't understand how far I stood on the outside of everyone else.

My relationships with men had been lacking as well. I was awkward and shy when men flirted openly with me but pined after the ones who showed no interest. If, by some miracle, the ones I took a fancy to did finally notice me and make an effort, I'd clam up completely. I was so out of touch, with no one around me to offer kind words of advice or slap some sense into me. It wasn't long after my hopeless blunders with men that he'd found me. I could never place why I hadn't cowered from his charming smile and ridiculously handsome face. Normally the better looking they were, the faster I'd run. Not with him though. He was a mystery as soon as I'd met him and as more pieces to his puzzle rained down on me, he became harder to solve. This is also what is ultimately my undoing with Eleanor. I'm so socially awkward and out of touch, I have no idea how to find out what's wrong with her.

Eleanor seems entirely different to me. That makes it more difficult to understand her story, as well as the beginning of her undoing. She was vivacious and forward with everyone she met. She'd strong-armed me into a companionship so quickly, I hadn't even noticed. A true master of how to be socially acceptable and adored by all. The small number of times we'd spoken, she'd sung her hellos to several people. The way their eyes had lit up as they noticed her had been telling. Eleanor was a bold fixture in this village, and both she and the locals alike loved it that way.

Seeing as I can't find her, I had thought it would be constructive to build a profile of what I think her predator would be. I'm no expert for sure. The only one I know is specific and moulded to me and what I respond to. It sounds straightforward: I just need to draw the line between what is a trait both would have, and what is one that will differ. It's harder than it seems as the growing pile of crumpled paper on the floor beside me shows. I've compiled a list of what my monster was made of, but looking at the blank page for hours on end struggling to comprehend another abuser like him is hard work. I'm a flailing little shy girl with nothing intuitive about me. Eleanor was the exact opposite and knew people like no one I'd ever encountered. I can't begin to understand the inner workings of her mind or how someone could manipulate it.

I can still recall how soft my flesh was as his talons dug into me. No hard exterior. No steel armour I'd layered over my heart and mind after years of betrayal. Not even a single wall built to protect me from the harsh reality of the world I lived in. I couldn't have been more of a let-down to women if I'd tried. I'd shown him exactly how facile it was to achieve his goal. No doubt I'd paved a way of hope for other sadists out there, waiting for a sign that their endeavours could be achieved with minimum effort. Although I feel his presence hover over me in this house every single day, it's the horror of endangering others through my naivety that haunts me most.

I tear the paper to shreds in frustration. I keep distracting myself with thoughts of him. It's been so hard to keep him out of them since the last incident. He invades every sense most days and I can barely focus on continuing to be my new self when I can feel that he's here living in the house with me. There are moments in my deepest despair, when I think I can see him sitting in his old chair – *my throne should*

I say – watching the same mindless crap on the television. I can even make out the reflection of the screen from the small parts of his glasses I can see from standing behind him. His face has a blue glow, the same one I was so used to studying when I sat next to his chair, legs tucked beneath me. I wasn't permitted to watch the screen, so I'd catch glimpses of blurry faces running across his glasses and watch how the glow illuminated his sharp features. He always looked so deadly then. A true ice-cold king with his slave knelt by his side.

By the time the memories have ceased taking control and I've lived through those years again, he's vacated the chair and I'm blissfully alone once more. He always leaves when I'm not focused on his translucent form. Not that I miss him when he's gone, but I crave the confirmation I can possess when I watch him depart. Infuriatingly, he knows me well and is enjoying the ability he has to keep that from me. My mind isn't doing well with accepting this new venture of his. It's not every day you rip out a beast's heart and find him still following you round months later. He's found a new method to send me still spiralling into that same madness. It's heartbreaking for me that I can feel that downwards plummet begin again.

No matter the dive my own situation has taken, I still have a task at hand to distract my warped mind from my problems. It's logical that I look at what drew Eleanor to me and go from there. If I build a person who would then appeal to her in the same way, it would write the profile for me. I'd needed assertion and a presence in my life that took control for me when I felt unable to. Eleanor is always in control. I think she was drawn to me the same way he was. She saw the vulnerability there that she could compensate for in the strange companionship she built with me. Her confidence was enough for both of us; my quiet, cautious nature exceeded my own enough to share with her. I would imagine she'd look for that in partners as well, potentially a man who would allow her to be the vibrant, sunny one. I was always the doom and gloom to her fair-weathered soul. It made sense that opposites would attract to an extent.

It's an unusual experience for me to think of being in her shoes when she was such a far cry from me in everything she did. In fact, the more I dwelled on what little I had learnt from her over minimal contact, the more muddled I became. It made absolutely no sense why she'd chosen me to accompany when she could have picked anyone. I was ugly, sickeningly skinny and unapproachable; her perfection and poise should have been repulsed by me. I wasn't exactly subtle in my nature. You could tell something was very wrong with me from the first glance. I didn't like the fact I was giving off that impression to strangers but, alas, it couldn't be helped. I couldn't have been more obvious unless I'd written trauma across my forehead to be honest. Funny how, despite my look, no one bothered to enquire on my well-being. It seems no matter where you are in this world, people are still more likely to ignore a problem than resolve it.

As I sit on the uncomfortable wooden chair hunched over my desk, I realise what I've been missing. It was only now I looked back that I realised the reason our acquaintance felt so odd was because she formed it for a specific reason. I may be overreaching, but my gut is telling me that this conclusion is absolute. Eleanor came to me because she recognised one of her own. She saw me as a victim and allied my battered body and mind with her own. She hadn't just started being abused;

she'd been neck deep in it from the moment I met her. She'd identified the common ground we shared and clung to it with a fierce hope that it would help her.

And I hadn't even noticed.

My stomach lurches backwards, knocking into my spine as the horrible actualisation of her situation punches me in the gut. She'd been crying out for help and I'd seen nothing. Heard nothing. Picked up on *nothing*.

I scream out in anger, throwing the glass on the desk at the wall. Clear, colourless glass shatters against that *fucking* magnolia wallpaper. Everything about this place drains the brightness out of me. I'm still as dull, dark and depressed as ever. Even the walls laugh at me now. Their laugh is just as bland as their colour. I swear I can hear him laughing too. Deep chuckles that rumble through the air dangerously like thunder. I don't want to know where the lightning is.

I'd been so wrong. So hurt, yet confident that I'd had a beaten mind but not a broken one. Now everything I'd known and held on to in longing had been pulled out from under me. I missed such a clear sign as to why she'd befriended me. I don't get it. I can't seem to move anywhere with this. Everything about this feels confusing and acerbic. It hurts how difficult this is and the agony gets worse with the revelation that I didn't know Eleanor needed me. My heavy breathing rings out loudly in the silence. I'm trying to slow my gasping but each lurch of my stomach makes my chest rises and fall unevenly. I can't even see Eleanor for what she is when she's stood right in front of me. I'm so, so lost.

The shattered glass winks at me from where it's scattered on the hideous cream carpet. It's got an awful yellow tone that has seeped through more and more over the years. Now

I can't stand the colour. All the colours in this place clash and look disgusting together. The yellows, grey shadows and the bright blues of the television screen when it's on. It all looks out of place and when the colours clash, everything just turns an unflattering shade of muddy green-brown. There are shades of fear and rot that I had never seen until my downfall. Ones that still adorn the four walls I've decided to remain in, regardless of how unnaturally messed up that decision is. Even for how sick and twisted I am, this is stretching the limits of what any person should put themselves through.

Looking back at the paper on the desk, it's still blank. I'm still at a loss as to what makes me appealing to Eleanor, except our similarities in suffering under the same evil. That doesn't contribute anything to how I look for someone fitting a description of her captor. I'm back at the same square one that I've been standing on through most of my life. When it comes to being something to anyone else but myself, I disappoint monumentally. I can't be the helping hand to Eleanor because I'm falling short on what I'm supposed to do. Like I always do when it's not all about me. It makes me question if it's because I don't feel the stakes are as high when it's someone else. That's not the person I want to be, but it's all that I'm capable of.

I clean up the glass instead of focusing on the task I can't complete. It seems easier to physically pick up the pieces of my destructive behaviour on the floor than the ones of my broken… well, *everything* I suppose. I scoop up the pieces with my bare hands. It doesn't hurt. I lost feeling in my fingers after he burnt off my prints so many times. My prints should grow back now, though, I'm waiting for that part of my identity to return.

The small shards roll under my fingertips, cutting my skin as they do. There are small red dots starting to grace the carpet but if anything, my blood gives it character. Morbid character, but still, it's an improvement. The red running from my cut fingertips still has the same comfort. It's got the same value of survival for me even though it's not him responsible for my wounds. Of course, this confuses me more because I shouldn't be depending on this like I had done whilst imprisoned. It's an adjustment, one that is larger than what I'd anticipated all those weeks ago when I decided enough was enough.

A piece of paper from the pile of screwed-up attempts catches my eye. My messy scrawl spells out the question 'Is there even an abuser for Eleanor?' I stop in my tracks, the glass still sitting in my palms. The question circles over my tongue as I read it out loud to the empty room. The more I sit on it, the more it starts to trigger more questions to circle around me. What if there isn't an abuser? What if she's not even being abused? What if I've just jumped to conclusions?

My brain moves a mile a minute as it hits me that maybe my crawler isn't my gut feeling, but my need to not be seen as the only one. This whole train of thought about me finding it difficult to adapt to this new freedom hits me hard. What if I'm looking at Eleanor all wrong? What if I just want someone to be in the same torment as me to latch onto so I don't feel so alone? It's no secret to me that I've been the most resentful of how much I stick out in this place. How different I am to everyone else.

My head is swimming in doubt and I can't pluck the comprehensive thoughts out of the water. The current is too strong and the way the snippets of my mind flash past my eyes makes it hurt too much to concentrate. The dizziness sends me to the floor, sprawled out on the ground, staring at the off-white ceiling. I'm not sure where the shards of glass went from my hands, but a small number of them sit wedged into the skin on my palms. I must've been clenching my fists at some point. I think that's the madness making me do that. It scares me.

I lie there for hours on the carpet, trying to understand my lapse in judgement with Eleanor's behaviours. It just leaves me with one thought.

Is something wrong with Eleanor? Or do I just want there to be?

CHAPTER THIRTEEN

Six years, two months prior

'm not gone yet. I'm not *fucking* gone yet. The purple of my bruises is deeper in colour today. My make-up doesn't cover them. It's almost laughable that I try to hide them today, but we're headed into the city centre to run errands together. I can't remember what for; all I know is, I don't drive. That means using public transport to get into town. That means people around us, people watching, looking. I need this. I need someone to see the bruises. I need someone to ask me if I'm okay.

I'm so fierce in my belief that I'll be out of this hell with him by the end of the day that I have to spend a few extra minutes in the bathroom to calm myself down. I can't skip out of the bathroom or bounce on the balls of my feet next to him as we wait for the metro. I need to be the same serene, calm Lora that I've slowly turned into since I let him turn me black and blue.

He's waiting for me at the bottom of the stairs, dressed cleanly, like he comes from old money. He looks up with a playful smirk on his lips as I descend down to the ground floor to meet him. A gasp lodges in my throat as I soak him up. His face, although dancing in the same shadows I saw six months ago when he left the first bruise on my neck, is heartbreakingly handsome. It's a face I would do anything for. I've never thought I would look for physical features over personality in a lover, especially with my past, but he conveys his mind, body and soul with his face. Love, warmth, light pours from him and it lights me up even when I don't want it to.

I try to swallow down my gasp but it stays right in the centre of my throat, mocking me. My small, pale hand slips into his tan one that he holds out for me expectantly. My cold fingertips warm alarmingly quickly with his touch and my whole body sighs in relief. I want to control myself, remind my body that he's the one that makes it writhe in pain, but it's useless. I'm lost in him.

His other hand reaches for my neck and I wonder in fear what I've done so early in the day to anger him. Surprisingly, the hand slips around my neck and pushes my blonde hair back over my shoulder. Right where there is a massive purple bruise sat upon my collarbone.

"Hm." He smiles and half smirks at it. It looks grey and dull under the mountain of concealer I tried to cover it with.

"I couldn't—" I start to stutter out an explanation.

"Shh," he soothes, gliding his fingertips gently over the tender skin. "It's okay. I know you tried your best." He kisses the corner of my mouth softly and I curse myself as my eyes flutter closed at the touch.

He takes my hand and guides me ahead of him to the door. I slip into a comfortable pair of shoes before stepping out into the street and waiting for him. He's behind me before I can let out the breath I've been holding since I pushed on my shoes and he remained deadly silent. He has a way of conjuring up a grave atmosphere around him without a word sometimes and it's the most terrifying thing he does. His hand sits on my collarbone and he pulls back the hair again so the bruise is on full display to the world. I start to get dizzy from how long I've held my breath for. I try to inhale but I can't. He's got me locked in this state until he says otherwise.

"Don't think I don't know what you're doing," he warns darkly, his grip on my hair a little too tight for comfort. His lips press against my bruise before he's gone.

I gasp for air. Luckily, the wind is so strong I doubt anyone can hear me over it. I choke and splutter as discreetly as possible with the panic in me rising. I'm in complete despair and spiralling as I stumble alongside him as we walk towards the metro. My eyes water and eventually spill out onto my cheeks thanks to how harsh the wind is. I can blame them on it if required.

He pulls me in sharply so I'm tucked into his side, my nose buried in the same beige coat I met him in. It puzzles me now that it's something that brings me fond memories and nostalgia rather than souring my stomach with the thought of how everything went wrong when I met him in it. I lean heavily into him, trying to show him some sort of reliance so I can lessen the beating I'm bound to receive later. He pinches my waist through my coat as an acknowledgement. I don't know what it means.

"Let's see how this goes, shall we?" His eyes are laughing at me as he asks me the question smugly. I look up at him confused until it hits me. He's talking about the bruise. The one that is so big you can see it peeking out from my undone coat and my scoop-neck top. Picked deliberately, of course. I'm no longer hiding.

My eyes steel over with determination as I scan the platform we're waiting on. No one looks over; they're either sipping on a morning coffee or reading a newspaper, waiting for the metro at this time. No matter. They'll need to look at me when I step on the train, no doubt.

As I step on, the wind lends me a helping hand and blows my coat open, revealing more for people to look at. My lips twitch, wanting to smile at the small victory, but I don't dare with him still firmly by my side. I turn towards him as I stand near the doors. Once the doors close and we set off for the next stop, I look around the carriage. Some people have noticed; a woman with her child gives me one look before focusing back on her child. Three young girls giggling in the seats next to us see me and stare, but all they do is look back and forth between each other before breaking out into fits of laughter again.

I hate those twelve-year-old little pricks.

I go to sigh in disappointment, but remember I'm with him, so instead I just huddle closer into him with my head down so I can't see what kind of look he's giving me right now.

Next stop. Someone will notice at the next stop.

A couple of older gentlemen get on; I turn toward them slightly, covering the manoeuvre up by acting as though I am moving out of their way. I practically push my chest out towards them as well. I don't care how fucking stupid I look. Their gaze lands on my bruise for a mere second before they move further into the carriage, trying to snag the odd remaining seat dotted around. I can feel myself deflating as much of the same happens with every other passenger who hops on.

As each stop passes by, I can feel the hope in my heart shrivel up and die. No one asks me if I'm okay. Not at the next stop, or the next or the one after that. No one finds time in their Saturday morning schedule to give a shit about a bruised girl with damp eyes and a quivering bottom lip. It's enlightening in the most painful way possible.

I can feel the huff of his breath in my hair as he watches on silently in amusement. They're all playing his game. They're flawless in their disregard to my broken state.

"Are you done yet?" he mutters in my ear, his hand on the small of my back as he guides me onto the platform when we reach our stop.

No. I'm not even close.

My determination has withered drastically but his words ignite a ferocity in me. I want to prove him wrong. I want to show him I'm not unsuccessful in this endeavour. There's a tiny hole in my heart that is telling me that this is going to end badly, but I refuse to believe it.

As we step outside into the bustle of the morning shoppers, I feel less motivated to try this time. We slot ourselves through the gaps of people on the pavement and not one person pays me any sort of attention. Their disregard stings: although I've never thought of myself as pretty, it hurts that I don't draw interest for an entirely different reason now. Maybe if I were more beautiful, they'd look at me and see the desperation for help in my eyes.

The first two stores we purchase items in start to carve out a pattern that's hard to swallow. Men and women who serve us or greet us as we enter definitely notice that something's wrong with my collarbone, but they choose to succumb to his charms instead of offering me a helping hand out of my nightmare.

The established pattern, of people's reluctance to behave the way I want them to, continues through the day until we're back at the house and he's shut the front door behind us. I peel the jacket off and hang it in the hallway. A strong forearm flashes in my peripheral and his hand wraps around my wrist, engulfing it entirely. He uses his grip to spin me backwards so I come face to face with his unimpressed glare. He looks even darker now, his dark rage oozing out around us, snuffing out the light that filters into the hallway from the windows.

"Well. How do you feel?" His teeth grind as he asks the question I really don't want to answer.

My mouth opens and closes but I can't get the words out. I can't lie to him and I most definitely can't admit how defeated I am to the person who wants nothing more than that confession. After a few seconds of heavy breathing between us, he pushes my wrist and slams it on the wall right next to my face.

"How. Does. It. Feel?" His grip on my wrist tightens to punctuate every word. The pain is unbearable but I slam my lips together so I don't let the cries of pain out. They make it so much worse.

"The longer I wait for an answer, the longer you suffer for. You should know this by now." His voice is taunting and playful.

He sighs as if disappointed but I know he loves it when I prolong these kinds of interactions. I uncurl my lips from between my teeth, trying not to gasp for air the way I want to.

"I-I-I can't say it," I half choke out. He's always admired my honesty.

From the way his lips curl as my head hangs in shame, I can tell he enjoys seeing me this way. Hurt and devastated. I feel more alone than before I met him. There's no one in the world who wants to help me. Not a single person from my old life before my parents died who would worry at the sight of bruises on my skin. Strangers don't care either. Today solidified that for me. People don't care about abuse anymore. They've learnt to mind their own business and the thing that hurts most about that is I would've loved people to have been this ignorant before him. I liked blending in with no nosy busybodies staring at me as I passed them by. Now I want the entire city to stare as I walk hand in hand with the most dangerous man I've ever met. But this isn't a TV show or film where the victim is saved before any real harm comes to them. This is real life and nobody gives a fuck about the victims here. I've given that startling realisation to him in the four words I've put out into the air between us.

"You say so much with so little." He sighs in satisfaction as he loosens the iron grip on my wrist.

I whimper quietly as my wrist is freed; my arm slides down the wall until it falls to hang by my side. His hand is suddenly cupping the back of my head pulling me roughly towards him. I stay there slightly off balance as he buries his nose in my hair and inhales deeply. He pulls back after a few seconds of awkward silence and I make the mistake of looking up into his eyes. They've darkened with desire. He's stripped me bare of my strength and now I'm soft and pliant ready for him.

My hair hangs over my face as he pulls me behind him, through the first door we find in the hallway. He twirls me round so we meet chest to chest. I keep my eyes low, focused on the hair floating around in front of me as I breathe out harshly through my nose. His large hand brushes the hair out of my face. He manages to do it with such ease, not even a strand remains falling over my face or tangled in my lashes. His hand stays firmly cupping my head whilst the other nudges my chin so I look up at him.

"There you are. All ruffled feathers and broken wings," he whispers.

I don't muster up enough strength to respond. What can I even say? He has me where he wants me and I'm not stupid enough to say no. I don't even know if I want to say no. He always knows how to turn a no into a yes anyway when it comes to this.

So I keep my eyes on his as he gently trails his hand down my body, pushing me back onto the desk my dad used to keep in the front room. The window blinds aren't closed and he smiles as my gaze lands on them, causing my breath to hitch at the possibility of someone seeing us.

"Eyes on me," he demands. He slots himself in between my parted legs, his hand on my chest keeping me in place. "You should only be thinking about me right now and all the things I want to do to you."

His hands come up under my top and I sit up so he can pull it up over my head. He uses it to wipe away the concealer over my bruise. The tender skin tingles under the material and I hiss at the roughness of it.

"Much better," he says mostly to himself. His fingers brush over several other bruises adoring my torso as they travel downward to remove my trousers. They slide off me with ease, as does every other item of clothing until I'm a naked, mostly blank canvas with ugly black, blue and yellow splotches all over my ivory skin.

"So pretty when you've been worked over," he mutters, his mouth dusting over each blemish on my body. He takes his time paying attention to every mark he's left over the past few months.

I know I shouldn't, but the warmth that spreads through my body with each kiss fills me up. I almost swear that each kiss makes the dull throbs of my injuries lessen enough to be able to focus on him rather than the pain. So, beyond my better judgement, I melt underneath him and succumb to this small taste of pleasure he's gifting me.

After however many hours it's been that I've been wrapped around him, he carries me upstairs, cleans me up and settles me on our bed. I notice something different. Little fingertips splattered over my hips all angry and red in colour. He's quick to pull the duvet up over me but it's too late. Even in those moments where he knows how to make my body sing and my heart to pound, he's marking me as his. As I recall our tangled bodies and how many times we fell apart all over that office downstairs, I wonder if the pain heightened my pleasure. I remember the pinch of his fingers on my hips several times. I even remember how exciting it was for him to come the closest to losing control when he gripped them like he couldn't get enough. I know seeing me surrendering to him and the game he plays gets him off, but the way he can't resist me when that happens is starting to feel like that's what sends me tumbling off over the edge with him.

Does that make me a masochist?

As I run my thumb over the marks on my hips and struggle to keep the smile off my face, I come to the realisation that I am. It also occurs to me that I'm only one for him. He's done this. Plucked at my strings and played me so well that I only dance to his tune now. I can't even bring myself to feel sick about how he's slowly making me thrive off the pain he causes me. My blood pounds in my eyes as I drift off. I'm losing more of myself with each day that passes with him, and I've no way out.

CHAPTER FOURTEEN

Present

The cobbled streets are especially slippery in the rain on this October morning. Dawn has long since broken on the horizon as I finally dare to leave my sanctuary at the later time of seven thirty. Now, forty-five minutes later and I'm flinching at every set of eyes my harrowing appearance attracts. I had hoped they would just have got used to the oversized coat hanging limply off my pale body and the same baggy bottoms I wear. It seems they haven't. It's not like I have an abundance of clothes to adorn my newly evolving figure with.

I'm hoping that I can catch a glimpse of Eleanor somewhere on these streets. It was evident from my failures at finding her that I needed to break my routine to discover if she'd broken hers. So far, the only thing I was achieving was extreme discomfort and making a spectacle of myself. I had no idea why I was willing to put myself through hell for this woman I barely knew, but I just pushed on anyway.

I suppose last night's revelations, that she was a potential victim too, spurred me on. I can't seem to forgive myself for missing that; I'm not yet sure if it's due to guilt or frustration. If I can't find her today, I know I will hesitate to do this again. This time my selfish nature didn't bother me so much. There were only so many limits I could stretch in my recovery period. This entire experience being one of them. I'm not ready for this level of exposure.

It's difficult for me to raise my head to look at passers-by, having to meet their curious gazes with my own. I have to, though, otherwise I'll miss something. There's a thread here that needs pulling; I can feel it weaving through the cobbles under my feet. I just need to find the end of it, pull it up through the crumbling sealant, sending stones flying. It should create the untidiness I need to shuffle all these puzzle pieces into an order that suits my comprehension. I just can't seem to put my finger on where or what I'm looking for. I'm *so* close, but I'm so unaware of what I'm close to, I keep losing it as it sits on the tip of my tongue.

The wind whistles harshly in my left ear as a particularly uncaring, busy local rushes past me. The catch of his shoulder on mine startles me and hurls me back a few paces, both physically and in regard to my fear of the outdoors. The innocent act, albeit quite rude, reminds me of the capacity for violence in every person walking this earth. It almost sends me into a black hole of worry and doubt. Perhaps being out here, amongst so many unverified faces and bodies hovering about my presence, is the stupid thing to do. The constant agony of wondering if my desperation to solve Eleanor is clouding my better judgment is excruciating.

I come to the end of the street. Well, the end of the shops that line either side. There's now a downward descent into private buildings and housing. I've never set foot down there, not that I can recall anyway. The small white, cream and red brick buildings all loom over the pavement in a charming way. The foliage around doorways, climbing up the wall and framing windows, is all beautifully trimmed. The leaves haven't yet turned brown but you can see the beginning of autumn colouring the edges of some.

I can't comprehend why, but the view before me looks dark and dangerous even as morning sun glints off the windows. The street looks beautiful; it's the perfect picture of how a rural, coastal village street should appear. There's nothing that's discolouring my vision, but all I can feel is dark grey as my sight line runs over every little detail in front of me.

The crawling awakens in my stomach and I know that as soon as I continue downhill, I'll find something that terrifies me. I press on anyway. Fear is not an emotion I'm unfamiliar with, so why not drown in it one more time? Every interaction I've had so far with Eleanor has unpacked a whole list of questions. Call it a misled need for finding a resolution to this, but I need to push on and face my fears. I need to know what's going on with Eleanor and why everything in me screams that I should be *paying attention.*

The cobbles slip and slide under the worn soles of my trainers until eventually they fade into flat tarmac. My calf muscles are thankful for the transition. They've been pulled, stretched and used way too many times this morning alone as I tried to manage uneven ground for such a long period of time. The constant wobbles and slips worried away at my weak ankles. They can't take the weight of my shaking legs most days so I'm sure some muscles have been sprained during this particular escapade.

My footsteps echo down the street. It's not as though it's particularly early so it does raise a brow when there's no sign of life down here whatsoever. I trudge on with my feet slapping loudly on the ground to try and carry me gracefully down such a steep decline. The echo starts to grate on me after only a few steps. It's like a huge siren beating down on me, reminding me of how alone I find myself now, even here, where there should be people milling around.

There's a flash of hair billowing in the morning breeze that I catch as it disappears past a perimeter fence on an especially pretty cottage. It's tucked between two larger homes that somewhat tower over it. However, the gorgeous white walls and trimmed rose bushes decorating the small path up to the front door mean it shines through despite its rivals either side.

There's a small body strutting up the path with quiet confidence, hair swaying in time to each step. I can tell just by the sound of her heeled boots who I've stumbled upon. It's Eleanor. Judging by the way she pulls the keys out of her pocket and unlocks the door, I've not only found her, but also her home.

Of course, this pretty, perfect little cottage belongs to pretty, perfect little Eleanor. Although she is slightly taller than me, I still stick with the first analogy. There's no drive for her car but I remember from when he made me house-hunt round the village that most homes supply parking at the back of the properties to keep up a certain aesthetic.

Although she doesn't own one, I can imagine she'd have a pristine little picket fence out here if she could. The whole outside view emits a dreamlike innocence which seems so much of a contrast to the personality I know. Eleanor was one that revelled in attention. Being her companion for those short moments outside of my prison had damn near beaten me again once over. The constant attention and spotlight she commanded when she walked through the aisles used to whiten my knuckles on the trolley.

I suppose, as I take in the house again, it is a striking beauty amongst the rest of the dwellings I can see. It certainly drew me in when I saw it. With Eleanor, I begin to understand her motives and how they're mainly all centred around appearance. The cottage looks like something picked out of a holiday catalogue. There's a stiff, controlled preciseness to how it's laid out here on the street. The roses almost look like they've been painted in vibrant pinks and whites. I've never seen roses look so clean before. The more I look at the small details, the more the house looks like one that Hansel and Gretel would've have fallen for if their interests had been small, quaint homes with stunning foliage. However, Eleanor is no witch, she's a victim. *Maybe.* I'm trying not to jump to assumptions, so the jury's out on that one still.

I'm grateful that there is still only me left outside. There's no one else to witness me doing something crazy, like stalking a woman who I could probably just ask what the problem is. The numerous windows surrounding me all look clear of the nosy neighbours that seem to collect and spread in these areas. It's not a thorough, one hundred per cent confirmation that I'm not being watched, but I push forwards anyway. I don't want to be out here much longer as the crowds build. Each minute passing is an increased chance of it being more crowded when I head home.

The front door is a gorgeous rich brown with black masonry. My fingertips gently brush over the keyhole and the knocker, exploring the beauty with touch. My bottom lip quivers as I process the fact that it has been my dream to call this kind of house a home. Instead, I live in a cold prison I can't escape. The thought of having to leave the walls that cheered as I killed my dream crusher just defeats my plans to move. It was as much my entrapment as it was my freedom. Whichever one of those meant I clung sentimentally to the property was a mystery. In an ideal world, I'd be living there and doing snow angels in the bloody carpets just to spite him. In truth, I was trying to separate myself from negative emotions regarding anything now, having been poisoned by them for several years. That prison, no matter how ugly, witnessed my first glimpse of positivity and I refuse to let it go. Now what I crave is the warm glow of contentment and long-awaited peace.

Shaking my head out of my selfish thought trail *again*, I push on the door gently and much to my surprise it swings slowly away from me, a view of an equally pretty and floral hallway emerging into my line of sight. Although it's poor weather all around outside, there is a warmth that feels like sunshine lighting up the rooms from within. It's devastatingly beautiful and certainly provides a clever cover to hide a more sinister evil lingering below. If that's what it's meant to do here.

As I creep down the hallway, I see the door under the stairs that's been left open. There's no light offered from the cellar that it leads to. As soon as I take the first step, my surroundings are covered in thick cloaks of black. The musty damp smell is worse than the one in my own cellar and I gag on the stench as it hits my nose with more strength the further I sink down into the depths. The staircase is steep and narrow and it's difficult to master with no railing for support. I lean heavily on the walls so I can ensure my footsteps are light and, more importantly, silent. I can't give away that I'm here or that I've trespassed on Eleanor's home without her knowledge. It looks crazy enough that I've been following and hunting her down these past few weeks let alone this on top. I silently say a quick thanks to whatever is giving me the good fortune I need to continue my endeavours undetected.

There's a creaking, almost like a rocking noise coming from somewhere behind me as my feet find the cellar floor. I keep my fingertips on the wall as I walk around and back on myself to find the source of it. There's some sort of light flickering faintly as I tiptoe further. It illuminates a shadow, although just barely, and I'm right. The shadow is rocking in and out of the light in a steady, panicked rhythm. The closer I get, the more unsettling this all becomes. It's too close to home for me, but I can't seem to order the thoughts in my head to understand why. As I get closer, there's a steady murmur I can hear as well. It's deep in tone but lightly spoken. The only way to describe it is as a guttural whisper.

"It's all meant to be. It's all supposed to be. It's all going to plan." I can hear the same three five-word phrases on repeat. The words sometimes whispered, sometimes spoken as the voice wavers on each syllable.

The pounding in my head, which started at the same time as this unsettling feeling in my stomach, increases in urgency. When I take a final step forward with the toes of my trainers touching a small candle on the floor, I see the cause. Eleanor is in a curled heap on the floor, pushing forwards and back on her heels in order to ease her flustered state. Her hair is still perfectly curled but pushed back off her face. Her face is still intact. She looks perfect except for the eyes that can't focus on anything and the swollen red puffiness around them.

It takes me a moment to figure out how this is the scene I've walked in on. It couldn't have been long enough after she entered her house and I followed her inside. How has this managed to happen so quickly?

I decide to focus on her instead of that question. I can always analyse that later in the safety of my own home. As I crouch down before her and observe her form more carefully, I sigh at how drastically different she looks in this predicament than I did. There isn't any discolouration on her skin, no sunken flesh around her pretty doe eyes or a collarbone that sticks out from the skin as high as Mount Everest. No, she's still beauty and grace in this moment. I know it shouldn't do, but it makes me sick.

How dare she look so stunning in the face of terror?

It's then, as my gaze slowly takes in the sight of her, my nose scrunched and lips pursed, that I realise I'm a terrible person. Absolutely awful. I know exactly how wrong I am but it doesn't stop the sour taste in my mouth that I crave to spit into her face. I'm not entirely sure why I'm like this, especially when my entire motivation has been to help her.

Deep breaths, count to ten.

I give in to the intrusive thought and reach out to slap her cheek. My palm stings, but her skin remains unblemished and the rocking continues. It's almost like she's having an episode. She's completely ignorant to my presence. I look around trying to grasp the situation in front of me and count one, two, three, four, five candles. I huff at the humorous thought she's put herself in a pentagram. It pisses me off that little miss perfect has put an odd number of candles around her. Even numbers are neater. The candles aren't scattered around her evenly in a semicircle. Well, sort of; there are three in front of her and the last two are sitting at each side of her hip. Luckily, it's not witchcraft, I think. I have the ghost of an evil incarnate haunting me; the last thing I need to happen is for this woman to whip out a Ouija board. It occurs to me that I have yet to understand what the candles are for and why she's lit them this way around her. It would have taken time, and yet she's in this dreamlike state that doesn't match the previous action. Maybe it's her abuser? Putting her down here with the candles as some sort of punishment or routine? It's bizarre at the highest standard. There are so many missing pieces to this puzzle that everything is messy and illogical.

The floor I'm crouching on is covered in thick layers of dust but I can't see any footprints illuminated by the light the candles offer. Not even my own as I turn to look behind me. The creases in my brow deepen further. The constant wrinkling of my forehead is going to give me a headache later. It's apparent that I'm not confident in my ability to deduce what's going on here in this cellar, because the more I take in, the more crazy it becomes.

I decide that maybe the tiny candles are my answer and concentrate on them. The flames lick at my toes as they're burning down the wick. I wonder how long before they burn out completely and she's enveloped in darkness. Will she still rock then?

There's only one way to find out.

A singular blow from my lips snuffs out the lights on all five candles. It would seem impressive, if I had the space in my head to feel that way right now. There's too much going on before my eyes to fathom anything else.

The murmuring stops. Eleanor is slowly coming out of her trance – if the creaking becoming less frequent is anything to go by. The noise is quite gruesome in the pitch black. My promise to not feel fear remains steadfast and I ignore the foreboding feeling that's creeping into my bones. Squinting into the darkness does absolutely nothing to help my vision; as logic would confirm, darkness is still darkness. The creaks draw themselves out, long and slow. Only now do I notice that a rocking motion shouldn't creak unless it's from something like a wooden chair, so what's creaking? I shudder at the thought that it's her bones making those wretched groans. The shudder continues to travel down my spine before it stops. In turn, so does the creaking.

A breath escapes my lungs and it's all that manages to leave me before claws bite into my throat, squeezing my flesh between long fingers. My head is thrown back by the force of it. I try to grab at the arm but it doesn't let up, just remains as it is, suspended in the air as it punctures through the darkness to grasp my neck. There's now a small stream of sunlight in the room but no windows for a source. The impossibility of it wakes up my crawler and I can feel it pushing back at the claws around my neck, doing its best to loosen the grip on my neck. No matter how hard it pulses in my throat, the fingers remain sunken deep into my flesh.

I let up, forcing my body to go lax as I give into the fact I'm unable to fight my way out of this. It's a version of 'play dead' that I put to good use when I became his plaything.

Disgust ripples under my skin as, once more, the behaviours I no longer wish to possess are now present without his force. It's me who wants my body to act like this, not him. To my bittersweet relief, the action works and I feel the grip loosen. I inhale sharply as I take in as many gulps of air as I can manage. The hand retreats back into black and I manage to remain standing on my feet, albeit stumbling slightly. I brace my hands on my knees trying to tidy my scrambled mind as I catch my breath. I'm aware something is looming over my hunched form, watching my every move. There's an overwhelming suffocation of *something*. I just can't name it. What's more, I have a feeling that, once I do, there's a devastating truth to uncover.

As I pull myself upright, straightening my shoulders so I stand as tall as I can, I catch sight of someone standing before me. Only they're taller by a few inches. The silhouette would be ambiguous to most, but to me, every curve and line of it looks exactly like the person it is. I've had years to understand the way he can exude darkness itself in the brightest of places, but in the dark, he shines. The crawling starts now on the outside of my body. Little spiders and centipedes scurrying over my pale skin, weaving under my clothing. Each tap of their legs typing out a morse code of their own.

You didn't think it would be that easy did you?
Did you really think he'd let you go so easily?
Why are you acting like you're free?
Your freedom will never be yours to control.
You're still in your prison.

I remain as still as I can, my eyes now the ones that are running left, right, up and down as I allow myself to give into the fear biting at my heels. I'm not just scared, I'm *terrified.*

My eyes ache as I try to strain them to see far into my peripheral. I can't turn my head for fear of upsetting him. Just as I think I might be seeing something lurking from behind, he steps into the light before me. The light I don't understand. The one thing in this infuriating, hostile cellar that I can't logically describe away.

The light comes from above and casts a dark shadow over his features, sharpening them. He looks more gaunt than I remember. He could fit right into a Tim Burton film if he had any charm in that grimace on his face. His eyes are black holes of inescapable fury and my eyes burn as I gaze into them. He stands right before me, his chest almost touching mine. My neck aches as I look upward, unable to look away from that face. He's never stood this close to me without bending his six-foot-five frame to meet my shorter one. He liked to crouch or lean or bend to my height as a preferred way to assert dominance. This, however, seemed more powerful than the other methods. I stand my ground, determined to show my new-found power and match his own. The left corner of his mouth slowly curls upward into a gruesome smile, his eyes twinkling in amusement at my efforts to deter him.

It's not working.

He takes a forceful step forwards, pushing his chest into my own and sending me falling backwards. I'm fairly certain a small gust of wind would've had the same effect with how fragile I feel. His hand catches the front of my coat before my back hits the ground. His thumb and fingers run over the material and I watch as the realisation hits that he's holding his own coat. I'm wearing it as a sick sort of trophy and he knows it. His other hand slowly reaches out towards my stomach, his cold fingers finding bare skin. I pull both my lips between my teeth, breathing heavily through my nose as he trails his fingers down further. The same process begins again when he thumbs the material of my joggers. His as well. He knows what this is, what I'm doing, and when I look back up at his face, he *loves* it.

I don't realise his nose is almost touching mine until it is. His hot breath on my lips startles me with how real this all feels. I know this isn't right, but I can't seem to remember why this is a delusion of my fractured mind and not reality. He hooks two fingers into my waistband, pulling my hips upwards towards his own. My whole body arches more and my feet lift, my body still bent back, mid fall, as he refuses to pull me upright. My toes barely remain on the ground, slipping as he fists the material in his hands to hold me closer still. His body is folded at ninety degrees and in turn he's managed to fold me backwards to match. My thighs are now pressed against his in an awkward, painful fashion.

My head hangs upside down staring into the gloom behind us. I do my best to keep my gaze there, trying to focus on how the shadows move rather than the pain and submission he's reduced me to. I welcome the sensation of blood rushing to my head, a good distraction.

"I don't think you're as immune to me as you think, little crow." His voice is low, menacing and *something else*. "I think there's a masochist in there somewhere who revels in my attentions." His hand lets go of my joggers and flicks my temple to accentuate his point.

I gasp in horror at his assumption and try to squirm my body away from his. He holds me steady where I am, until he releases both his hands. I let out a small scream in horror, falling towards the ground again before both large hands find my hips and yank me so I'm plastered against his body. I grunt in shock, not sure how I've managed to be pulled upright at the same time, nose nestled into his shoulder. My eyes peek over his firm body but all I can see is black still, no way to escape.

"Shh, it's okay, little crow, everyone has a darkness inside them. It's okay if you enjoy it." He soothes me but it doesn't calm me even in the slightest. Tears spill from my burning eyes as he rubs my back.

I don't get a moment to compose myself before he leans back, pushing the hair from my eyes and doing a poor job of wiping the tears from my face. He pouts mockingly at me as my upper body starts to shake. I cry harder and harder as he watches, enjoying the show. It took him seven months from the day he met me to make me cry, and since then, even though he does it frequently, he likes to watch my tears fall every time. He says he considers it one of the greatest achievements in our time together. Abducting and torturing a woman shouldn't be whittled down to a simple 'time together', but that's what he calls it.

His hands move up to my waist, taking the hem of my baggy T-shirt with them. I silently thank my past self that I put one of my own on this morning, not his. He doesn't inspect the T-shirt like he did the coat, which I realise now is not hanging off my shoulders.

Where did that go?

His fingers bounce off my protruding ribs and his hands climb higher. Since killing him, I can't seem to gain back the weight I lost and he's laughing at it every time his fingers knock against one of my ribs. His thumbs dig into the flesh just under my ribcage to further the point he's making. He's pushing down at the flesh to make my bones push against my thin skin even more.

"You're so beautiful," he whispers, in awe as he stares at the body he's created. The decline of nourishment he's caused. He's looking at his masterpiece.

My eyes look upward to the ceiling and more tears burn as his hands climb higher still. The unwanted nostalgia floods back and overtakes my body as I remember those moments in my darkest hours when I'd revel in his affections. His attention to every curve, every bone that stuck out more prominently than when I'd met him. He'd caress and kiss each one, muttering his approval and admiration as he went. Although I knew it was only about him and not me, I'd been so deprived and so *tired* of being beaten. It felt so heartbreakingly wonderful to be adored, in any form. I battle with that same need now, but as I lose the T-shirt and joggers to the darkness, I lose everything. Oblivion comes to me and I welcome it happily.

I don't come back round until I'm alone, panting on the floor, shedding more tears as I come to terms with how lost I truly am. My sobs echo in the dark cellar, but now I can see the dim light spilling from the door at the top of the stairs. I'm not drowning in darkness anymore.

It's then that I'm reminded of why I'm here in the first place. It's not about me.

The singing in my head starts again.

Something is wrong with Eleanor.

CHAPTER FIFTEEN

can't face my reflection anymore. I'm sure I never really could, but now that I've been pulled underwater again and enjoyed it so, I can't bear to look into the eyes of a traitor. Not to mention the bruises on my hips, neck and ribs. The purple clashes with red and it looks ugly at first, and then almost comforting. I can't control my emotions anymore and they're betraying me at every turn since I visited Eleanor's house. I won't go near the cobbles, now that I know what happens after them. I've steered clear of anything familiar to Eleanor as well. I can't bring myself to plunge back into her mystery after what's occurred. Everything is too dangerous for me and my health now. I used to think that I'm not mentally sound and proud of that. It's logical that I wouldn't be after what I've endured, but I draw the line at that. Nothing further.

Please nothing further.

I've moved bedrooms. I can't sleep in the bed knowing it's more of the same messed-up emotions. The sheets don't smell like him in the spare bedroom. The wallpaper hasn't absorbed his musk, allowing his scent to linger in the air above me. I've masterminded that his scent amongst other things could be to blame for the hauntings. That's why this week, I emptied out the entire kitchen cupboards of all the cleaning products and used every single one until the last drop. The floors have been mopped six times over. The cupboards have been emptied, cleaned and rearranged four times. I had to keep revisiting the organisation of foods and products when the orders reminded me of him. Eventually I settled on categorising them and turning the labels away from me. Labels facing forwards is my obsessive compulsion but it was a trait of mine he let me keep as my own. It unnerves me that I've gone against it but I want everything to be opposite. It's the only way I can exorcise him out of my life.

My eyes burn sometimes when I walk into the rooms that used to be our most used. The chemicals I'd emptied onto the walls and floors were extensive and the fumes still linger. It's humorous to me that the place is cleaner than when I'd murdered him. Others would be more inclined to believe I murdered someone now, with how obsessive I've been over the last few days. I dedicated a full twenty-four hours to each room to ensure I'd gone over it enough to guarantee excessive cleanliness. The fumes made me sick some days but my heart and soul felt happier the more I persevered. The bed rest after was worth it; not only that, but it was nothing compared to the torment I'd feel when his ghost visited me. A trade I could live with. I remember that I smiled as I threw up my stomach contents. I guess there is happiness found in everything if you work hard enough.

There were small moments of complete insanity, when I looked at the bottle of bleach in my hands and wondered if I should drink it. The darker thoughts in my head are scaring me now, but I can't stop from straying to the darker corners of my mind. It might be easier to end this all now. I'm not living the life I promised to myself that night in the bathroom. I'm haunted by the man I killed, the abuser I beat, yet I'm still his toy to play games with. The only thing that shook me out of my contemplations of death was the hope that the new cleaning endeavour would work. Now that the task is done, I feel happier. I possess a high amount of optimism for my future.

Today, I've opened the windows to let in some air and ease the intense scent in my home. The crisp air that swirls around me makes me feel like I've got a fresh start in the making now. The walls don't look so drab anymore either; they've faded from an awful yellow tone to an almost sharp white. The floors shine and the carpet is a soft brown now. I'm so thankful the only yellow I'll see now is in autumn leaves and sunshine. That's the only place it looks perfect to me, and that's how I want everything to be now. Perfectly perfect. I want to make this home exactly what Eleanor's was, except more like a warm, welcoming, lived-in home. Not the eerily still perfection she revels in. There are some shades of perfection that chill me to the bone and her house is a prime example. My abuser's presentation of himself was also a sickening type of perfection I would be grateful to never see again.

There is, however, the matter of the bloodstain in the sitting room upstairs at the end of the hallway. The one with my throne. The sticky patch just in front of it is where I killed him. With all that's going on with him haunting me, that dark stain is the only thing that gives me the confirmation he's dead.

After making sure every window is cracked on the upper floor, I head downstairs. It's not used much as he didn't want prying eyes of busybodies trying to catch a glimpse of what went on inside our dwelling. Our lounge is one of the bedrooms converted, the kitchen is at the back of the house so we still used that. I don't like the kitchen much, even now. Not that any normal person would observe this, but the kitchen is the most dangerous room in the house. The knife block, gas hob and heavy pots and pans. Each inflicted damage on me in the past that is irreparable. The trauma of each injury still lingers in that room.

I stumble into the kitchen, blindingly reaching out for a cupboard handle. I'm still lightheaded from the stench of bleach. Finally, I grasp the cool metal handle and yank on it. I'm met with the sight of all my cereal boxes and baking ingredients facing forwards, glaring menacingly at me. In my shock, I jump back and end up leant back up against my kitchen island, breathing heavily.

Wait a minute, kitchen island? When did I get one of those?

My fingers spread out behind me slowly, trying to understand what material this is. It feels glossy and smooth, which is nothing like the worktop I have. I have matte-grey, textured worktops in my kitchen with cream cupboards, don't I? I lean heavily on my left arm and use my right to push my hair out of my face. As I look up, the products are still staring at me, their labels perfectly level and looking right at me. Only, the cupboards aren't cream, they're white. There's no way I cleaned them that well the other day. No, they're completely new. With black hardware. The cold metal I felt earlier was the new handles, not my old chrome ones. It's then that I turn around to inspect the island behind me. It's small, with a shiny black worktop covering it. The kind of material that you'd easily see a single speck of dust on in certain lights.

When did I get a new kitchen? When did I redesign this room?

I don't remember having the space in my head to even think about renovation. I hadn't even looked at getting a phone or a laptop yet. I wouldn't do this. It's only been three months, not enough time for me to start making such drastic changes. I don't like it. I like the old kitchen with the creaking doors and dull greys. I wasn't ready to part with it. I made my first meal all by myself in this room not so long ago. That was without a pair of eyes lurking over my shoulder. Now it's just a memory and the slate has been wiped clean. It feels unnatural and unwelcome.

It's not right.

It's as my eyes roam further that I notice the figure in the room. The long locks curled round a tall, slim frame. The perfectly fitted clothing her body is wrapped in. It's like they were tailored for her. The sunlight shines through the patio doors like a halo over her head, making her features from her shoulders and upwards a dark silhouette as she turns to face me. She steps forward with her hands wrapped around a mug that I don't recognise. It's a gorgeous rustic mug that I wish I'd had the courage to buy myself under his watch. The bottom half is a matte finish in an off-white, with a pale-blue ombré glaze on the top. I swallow down the sadness I feel on watching this woman take ownership of my kitchen in the way I wish I had.

She eventually comes to a stop on the other side of the island opposite me, her body now blocking the light completely so I can see who has intruded in my home. The straight white teeth and plump lips give her away almost instantly. Why is Eleanor in my home? And when did she do this to my kitchen?

"Don't you think this is so much better than that disgusting hell hole you were living in?" she asks softly, almost affectionately. The tone mixed with the brutality of her words is misleading to the fragility of my mind.

"What do you mean?" I whisper, trying to keep the hurt at bay. I blink rapidly as I feel my eyes start to water. "I... I liked it the way it was."

She smiles in a way that should convey care but all it does is patronise me. My words have fallen on deaf ears. She sighs mournfully at my inability to give an acceptable answer. My bottom lip wobbles at how lost I feel. In my own home as well, of all places, and she feels comfortable enough to insult me. The thought sets off a siren ringing out through the silence. I realise as she inspects the worktop in front of her, brushing off bits of imaginary dust, that she's in my home. Uninvited.

"Eleanor." She ignores me, still inspecting the kitchen decor. "What are you doing here in my home? I've never told you where I live." I feel more confident now, the annoyance directed at her monopolising my emotions.

"God, look at those fingerprints on here already. This worktop is a policeman's dream," she mutters to herself. Her brow furrows slightly before it goes completely flat. I can almost hear the creases flattening out on her forehead as the room goes silent and cold.

Eleanor takes a shaky breath; her mug is placed on the worktop cautiously. Her arms have a weird tremor running up and down them. My head tilts as I watch her posture and body language shift. Combined with her unsteady breathing and the slow curl as her shoulders hunch over, I know exactly what that metamorphosis into a new persona means. She's sensed him too. Her eyes lift slowly to look up directly behind me. My back tingles as I realise he must be standing exactly where she's looking. It's her turn now for her lower lip to wobble.

I turn to look behind me. I've faced his ghost so many times now, I don't have the energy to fight against the inevitable. He'll fall into my line of sight one way or another, why not control it as much as this small action allows? It thankfully turns out not to be an anticlimax because his presence behind me is non-existent. I let out a laugh of relief, in doing so releasing the breath I'd been holding. I shake my head. What am I even doing, acting like I'm being haunted in front of Eleanor? Do I want her to be the last person in this village to think I'm crazy?

I turn around to turn my attention back to Eleanor. "Sorry I…"

Eleanor's not there anymore. Nor is the sunshine streaming in through the windows.

His taller, more menacing figure stands in her place, his large hand resting on the island as he smiles at me. There's so much darkness in my heart and head when he's around but now even the rooms lose light when he visits. My anxiety is always morphing into a black hole of terror and hatred when he resurfaces. I'm dubious whether I can stomach this in my life for much longer. I've had seven years of feeling completely and utterly flattened under his thumb. Seven years of these emotions weighing down on my frail bones when I can't even carry the weight of my body, let alone the burden of my trepidation. This is too much pressure on my glass mind.

I shake my head as the tears that were threatening to fall earlier finally burn the familiar trail down my cheeks.

"Please, just leave me alone," I whisper. His smile widens manically.

"But why would I want to do that, little crow? You're so close to being exactly where I want you." He trails his fingers on the worktop as he rounds the corner of the island to get closer to me. I cling to my edge possessively, refusing to move or show him any signs of how close to falling I am. My fingers are hooked under with just my thumbs on the top. They're almost white from the pressure of how hard I'm pressing down on the counter.

His fingertips rest inches from my thumb when he finally stops. There's only the corner of the recently acquired island in my kitchen that separates us.

"What do you mean?" I whisper up at him. I don't understand what he's talking about. I haven't done anything differently enough to warrant that I'm being moulded into something for his purpose. If anything, I've been banging my own drum for months, heading down a pathway I'd carved out for myself.

"You don't see it, do you?" He curls his forefinger and uses it to hook under my chin and tilt my head upwards. The thumb pulls at my bottom lip; his mouth twists in disappointment. "I thought you were smarter than that, little crow."

I frown. He thinks I'm smart? Since fucking *when?* This man has ruined my self-worth more times than I can count. Taken my purpose from me and made sure I knew I'd never amount to anything but something on the bottom of his shoe. I've had years of infected wounds and mind-bending to become his ideal woman and somehow I'm now smart?

How dare he?

I push at his body trying to throw him off me but he remains standing firm. Not even a small shift in position for the finger under my chin. My face remains set in pure hatred and disbelief in his antics. He uses his finger folded under my chin to manoeuvre my head around, his face inches before mine to inspect it. A deep chuckle sounds near my ear. He's laughing at me. His throat is so close, I can feel the vibrations as chuckles rumble up it to escape from his lips. I hate how well I know him. Even though I can't see it I know exactly how his smile looks as he laughs. I even know what his throat looks like in this moment as well. I can see his Adam's apple bob under his clean, smooth skin. Not a blemish on there; even in death he only looks hollowed out with some of his features. Much like I do.

"My, my. I almost thought she didn't have it in her anymore. How mistaken I was." My eyes widen in fear. I can't believe I've shown him anger. An emotion I don't have the privilege of being able to express in his presence unless I want to be victim to his chaos.

The hand that's currently under my chin creeps round to the back of my head and I know what's next. I screw my face up ready for the inevitable impact. The last scrunch of my eyelids barely finishes before he pulls me forwards and down, smashing my face into the countertop. The loud crack and the searing pain in my face and my eyes confirms he's broken my nose again. He holds my head there, pushes it in further to emphasis his disgust. Then his hand is gone and it doesn't feel as cold anymore. Maybe that's because my blood is so warm.

I sink down as my upper body slides off the worktop and crumples on top of my folding legs on the floor. I rest my head on the cupboards in front of me as my blood pours from my nose. I don't bother to wipe it, just let it run red rivers onto the new tiled floor that I never wanted. It tingles and burns as it runs down my nostrils but at least it's not inflicting further stinging. I rotate my head left at a snail's pace to see his legs still there before me. They blur as tears pool in my eyes but refuse to spill over. Even in my state of shock, I know this is different. He normally leaves when he's won.

I must be fading in and out of consciousness because suddenly his legs are gone and his face is now in my view. The edges of my vision are even darker than my surroundings and I know that means I'll pass out soon. My nose is still pouring blood and his face is smudged. My ears are ringing so I can't make out his muffled words either.

Before I can try to decipher how to get myself out of this scene, an elastic band snaps on my brain and he comes fully into focus. He grabs my body and hauls me in front of him so his hands are on my shoulders. I can't quite hear him yet, but the vibrations on my ear drums are more prominent, which makes me assume he's screaming at me. That or he's just very loud. Loud enough for my ear drums to shake uncomfortably.

My crawler is rattling around in my head trying to decode the vibrations for me but I feel so far gone I'm not sure I'll survive to hear what he has to say. Not that it will be anything I'm longing to hear. I don't have any expectations of what I want from him. There shouldn't be a single will or motivation in my body to want to know what he so desperately is trying to convey. His hands are cupping my head from the back of my skull, his palms covering my ears, and the ringing stops.

"Tomorrow, you're mine."

I muster enough energy to flail out of his arms and land on the tiles. My back screams. The ceiling above me fades to blue, then grey and finally black as I pass out, choking as the blood pouring from my nose shoots back up from the motion of my fall. As it burns back up my nose, I choke and splutter. I don't have the energy or the want to try to stop it. If choking takes me before he does, so be it.

CHAPTER SIXTEEN

"Time to wake up," a dark, low voice whispers in my ears. My eyes snap open and I'm staring at the same ceiling I passed out under. My eyes scrape painfully; I can feel the spiders sitting behind them scratch on my eyeballs with their long, needle-thin legs. I wish they'd skewer straight through them at this point. I don't want to experience any more fear-inducing scenes as they play out before me. I'm tired of feeling more trapped by him in his death than I was when he was before me in warm flesh and blood-filled veins.

My neck and back ache from the movement and my face screws up to suffer through the pain as I take in my surroundings. I turn to my left and prop myself up on my elbow, surveying the hideous new decor. My body twists further left, so far that my right arm now rests a shoulder's width away from my elbow, preventing my upper body from clashing with the floor again. The position is awkward and the discomfort of my twisted torso screams. Unfathomably, the pain is longed for by my spiralling mind.

Awful situations such as this crave emotional turmoil and my anger serves me poorly, giving into the frustration it has orchestrated within me. For some inexplicable reason, I repeatedly purge emotions like this with my own infliction of physical abuse. Even more so, I did it before I was his.

The throbs of pain slow and fade off, allowing me to place my focus back on the room itself. I wasn't dreaming or imagining this change. The kitchen remains the same as it was. I pant heavily as the panic sinks in; the house is *wrong*.

It takes several minutes or maybe a couple of hours, who knows how much time passes. I can't even process if it's dark outside or just dark because I can feel he's still in the room with me. My brain is foggy, probably from the blood loss. I can feel the blood crusted around my nose, lips, chin and all over my cheeks. My face looks like a bloodbath of the sinister kind. It seems only fitting when it was done by even more sinister hands. I'm standing, or leaning may be a better word, on something but the room spins and I can't make out what. My head spins as I push off from whatever counter I'd been using as support and I head through the house.

As I step into the front room on the ground floor, I'm blinded by bright florals and ebony upholstery. A prim, proper sort of room that would be enviable to the busybodies peeking inside from the street. The huge bay window has been cleaned and repainted. It's now so easy to see through into the house, I may as well hook up a live CCTV feed to my living room for the whole village to see. *I hate it.*

I use my shaking hands to wipe at the blood that's long since dried all over my face. The sprinkles of it that I dislodge from my tingling skin flutter onto the new floor and the way they tarnish the new carpet gives me small satisfaction. But the room is still *wrong*. Upon that thought, my unhinged desperation takes complete hold of my functionality and a plan is executed. The letter opener on the new side table slices my palms open, the act painless. As more blood pours, I make use of it. The walls and florals are smeared in maroon. The last throw blanket I manage to grasp is taken with me as I continue the journey through my home.

The hallway is all sunlight and ornaments. Not once has this hallway been so bright. On my way to the stairs, I viciously whip the throw at the ornaments, revelling in the sounds of the broken pieces crunching under my bare feet. The feel of jagged pieces burrowing into my soles stings, but I enjoy the pain. It's no matter to me anyway. They've seen worse.

My free hand slides up the bannister painting a pretty pattern of specks and spatters as it goes. The pieces of pot and ceramic thud softly on the carpeted steps as they dislodge themselves from my sole. The landing is my main focus as I see my whitened cream walls have been replaced by dark blue. Blue?

Blue is all wrong.

Blue blends too well with his darkness and is the one colour he basks in when he's here. Blue is his colour. Why is *my home* in *his colours?*

Finally, I'm on the landing, bloody footprints proving my arrival. There's more blue and stupid little side tables with those wretched ornaments adorning them. I pick up a small stone ornament; I think it's meant to be a contemporary version of a human figure, maybe? The rough surface scrapes along my cut as I launch the decoration at the wall. It's breaks into three large pieces and leaves a spectacular dent in the wall. The pale cream colour underneath is showing through. It's not anywhere near the level of untidiness I wish to cause, but it's a promising start. I move on forwards. There's much more to do.

My bedroom door slams against the wall as I kick it open. My dark hair billows off my lips every time I breathe. My room doesn't have a bed. The clothes I'd kept folded in small piles on the floor are gone. I drop to my knees. Blood still drips off my fingertips, the soaked throw discarded beside me. More blue. I crawl forwards trying to find a speck of dust or a patch of brown carpet that looks like mine but fail miserably. My eyes water.

The entire room is empty and, by default, my existence. The walls are that awful dark blue and it's making the corners he hides in more ambiguous. There's so much darkness in this room now. So much of him painted into the walls I'd scrubbed clean. No matter the work I'd tirelessly done to erase him, he had a way of returning back tenfold.

I push up off the floor, red outlines of my palms left in the now almost white-grey carpets. I slam my palm on the wall, furious. My palm stings but the feel isn't as brutal as it needs to be and the splatter on the wall around my handprint isn't as much in disarray as it should be. So, I pound on the walls, maroon flying, blue turning to brown as I punch, slap and scratch at the walls. Once the appropriate amount of soiling is done, I move on with purpose. I need to see what else he's done, how far he's gone.

Every room I storm into enforces the same ear-pounding, gut-wrenching affliction. His laughing face burns in my gut with every stab to my chest. The stereotypical vivacious colours and decor are stirring up nausea in my stomach. There isn't a piece of me left on any of the four walls I stand within.

The living room feels like a hand has punctured through my skin and bone and wrapped around my stomach. There is no television, nor his famous armchair.

My throne.

I stand in the exact spot where it would have been. I can almost feel the ghost of the seat cushion around my legs as if the soul within it remains even if the actual object doesn't. The walls in here are red, so my blood unfortunately can't taint them.

Blood.

I look down to the bloodstain I always stare down at from my throne and find it gone. The grip on my stomach relents and it falls fast and hard to the floor.

"No, no, no, no, no, no, no, no, no, no, no, no, no, no," I mutter anxiously, clawing at the new carpet, trying to find a shade of red that I'm not inflicting myself from my bloody hands. The small fibres that loosen stick to my skin and under my nails in my efforts as I dig helplessly.

I don't know how I manage it, but it's as if I will my hands to dive under the carpet and pull it apart from underneath, and they do exactly that before my disbelieving eyes. I don't have much time to comprehend the action as I rip the carpet back a few paces and then run back to the patch where his blood should be. The floorboards underneath shine in excitement as they watch my face fall. They are as pale and brown as I had greatly feared. Not a drop of blood has spilled over them.

This can't be happening.

I remember killing him right here. I remember the blood as it soaked the carpet underneath him. I recall the uncomfortable crunch as I wedged the blade into his stomach further. Each layer of organ, vein and flesh making its own sound as it was sliced through. It would have *had* to have stained not just the carpet but the floorboards underneath. Why does this house now not know the metallic taste of death?

I know my reality is slipping away from me. I scrape my nails across the floorboards as my fingers scramble to pull away more carpet. No blood. *Pull.* No blood. *Pull.* No blood.

I fall back, a silent scream in my throat as the mass of black moves over the floor. I can feel the long legs hurry over my damp skin as they crawl out from behind my eyes, the spiders that sit behind them now crawling over the carpet in formation. They start tittering in amusement at me as they start to double, triple and then quadruple in numbers. The sound is almost melodic. They nearly completely cover my bare legs splayed out on the floor in front of me. I scramble back, eyes wide and my body shaking in fright. The laughing gets louder and the crawler in my stomach wakes up.

Something is wrong with you.

I shake my head violently in denial and run out of the room, brushing off as many spiders from my arms as possible. I flick away a small one dancing about in the blood on my palm, shuddering in horror. The door swings shut with a loud slam and the laughing stops. I halt in my movements, body still hunched over from inspecting my hands. My heavy erratic breathing is deafening in the silence of the hallway.

The walls are still slanted before me. Sometimes when I'm particularly traumatised by his abuse, my vision is compromised. The walls blur in front of me, the edges of my sight darken. My eyes burn but I crush the heels of my palms into my eyes to prevent the tears.

It doesn't make any sense.

"Confused, little crow?" He's leaning in the door frame to what once was our bedroom with a devious smirk painted on his pale, deadly lips.

My mouth opens to answer but I close it. I can't engage anymore. He probably keeps showing up because I'm reacting to him and providing good entertainment. Instead, I look away from him. He laughs and I can hear his arms unfolding from his chest as he stands to his full height. His boots fall heavily on the floor as he approaches. A gentle hand trails from my shoulder to just above my elbow and guides me towards the doorway along the wall. I gasp when his hand leaves my elbow and pushes my shoulder hard into the wall. He uses the shock to quickly situate himself right before me. His hand trails the rest of the way down my arm and diverts its direction of travel. Both hands are on my hips, his thumbs digging into my skin as he pushes them back against the wall too. I swallow my fear at the aggressiveness of the movement.

"It's time for you to wake up!" he growls, palm slamming down on the wall right next to my ear. I flinch and whimper at the action. I press my hands flat into the wall so they don't do something stupid like try to cover my face or push him off.

"I don't know what you want," I mumble, my lip starting to wobble again as his eyes set ablaze in rage.

"You know exactly what I mean, it's just deep down in that tiny, useless little head of yours." His finger shakes from how hard he pushes it into the side of my skull as he spits out the words to me.

Much to my horror, I start to weep at the overwhelming events I've been dragged through in the last few hours. The guttural wailing and groaning vibrating up my throat sound foreign to me. The cries of anguish grow louder as I finally come to terms with the fact he's unlocked an immense sense of defeat in me. One that I never thought I was capable of or even knew that I could possess. I feel my insides crumble away into a pitiful arrangement of organs and frail tissue. I'm irrevocably weaker, milder, and a more pathetic woman than I thought possible. I've created a masterpiece of an irreversibly tragic downfall of a victim who remains abused even when the tables have turned.

He is stronger, more menacing and more heartbreaking in death than I could have ever anticipated. As I hadn't planned for his return from the depths, I couldn't fight his stifling presence sucking every aspiration I'd had out of me. I'd only managed to kill him because I'd learnt how he acted over the years and planned the attack in accordance.

Silly, foolish, unweathered little girl.

How could I possibly understand his reckoning and what would become of it when I plunged that knife into him and dragged him under. I was playing with a concept of an evil I didn't understand.

"Shhhhh. Don't worry your frown lines like that, little crow." His punishing hands now push the hair out of my face. He affectionately tries to clean me up, gently wiping my face with his thumbs. "It's okay if you don't understand. I promise you, it will achieve the same outcome no matter how confusing all of this is to you." He gives me a reassuring smile that my crawler hates. I can feel it dancing on my heart trying to put a stop to the pangs of longing he's drawing from it. That smile still unfortunately stirs up heated emotions in me that he's designed.

"It will all be over soon; you just need to wake up." His thumb runs along my jaw lovingly but I can feel the dangerous tremor in it that promises my undoing if I don't follow his order.

"You can't make me do anything now. I got rid of you once and I can do it again," I say through gritted teeth. His smile grows with every word.

"I was hoping you'd let me have one last bit of fun before you go." He smirks and backs away, leaning on the wall opposite me in the hall. "Go check our bedroom why don't you, little crow."

I frown at him in confusion and look over at the only closed door left, except it's now open. He was standing in that doorway when he first spoke. I'd left that one purposely unexplored. It's a room I shouldn't care for. It was *our* room and examining its changes would stir up complicated emotions that I didn't want to face. What if that room broke me the most? What if that room hurt more than the others? What would that make me then?

"Tick tock, little crow. I'm not here to spare you the time to dawdle." He snaps impatiently.

I swallow down the lump in my throat and push off the wall. I keep my eyes firmly on the door and don't let them flit over to him. I don't have to see to know he watches me closely as I move. I can hear him push off the wall moments after me and know he's walking only one pace behind. I'm sweating so much already that I can feel his soft breaths on the back of my damp neck.

My hand rests on the doorknob, my heart pounding. More hair has fallen out of my bun and blocks my sight. I hastily push it out my face, thankful for a reason to delay my task. Most of the blood is drying now but I can still feel a few damp specks on my cheek and ear as I tuck my hair away. I manage a deep shaky breath before I shove the door open. I was always more of a 'rip the band aid off' kind of person and this was no exception.

There's a bed in front of me. Brand new and bigger than the one we'd shared only months ago. The decor is much like the other rooms but I have no time to observe further before I hear her small cries. Eleanor is tied to the bed, hair splayed out beneath her, gag in her mouth and naked. I watch tears stream down her face as she looks at me desperately. My mouth opens to emote in some way but I come up short. Nothing comes out. I can't move. I just can't do it.

I know what I should say or how this should make me feel but I can't bring myself to do it. Every time I try to go to help her, I stop short. My fury at her doesn't allow me to proceed with a kind heart.

That should be me.

The cold, hard truth of the venom I inject into that statement circling over and over in my head completely breaks me. It's not the welfare of a friend that sparks concern or the relief of seeing he has a new victim that then drowns me in guilt. It's the red-hot rage at seeing her in our bedroom, tied up for my abuser that introduces an emotion I'd never felt in this kind of context.

Jealousy.

The crawling begins on my heart as it tries to warn me of the unhealthy attachment that's causing it to break. Luckily my eyes are already wet so he can't see if they start to water again at the sight of another woman laid out for him like that.

"I knew it," he whispers against my neck. I can feel his lips curl into that awful crooked smile he gets when he knows he's right. A soft kiss is placed on my neck. "I knew you wanted me for yourself. You're exactly what I wanted you to become, little crow."

My stomach heaves and I vomit on the floor. My bloody hands smear on the door as I grab it for support. His laughing is ringing in my ears and rattling round my brain. I'm pretty sure I can hear the vibrations of it rumbling through my chest. It's like he's blended into my DNA, woven through the strands in a pattern that completely rewrites me from Lora to his little crow. I'm not my own person anymore, I'm a blend of the weak parts of myself and the ominous parts of him.

"No!" I scream and whirl around to face him. He frowns as he looks down at the finger I have pointed at him in determination. "You don't have me, if this is what you've made I'll make sure you never have it." My fingers wrap around a vase situated on the desk just beside the door frame and I smash it over his darkened face before leaping over his body and running out of the house.

I run, eyes panicked, feet bleeding and bare as I run back over the mess downstairs and out the front door. I stumble over the uneven ground of the winding paths all the way up to the cliff side. I can feel his footsteps pound in my head behind me and I know he's following. He's *scared* of what I'll do next. I have to make sure I get to my destination before he catches me. Even in death he may be faster than I can ever be.

I jump and fly through the rough terrain and overgrown grass. My hair flows in the wind and lashes around my face violently as I run, my hair tie long lost in my escape attempt. The cardigan I'm wearing has fallen off my shoulders but I can't stop to pull it back up over my bruises. Not when it won't even matter in a few seconds.

I slow as I come to the edge of the cliff, one that I know looks out over the beach from over twenty-five metres above sea level. It's a height that is going to do the amount of damage I need it to.

I whip around in the cold air. The rain starts to fall and I can't help but think it adds to the mood of the spectacle that's about to take place here. He's standing only a few steps away staring at me, his head cocked to the side. I look back behind me to below; no one is there so there's no chance of traumatising anyone when I make my final move.

"Little crow, even for you this is a new shade of stupidity." His hands remain sunken deep in his pockets as he shrugs at me and smiles at how stupid he believes I am. I don't miss the twitch in his eye, though. He's nervous.

"Is it?" I ask. "Is it really that stupid, or is it a sacrifice I'm willing to make to ensure your unhappiness?" I take a step back.

"You're being *stupid* because you can't accept that you need me as much as I need you."

I shake my head and the tears fall again. I've cried rivers today. "No, you've twisted my head," I shout smacking my head for emphasis. "You've done this to me and I can't undo it!"

"Maybe because you don't want to," he states firmly, glaring right at me with those furious dark eyes. I feel them willing me to accept that.

"If that's true then it's all the more reason to do this." I step back again and my heels are now hanging off the edge. My balance is unsteady and I sway as I say my final words.

"Fuck you, creator."

I push my middle finger up and smile, the last tear falling from my eye. In turn, my body sways back with more force and I welcome the plummet down to my sweet death and freedom.

*

I don't land on my back. My palms burn as they slam down into the sand. My body is light and no ache or pain flows through my joints. My knees don't creak as I rest on all fours, staring at the sand below me through the curtain of dark hair. My hand curls in the sand and I lift it, watching it pour back to the ground. Grains of sand nestle themselves into the split skin of my palm. I frown and turn my hand. I'm... not dead. *How?*

The crawling under my skin runs all over my body before finally finding its way up my throat, behind my eyes and into my skull. It's telling me something but I can't quite figure it out. Its legs pound harder on my brain sending searing shocks through my head. I curl into a ball with my hands over my head, trying to make it stop.

One. Two. Three. Four.

One. Two. Three. Four. Five. Six. Seven. Eight. Nine.

One. Two. Three. Four. Five. Six. Seven.

D

I

G

Dig.

My fingers twitch in compliance.

Dig.

My hands slam down on the sand with a force so phenomenal I can only watch in shock as my fingers sink below the surface, grains burrowing under my ragged fingernails.

Dig.

Sand flies as my shoulders rotate and my fingers claw at the sand.

Dig.

The sand turns black and weeps blood as I go deeper.

My hands shake as I pull them up to my face to inspect. My cuts are gone. My skin is filled out around my fingers, my bones not as prominent as they were. My arms are bare and pale, no purples or reds adorning my skin. I instinctively grab desperately at my hair and bring it in front of my face. Blonde. My hair is a gorgeous, silky sunshine blonde again. I run my hands over my body, checking for what I know is now there as well. A beautiful pillow of flesh on my stomach, parts of my body I can grope at and not feel bone or thin skin stretching. I cry tears of joy, my breathing erratic as I process this incredible revelation.

"*Lora. Dive.*" I gasp at the sound of an urgent voice that sounds like my own. I look around, hands digging into the black sand I'm kneeling in, and see nothing. There's only a dark sea surrounding me, waves lapping soothingly at the shores of my little island.

I frown and turn back to the hole and scream at my face staring back up at me from the hole. My eyes bloodshot, skin bloody and hair greasy black sludge on my scalp.

"I said *dive*," the face growls at me, the bloodshot eyes igniting with fire. Red veins flicker in her eyes and become orange and yellow flames licking at her irises. Before I can respond, two bruised arms reach up out of the sand, grab my shoulders and drag me down in to the depths of the hole I'd dug with my bare hands. My mouth, nostrils and eyes fill with sand and the lights all go out.

152

PART TWO

PART TWO

CHAPTER SEVENTEEN

The air around me is cold, damp and stagnant. It doesn't feel at all like what I was expecting when I dived through to the other side. I had hoped for a warm breeze as my body was laid upon soft grass in a meadow. My quiet optimism leading me to believe that I'd end up in a place far away from anguish and regret. It seems even in death my fantasies don't come to life. My closed eyelids pulse with impatience. It's not that I don't want to open my eyes, it's just that the crawling is back. Its limbs are rippling under the lining of my stomach and gut, warning me that something is still very wrong.

My body feels different as well. Heavier. Sunken, even. It feels like my flesh is melting off my bones, pooling underneath me. The fragility of this new development means I don't dare to move my body an inch. I can't begin to compute where I am or why this is happening. I should be done with the darkness but it seems I'm still suffocated by it even now.

In the next breath, some kind of light turns on right above my face. Naturally, it jump-starts me into action and my eyes snap open. That's when the strange things start happening. I'm staring up at my basement ceiling. I can tell because the broken bits of plaster look exactly like ones I'd make shapes out of when I was down here for punishment.

Luckily, the basement has had no further improvements made to its appearance, unlike the rooms above. It's still as cold and unwelcoming as it's always been. Awful light strips on the ceiling that can only blaze a clinical blue-tinted white. The wall to my left is still lined with the same tools as before. I always say a silent thank you that I've never known the damage they can inflict when I see them still perfectly in place, gathering dust. My mind starts working out my surroundings as I stare. If I'm right by the tools, that means that I'm currently laid out on the metal table in front of it. Why am I laid out in front of it?

What the hell?

I hold back a gasp as his perplexed face is suddenly taking up the entirety of my vision. His frown deepens as he pushes his glasses further up his nose. His head bobs in and out of sight and it looks as though he's examining my body. I'm more concerned with how there's no reaction to my conscious state. From what I can piece together, with my memory of the cliff side and me falling to my death, he must have dragged my dying body off the sand, carried me through the winding paths back to the house and hauled it onto this table. Surely, my erratic eyes absorbing my change in surroundings should alarm him.

"I'm sure you moved. I'm sure I saw your chest rise and fall," he mutters to himself. His arms reach over and although it looks like he's prodding at my body, I can't feel his fingertips sinking into my flesh.

"I just can't figure you out," he sighs defeatedly. His hand reaches tenderly for my face; my eyes follow it cautiously. I can't seem to move my head so I just remain deadly still as he continues.

His left forearm rests flat next to my head and he leans right over so his face hovers above mine. I blink rapidly trying to determine if I'm actually seeing his lip wobbling and eyes watering. It's a new development in how he can use his features in an order I've never seen. I'd venture to guess I'm in some version of heaven to weave that distress through his frown lines, although something about this feels like it's happening back in the reality I no longer breathe in.

"It didn't need to be this way, little crow. I could've given you everything if you hadn't tried to kill me," he stutters in anger as the arm next to my face lifts and his fist slams back onto the table. I can't even flinch in response. The only things I can operate are my eyes.

Hang on. Tried to kill him?

"I'm sorry, I'm sorry. I know I agreed that I'd let you rest in peace down here. I shouldn't have lost my temper like that." His lips purse and advance towards my face. I really wish for the functionality of my limbs in this moment. Thankfully he veers upwards and my eyes stare at his collar whilst he places a kiss on my forehead. The material of his shirt is painfully smooth even as he's twisted over my body in an awkward fashion. The sight of the neatness of him makes me want to shudder. Normally, this kind of gesture would urge me to fold to his affections, but as I still can't feel anything, it's just an awkward silence that I endure.

Much more preferable.

I'm still trying to calm the crawling in my gut but something about this environment and the sequence of events has increased its intensity. The way it dances to its own tune makes it hard to breathe. I need to focus on the core issue but it's so hard. I feel disorientated and under immense pressure. That combined with the inconvenience of my inability to move isn't the best recipe for an advantageous outcome.

His collar fades from view as I contemplate why something feels off. His face is now back to being suspended above mine.

"God, I miss playing with you," he whispers mournfully.

Yeah, it must be so hard to be you.

"Even in death you're still the most beautiful thing I've ever seen."

My mind races. In death?

In death?

Death as in, I did actually die when I jumped from the cliff? My mind races as I think back to the bizarre events at the bottom of that cliff. The black sand, the blood. So I'm a ghost, which explains how I can't feel what he does to my body. The crawling in my gut becomes more vicious and irate.

Something still isn't adding up.

I'm so enraptured in my swirling thoughts that I don't see him advancing on me until he's kissed me. I just stare up at his closed eyes behind his lenses, pondering on this new personality trait. Is kissing my dead body more psychotic than I expect of him? I suppose not. The moment he pulls away, the plot thickens. His lips are tinged grey and a weird texture. I can't really explain what I'm seeing but the room feels like it's closing in on me the more I stare. The air around me hums as my wide eyes watch him wipe his lips clean.

I've been dead twelve hours at most, probably not even that. My decomposition shouldn't have begun yet. By the fact I can't move my body or feel anything, I assume my body is currently experiencing rigor mortis. The inexplicable thing is that my lips shouldn't crumble under his kiss or transfer colour until much, much later. My body would have to be long gone for what's just occurred here.

No.

No.

This can't be happening.

"I can't keep you here any longer, my beautiful little crow. I have to bury you now," he whispers unsteadily. I can tell by the way his throat moves around the words that he's struggling with this.

I want to reach out and hit him, strangle him. Do *something* to vent my emotions but the body my ghost is buried in doesn't budge. He's got his left hand covering his face as he tries not to cry, his right propping him up over the table as he processes the loss.

I want to cry too but my tears don't escape. I wonder if I lost that ability in my demise? I can't stop the questions as they rain down on me. Have I been dead longer? Did I die? When? Have I been roaming the house and the streets only in spirit? I'm consumed by questions and no answers come. I hate him, but as he remains looming over me, I have to focus on his words. He's the only one who can help as he talks to me in his insanity. But I struggle to grasp the circumstances, too caught up in my own issues.

It's not that I didn't understand when I first saw him, what it meant. I think I'm just slow on the uptake, as some might say. I can see him living, breathing, crying even, over my dead body and I'm not actually *seeing* it. I'm just watching as he puts on a bizarre display of emotion right above me. I think it's stranger that he can't see *me*. He's the one who's been haunting me all these weeks, surely he should be overjoyed by me joining him in the afterlife?

Every word he's spoken since I've come to starts to swim in my head, pounding behind my eyes painfully. It's excruciating, but even more so is the frustration of feeling as if I'm five steps behind. I know that my head is far gone with everything I've discovered in the past handful of minutes but I still berate myself for not being able to think clearly. He seemed so… real? Almost as if he was alive. I squeeze my eyes shut as the swirling in my head becomes more violent.

My heart pounds as the more logical thoughts begin to surface amongst the chaos in my head. I think back to that night and start to understand how wrong it is that I can't remember anything past stabbing him. I'd never even noticed how odd everything was until this moment. Even now, trying to think back to remember him dying is hard. I can't comfort myself with memories that I can't find of him when they're not there. There's nothing I can remember that can convince me that I did kill him that night. It feels like I'm going crazy.

I want… I want so much to be different, so much to not be, as my eyes flit around, looking for something to disprove what I know deep down inside is right. The crawling in my gut has eased off; I can barely feel it. I know now why that is. I've finally listened to it and drawn the correct message from its scattering around my insides.

I never killed him. I never got freedom or hope. I never got to smile for a moment that was true. Even worse, I took his place as the one who died that night and I've been living a lie as a ghost all this time.

I've failed.

I've fallen.

I'm *nothing*.

"I… I can't do this now. I'll come back for you later," he says, pushing himself completely upright, his composure back to his usual perfection. I watch his chest rise and fall, confirming he's in the land of the living. My rage burns. He turns, shaking his head and turns towards the stairs that are opposite my feet, north of my body.

I realise then his first words. He could see my chest rise and fall when I took a breath earlier. I could only do that if I could pass through to communicate with the living. That meant I could control this body to do so.

But how?

I close my eyes and focus, taking another deep breath. Victory surges through my veins as I feel the heavy chest move with me. I scramble to continue, aware that he's walking towards the door and I only have this one moment to induce in him the terror he's subjected me to during my time with him.

My back arches slowly, bones cracking loudly in the silent room. Unintentionally, my mouth opens and sounds off a high-pitched, slow intake of breath. It sounds terrifying even to me, and I'm the one controlling it. I can't see him stop but I hear his shoes scrape to a halt on the cement floor. It also confirms that, in some way, what's happening as I channel myself through my dead body is one hundred per cent real. It's occurring in present time right before him.

It takes great effort and a surge of energy that I muster from sheer will and determination from my core, but I manage to haul the body so it's sitting upright, staring straight at him. I'm not sure what I'm doing and the action is anything but smooth. My upper body jerks and twists awkwardly to its position. His broad shoulders are hunched, riddled with tension. I can imagine the cracking and creaking of a decaying body is enough to shake him. He only likes the horrifying side of life when he manufactures it. I smile, unconsciously pulling my dead lips with me as I go. This may turn out to be a lot of fun.

He takes a sharp breath, most likely hyping himself up to turn and look at what he thinks can't be behind him. I can't wait to prove him wrong. He turns to his left only slightly. He stops himself before he goes too far, and I know it's because he feels it. He knows this isn't a moment under his control. It's not a carefully curated piece to play in the game he's mastered. I *love* how the joy rattles through my body ferociously. The fire within me burns bright, finally ignited within me as I understand why I'm here. Why I've suffered. I can see my face in the cracks appearing around his usually flawless composure.

This is my calling now.

He eventually turns, forehead creased in scepticism. I enjoy watching his jaw slacken, his eyes widen and his forehead unravel from inquisition to fear. In that moment, as he's stumbling back from me, mouth open and arms flailing, he looks so *fucking* beautiful. I understand why he loved watching my fear and distress so much now. It's just wonderful to watch him crumble, stutter and choke on his horror, knowing that I'm the one who's pulling the tears out of his eyes. I'm ripping those awful half gasps out of his throat. I'm the one squeezing his lungs so it feels like he can't find air. I'm his creator and now that I have this power over him, I'm far from humble with it. I'm going to use every single surge I have to take this motherfucker down and when he's finally six feet under, I'm going to be the one waiting for him in death, ready to torment him all over again. I can learn this world better than he could, and I'll use it to not only turn the tables on him in the afterlife, but to slam them down on his throat.

I cackle in delight at my new position, the body I'm possessing shaking as I do. I'm struggling to hold it now, so much energy has already been used just to pull it up. Something gurgles in the throat and the sound it makes is deliciously sinister. It's enough to force him into a fit of terrified screams and shouts.

"No! No, no, no!" he shouts even more aggressively than he did back when I used to disobey him. It seems I've unlocked some delightful new emotions of his to play with.

I leave the body, unable to hold it any longer and it slams ungracefully back down onto the metal table. I don't turn to see it. I know I won't be able to face that now, so I just stand there next to it, facing him. I step over to stand in front of him, watching him closely as he strains his poor throat. I crouch down, trying to get a better look at this face I've never seen him wear before. His whole body slows down and I watch as his face is trapped mid scream, eyes watering and bloodshot, his neck bright red to match. His hair is drenched in sweat from only a short minute of the events occurring. How strange. He's so quick to crumble. It's almost disappointing that this isn't going to be as much hard work as I thought. I was hoping to accept some small challenge at least.

Still, regardless of that, I'm buzzing with anticipation. This is still going to be so much *fun*.

CHAPTER EIGHTEEN

've not yet been able to look at my dead body. I left it rotting below, face contorted into a sinister smile for his guilt-ridden eyes to fall upon. I'm euphoric looking at his broken composure as it flits from room to room, knowing that I'm responsible for it. The smell is creeping up onto the ground floor, lingering in stale air, reminding him of what awaits. He still refuses to venture to what lies beneath the newly laid carpets. I hold onto the moments I get to witness his deterioration to distract me from the inner workings of my own body.

My new form is not unlike my living one. It's undeniably human in some ways but I feel lighter, more powerful in the afterlife. My bones don't feel as much of a burden within my aching limbs. My muscles don't scream when I roam around the house, quietly observing. It's been so intense to discover what a healthy, pain-free body feels like, let alone a dead one. The times I wandered the streets thinking I was almost healed is nothing to what I feel now. My body is warm, soft and bends to my will with no protests. I can't quite accept how promising my death looks, but I'm discovering that I've never been so fulfilled than I am now.

Despite the positive, there is a cause for concern within me. Something buried deep in my guts that is waiting to pounce. I can feel it squirm every time I near the second floor. I've only stomached a total of seven steps towards the truth of what happened that night. The pain becomes unbearable and there's a dizziness that swamps my head if I push on. It's terrifying to feel like I'm being pulled out of the place I'm in to somewhere else. I'm not ready to leave this house behind, not when I've discovered what I could be capable of here.

He doesn't travel up to the second floor either. Something that I grasp onto as a small win. If even his hands shake at the thought of what now lies upstairs, it's okay that I struggle with it too.

The days have blurred slightly and I don't have much of a concept of time. We never had clocks in the house, a form of punishment he tailored for me that was arguably one of the most debilitating. Knowing time was wasting away from me, and being unable to know just how much, was its own torture. Now I have infinite time, it's interesting. Each day slips into the next and nothing in me changes. Although I love my new ability to haunt him, I've not been able to do much since and every day of being able to do nothing but watch is starting to grate on me. I could attempt the stairs again but I doubt my strength and my capacity to stomach the truth.

Today feels different than the ones since I discovered the truth. There's something lingering in the air that makes me want to heave. I can feel it curling around my neck as I aimlessly wander through the house. I haven't been able to describe it until now as the sun peaks in the sky whilst I stare out the window. It's a noose doused in kerosene tugging on my neck, pulling me back to the stairs. The stench of it makes my eyes water, but it doesn't smell as it should; the scent is infinitely more dangerous than a flammable oil-soaked rope lying too close to an open fire. I wish for the flames so hard today. I don't want to be here to face the same problems that remain. I just want to be free.

As I step back from the window, trying to ease the burn of friction every time the noose tugs, it yanks harder. I stumble in shock. My hands fly up to try to wedge my fingers between my skin and the rope, but the pull continues until my helpless body is dragged backwards out of the room and upwards. Every bump and scuff that my back suffers from the stairs stirs up a foreboding feeling in my gut. I barely have time to acknowledge the growing intensity of it before I'm pulled upright harshly and standing in front of the mirror. I know exactly what mirror this is.

The noose falls away and purple and red blooms over my skin as time is turned back to that night. I watch in horror as my eyes sink back and my skin darkens to a sickly grey I haven't seen in months. It's the same pattern of violence that decorated my face the night I decided to murder him. The night I thought I *had* murdered him. My hands shake and my heart pounds. I feel sick. I *know*. I just *know* that I'm about to discover what truly happened that night and I can't do it. It's been painful enough to know I lost; I don't want to discover how.

"Please," I whisper, trying to hold back a sob. "*Please. Don't do this.*" My reflection just continues staring at me with this pitiful gaze. She continues to inspect her face as though I'm not there.

The more I watch, the more my desperation surges up in my chest. There's a huge weight pushing down on my stomach that is sending red-hot panic shooting up through my core. It clambers up my neck and sits heavily at the top of my throat so my attempts to vocalise my panic are futile. My shaking hands are scratching at my neck, breaking skin to try and distract me from the anxiety building rapidly. I try everything to prevent the next sequence of events but, before I know it, I've grabbed the shower head and ripped it loose from the wall. My stomach lurches and I swing round and throw the shower head at the mirror with all my strength.

It's only when I open my scrunched-up eyes that I realise it's not the shower head that's broken the mirror, it's *my* head. In that exact moment, I realise that I've lived this memory before. Only, I thought he was haunting me, I thought he was hurting me in the present from beyond the grave. I gasp for air as the overwhelming feeling rushes over me that I've been haunted by my own memories trying to get me to understand what I didn't want to. I've been a ghost in this house for months, blind to what was happening around me.

The hand pulls me back sharply and he's right behind me like he was when he found me plotting in here. He's disappointed, he says, in how weak I'm becoming. It's upsetting that I'm more fragile than before and have to spend longer cleaning myself up. It's infuriating that I've not even started to amend my appearance judging by the blood still puddling on the floor beneath me.

My body follows his words to the letter as he fists his hand in my hair and guides it in to his desired position.

I'm his useless doll like I was all those months ago and I'm unable to do anything but reside in my body as the memory of that night plays out around me. I try to listen to the muffled voice and take in what's happening, but before I know it, my head's hurtling towards the mirror again and then it's dark.

It takes me a few moments to realise I can step out of the body I had in this memory and instead watch it laid out on the floor. It's bent at an awkward angle as I already know it will be. My eyes water, looking down at what I'd become after all those years. My battered skin glows under the moonlight. It's almost like a silver colour. I'd have said in any other circumstance that I look ethereal, but I look like Dracula's last meal instead. Drained of all colour except from the blood pulsing under patches of skin blemished by fists and feet.

I crouch down and carefully push the matted dark hair off my past self's face. She looks so sad even in the peace of unconsciousness. I screw my mouth up as I try not to shed a tear for her. I don't remember ever feeling as much of a victim as what I look like there on the floor. I thought I was better off than others, a comfort I selfishly indulged in, imagining the horrors I could have faced but never did. Looking down at my crumpled form on the cold floor, I wonder how I survived so long. I don't look real. I look like a dead body and it terrifies me as much as it chokes me up.

I manage to keep my tears at bay, and just gently stroke my unconscious face in an effort to try and soothe the frown lines decorating her face. Her grey skin against mine now is a huge contrast. I frown at the appearance. I'm not sure I remember being this tanned even when I thought I was still alive and healing.

I'm conscious I'm still in the memory, so I quickly look down at my legs peeking out of the long slip dress I'd been wearing that night. It matches the one she's wearing, only the one adorning the broken body on the floor is ripped and stained with blood. Mine is a clean black now, no bloodstains or rips. As I reach up to check the straps of my dress are still there, my hands tangle in smooth hair. I pull it so I can see the ends in front of me and drop them immediately as I see blonde again for the first time in seven years.

I remembered seeing the change in myself when I landed on the black sand after jumping off the cliff. I'd never imagined that what had washed off me there had taken a permanent effect. There isn't as much relief as I thought there would be about my return to who I was. The blonde locks frame a face I don't recognise. Perfect skin wraps around eyes that have seen years of torture. They stick out like a sore thumb and nothing fits with the person I am now, even if I am just a ghost. I don't know if I'd be happy still looking like his little crow either.

I turn back to the body on the floor when its limbs start twitching. I'm waking up. I swallow a lump in my throat as I watch watering, bloodshot eyes look around frantically for danger. She finds none and I watch her body deflate into the floor.

Was she tensed like that the entire time?

I know I should know because this was me once, but all I can relate to is her fluctuating anxiety as she lies on the floor wondering what to do. I can't remember what happens next so I just remain hunched over her form, quietly observing whilst I wait to watch my death.

CHAPTER NINETEEN

The dull clicks from bones snapping into place fill the silence. Although I wanted to break it, listening to my past body creak and groan as I rise up from the floor isn't my preference. They're still the sounds that plunge deepest into my soul. I always detest my ears and how they convey so much by doing nothing but their job.

My past self makes small, sad noises as she pulls herself up. I know my past well enough to know she's forcing herself to get moving as quickly as possible so as not to frustrate him. It's eye-opening to watch the struggle as an outsider. For some reason I imagine the pain to be even more excruciating than what it actually was. She stumbles and takes in a sharp inhale of breath in discomfort. I reach out for her, but although I can feel myself holding her up, she still rocks unsteadily on her feet.

Eventually, after trying and failing to prop her up, she leans heavily on the sink once more. Blood leaks from her mouth, but she's too out of it to spit it out. We both just watch her reflection in the mirror. There are unshed tears balancing dangerously on the lower rims of her eyes but she refuses to let them fall. Instead, she just presses the heels of her hands into the sockets trying to push them back in.

I give her a moment as I look in the sink at all the blood and broken shards of glass mixing together. Its only then I see a shaking hand reach for a particularly sharp piece that I snap out of it. My past self grasps it half-heartedly, inspecting it. 'It won't do the job,' I want to tell her, but there's no use. I'm too aware of the decomposing body under the house to know it's already done. No amount of trying to break through the wall into the past will make it become undone. She's lighting up inside with a hope that I can't squash, and it's ripping through me viciously that I'm watching this small hopeful little victim go to her death.

Her hand still shakes, compromising the grip she has on the shard as she carries on down the hallway to the lounge.

I thought it was a knife?

I don't know if the small memory I have of stabbing him is completely fictional, seeing as his death was. I guess it's something we find out now. I have only a small moment to contemplate how powerful the mind is to rewrite and even erase memories without my say.

He's sitting in that armchair of his, staring ahead at the TV. He doesn't react to her soft footsteps as she enters the room. Even I can hear the difference in their pitter-patter on the floor. The beat is the same but each press of her sole is that little bit firmer and sharper on the ear.

"Tick tock, little crow." It means I'm late. I am. I *know*, I want to scream.

I know it's too late but I can't rewrite it.

My past self doesn't falter in her steps. She pushes further into the room. The shard of mirror doesn't reflect any light, but as she moves further, the glow off the TV makes my stomach stir with unease.

It's the first glint of the shard that gives me away that night. A particularly bright scene on the screen fills the room with light and the shard starts bouncing rays around the room. He's sharp then, he sees the obscurity and is immediately up off the chair.

The struggle between the two of us is surprisingly silent. He doesn't utter a word, only grunts as he tries to control the raging adrenaline I must have as I watch my tiny malnourished body deflect his moves. My defence isn't perfect but it's enough to confuse him. I realise that his shock is hindering him in his attempts to tame me but is doing wonders for my delusional confidence. I can see how quickly I start to believe that I can fight him off and kill him.

My gut clenches as I watch her eyes gloss over in awe of her new-found strength. She shoves him to the ground after he loses balance by knocking into the same armchair he was sitting in. They tumble to the ground and I watch the shard slice through his side, just as I remember. I remain still, hunched over him, watching blood ooze into his clothes.

I can see the release in my shoulders as I believe he's truly gone and I'm free. There's a lump in my throat as I wait for what happens next. It feels more monumental to learn how I die from here. I'm terrified to relive a memory I can't find.

I don't really take in the scene in front of me. My eyes flit nervously around the room, trying to look for the warning signs. My heavy breathing almost deafens me as I look around. It's so loud and distracting that my focus is off. The TV continues on in the background and I can hear a man laughing. I know, even though he doesn't know I'm here reliving this memory in the room, that he's laughing at me. He sees me for what I truly am, a hopeless victor, and he just can't help but break through the fourth wall and the screen to let me know how far from the truth that is.

My knees thud on the floor and my body folds so my cheek rests on the blood-spattered carpet. His hand is directly in my line of sight and I settle in, waiting for it to twitch back to life as I already know it must.

The laughing has died down to a faint hum in the background and my past self has stayed with the shard embedded in his side, almost stoic as she watches his face with deep fascination. I know from the way she doesn't blink that she's having trouble believing she's succeeded. I feel like grabbing her shoulders and shaking her, to warn her that she hasn't. To my dismay, I can't and I know it, so I just focus back on his hand and wait.

It's only a few seconds before his hand stutters back to life. Although gaining consciousness must be alarming for even him, his movements remain calculated. I watch his strength flood back through his veins silently but he barely moves. His hand curls into a fist, his arm shakes with silent rage. Tears roll down my face as I watch from the carpet as it moves slowly upward to the body still straddled over him.

It happens at lightning speed as he pulls the body off him and slams her on the ground. I have to roll out of the way and crawl backwards to avoid being thrown into the mix with them both. His knee is pushed into my stomach and I flinch as I imagine how painful that must be. Her legs flail helplessly, tears roll from both our eyes, knowing the bitter truth that she's not strong enough to fight him off. It's breaking her heart and mine knowing her body still fights, despite knowing she's already dead.

There are cracks of bones, powerful thuds as fists and feet meet flesh, and soft whimpers as his fingernails tear pale skin. I just watch helplessly, unable to stop the waterfalls of salt burning down my cheeks from my wide eyes. The sounds and actions are nothing I haven't heard before. He's always hit with a power I can only describe as nothing short of god-like. Whether that's because the pain is phenomenal or because I can feel manipulation ripple over my bones each time he makes contact, I don't know.

As I realise that there's no knife, or shard or object that kills me, she turns her head to stare directly at me. She looks so small, so *tired*. I get it; looking into her eyes, I completely understand. I throw myself forwards through my own tears and move through the room towards her. I didn't realise how far I'd retreated from them until I pick my way through the carpet to reach her side.

I cradle her face in my hands, hunched over her head. My body shields him from her mostly but I can tell he is still delivering those mortal blows from the jerks of her body. I don't pay it much mind as I focus on her eyes, hoping that somehow I can push through the barrier and be present for her even in a memory. I need to reassure her. Her mouth is screwed up in pain but I know she's clamped her lips together to muffle her tortured cries. Anything to hide her agony makes her feel better on the inside, knowing she can still control that much despite his inflictions.

"It's okay, it's okay," I mutter over and over. I'm not sure if it's more for her or me. She looks up at me but I can't tell if she actually sees me. There's salt pouring onto her tear-stained cheeks and I realise that it's pouring out of my eyes for her. They burn painfully as though too much of it is pushing out of each socket.

"I could have given you everything. You were so close. So, so close," he spits out in anguish. I can feel the change in the air as his hot breath leaks out and slithers over my damp skin. I don't want those words to be the last ones she hears, even if I know they won't be because I'm her and I'm still here.

"No!" My nails bite into her skin as I try to drive my words home. "No, you weren't close because you *fought back*. You hear me? You were never close to his end goal, I promise you." I'm a wreck as I lean over her. The horror of watching my death but having no real comprehension of it is battling with my steel determination to comfort my past self. My mind is scrambling around both emotions, making my head pound.

I'm so entrapped by my own inner turmoil in the situation that I almost miss the final blow. My body runs cold as two fists hurtle down through the ghost of me and land on my past self's chest. The heart to be exact. The dull crunch under his hands is deafening. I suck in my breath as though I can feel his hands crushing through my bones as well even though I can only watch from my position. A final tear runs hot and fresh down my cheek; it splashes down onto her open eye. She doesn't blink, doesn't look at anything around her. The sound of her final breath leaving her mouth grinds on my eardrums. Instead of the silence of death, all I hear is noise. I hunch further on top of the dead body below me as the sound of my death rips through my head, gritting my teeth as I suffer through it.

My shoulders sag eventually after a few moments but remained tensed. I know she's gone now and that this is the end of the memory but I feel closer to insanity than I did without it.

"Don't let him get to me," a small voice whispers from below. My head slowly rises as I look upon the dead face before me.

Two bony hands grab onto my shoulders and pull me sharply downward. My nose is millimetres from hers. Her eyes are now a silvery blue, not grey. Her hair is back to the pale blonde it was before my attachment to him. My features look fuller, younger. I realise I'm looking down at the naive little girl she was before he started pulling her apart and reconstructing her to fit his needs.

My breath slows; everything around me shuts off. His fists are no longer beneath me, buried in her chest. My surroundings are pure darkness, even more so than what he had cloaked the room in for all those years. It's just the lost ghost and the unsuspecting woman now.

"*Don't* let him get to me," she whispers more harshly, her eyes filling with crashing waves of desperation.

"He can't anymore. You're free," I stutter back. Even I don't believe those words. She doesn't either.

"*Listen to me*," she grits out. Her tone is sharp but uncontrolled. "You're not free, you won't be until you fulfil the purpose."

"What? What purpose?" I'm the one grabbing her shoulders now, clutching onto the material of her slip. My hands shake but my grip is strong.

She smiles sadly at me and shakes her head in defeat. Those waves in her eyes finally crash onto the stone surface of her greying skin. I know she's looking at me and sympathising with my hopelessness.

I know I'm without hope.

I know. I've lost my mind, probably never even had it. All those beautiful sane thoughts I used to own that hadn't been tampered with by his hands. Now they're rolling around all over this house, escaping from me down cracks in the flooring and holes in the walls. I've not had a real understanding of anything since I died. There's nothing I can offer her.

"I know, *I know* I'm not what you want me to be. But I'm trying," I sob. "I'm trying *so hard.* Nothing fits. Nothing makes any sense here." It's pathetic, but she's the only confidante I'll have. There's no trust anywhere else. Not even when I'm dead.

It all rolls over so quickly. I'm thrown off her body and dragged underneath her as she now holds me down instead. Her eyes are bright with a fury I didn't know she could possess. My jaw drops in shock as she looks over me. One hand fists my dress in her hand, the other sits behind her back. She's breathing heavily and although I thought it impossible, her rage grows and burns brighter with each second that passes.

An ear-piercing scream is let out before her hand pulls out from behind her back and slams down by my head. I turn to the right, following it, and see my own panicked face staring back at me. It's the shard of mirror that I'd used to stab him. I pant erratically, still reeling from the shift in events when I feel her breath against my ear. Her hair tickles my eyelashes as it falls from her hunched shoulders and onto me. I don't dare look away from my reflection as her lips brush my ear.

"*Something is wrong with Eleanor,*" she whispers. Then she's gone and I'm alone in darkness, wondering where I go from here.

CHAPTER TWENTY

Days pass by and I become a hideaway rather than a haunting presence in his home. Confusion bleeds through the hours, falling from the newly painted ceilings and flooding the walls I curl into. No matter how much I shrink away from my surroundings, it doesn't make them disappear. Much to my frustration, the rooms are still immaculately decorated in a new, bold style that I hate. I don't long for the old crumbling beige ones either, though, so I'm at a loss about what I want. Nothing pleases me, but I allow myself to reason that I'm allowed to feel this way. I worry that this reasoning is wearing a little thin now. It won't be long until I'll be stuck with the fact I'm just misery regardless.

The small lounge on the ground floor has been a welcome solace for me. I don't see him here as he follows old routines and habits. It's almost as though he was released from his fear of the upper floor the second I was pulled out of that memory and back into the house. I recall the dizziness my reeling mind gifted me as I landed hard onto the floor, my eyes focused on the outdoors like they were prior to being dragged back through the house to face my past. I don't understand where I am anymore, which is why I'm hiding. Pretending to know what the afterlife would look like is presumptuous, but it's not like what I imagined at all. I thought that being a ghost haunting my murderer, I'd have some control over my movements. The events that unfolded mere days ago disproved that theory in the cruellest way.

Occasionally, I hear the footsteps creak above my head as he wanders into the room upstairs where our old lounge used to be. There's little movement in that room, which is normal. It's the same trail his feet follow, telling me he's gone back to his way of existing effortlessly. It's balancing on the tip of my tongue about why that's so concerning to me, but I haven't injected much energy into that. I'm more than happy to sit in this room that remains without purpose for the occupant. It's a window display to portray to curious locals an impression of a lovely home within, which does its job well. I feel such bitterness for this room, knowing it helped to hide the horrors I suffered just a floor above.

If I hadn't already known, I know now how much I hated this house. Hated everything it stood for, everything it had put me through. Even how fickle it was with me, changing its insides to match his next desired look in the home that is in *my name*. It serves to deliver a slap to my face that this horror house is owned by me. Every wall that shielded the world from my torture, I'd bought with my own money. I'd traded my parents' beautiful home for this torture chamber hidden in plain sight. I can't stomach this place. I can't stand the fact that I ended up here almost willingly. My traitorous mind convincing me that there'd be a way out further down the line. Well, there isn't. Now I'm stuck with a brain inside my skull that has been against me since I laid eyes on him.

There's lots of things I've learnt even hidden in this room, my body curled into a small ball, eyes wide, watching for the next surprise I'm in for. Some have been difficult to bear, and the weight of some revelations sit heavily on my fragile shoulders. I would've thought that, in the six and a half years living here, there wasn't much left. Unfortunately for me that's not the case.

The tether between me and him still feels as strong as ever, that's the truth I struggle with the most. The golden thread that he followed to find me. That's what he had claimed way back when he was romancing me. I'd blushed under such a compliment and the implication that he viewed me as his soulmate, courtesy of the string theory. Looking back now, I still recall how his eyes darkened when I held his hand, telling him I could feel it wrapped round my heart. Whether or not his reaction was because he loved that I was confirming the construction of my tether to him or because he wanted it wrapped round my mind instead, I'm not sure. We have to remember that even when he gets what he wants, it needs to be by his design, his will. The violence of his character reared its ugly head not long after that conversation. Interpret that as you will.

Although I know that staying here within the house I hate so much is proving that I am still attached to him, I don't try to exit through the door. It's not that I don't want to, I just can't. It's like there are invisible walls within the house that keep me contained. The thought has occurred to me that it's my backstabbing brain that's making me think that, but even a thought that feels like my own can't be trusted. The conflict battling around within me would be enough for someone to contemplate whether or not it's worth living with this. To my despair, I don't have any other option, seeing as I've already died and tried to kill myself whilst dead as well. I'm stuck in purgatory.

There have been a few small tantrums in this room over the last few days. I'm adamant this isn't fair and that I don't have any sins to atone for before I'm allowed to leave this place and find my peace. I've gifted myself the immature outlet of my emotions, trying to be kind to my soul. I've spent so many years with pent-up emotions and turmoil that I don't want to do it ever again. Every irrational and uncalled-for reaction will be on full display to work through. No one can see me anyway. Why can't I feel things more freely and make a fool of myself? There's no such thing as being an embarrassment if there's no one to witness your failures in composure. A small voice is disagreeing with me, stating I've always been an embarrassment to myself with what I became under the crushing pressure of his thumb. I pay it no mind though and shake the degrading thought off.

The sun starts to creep in through the windows; it must be mid-afternoon by now. The light causes me to catch a glint coming from the disgusting coffee table positioned a perfectly equal distance between the two ebony sofas lining two walls. Even in my curiosity I can't help how hard I glare at the unwelcome glass-topped furniture in front of me. It's never reflected light quite like this though. I'm tempted to ignore it, but I huff in annoyance at my stupid inability to leave small things like this alone.

It's not long after the annoyance has fled that I'm moving towards the table. There's just a small book slotted underneath the glass. The cover has long since lost whatever shine was meant to adorn it. It's unsettling that it's worn down enough that it shouldn't have caught the light like that. Although I spend most of my time here frowning, I feel my features turn downward into that same pattern regardless. Another mystery to solve in this hellhole.

Lucky me.

I roll my eyes as I bend down to swipe the book. I'm still sighing from all this effort that I'm reluctantly but also willingly putting myself through. I think it's more disappointment at myself for getting sucked into this mockery at my expense. I'm dead; I deserve to be dead in peace at least. I flip the book open and a passage at the very start has been bookmarked. The second paragraph catches my attention; my crawler pinches my gut cruelly when my gaze falls on it.

Who among the gods set the twain at strife and variance?
Apollo, the son of Leto and Zeus; for he in anger at the king sent a sore plague upon the host, so that the folk began to perish, because Atreides had done dishonour to Chryses the priest.

I don't read anything further. Something about the way the words beg for my attention urges me to resist delving through the marked pages. My crawler shudders deep in my gut. The book falls from my trembling fingertips.

When did I start shaking?

I step backwards towards my corner. The room feels colder than before, the sun having passed on since I moved. I frown at the unnatural passing of time. I'm not sure how my concept of time differs from when I was alive, but the question of why certain parts of the day filter through me with little acknowledgement adds to the overwhelming experience of haunting the house.

I return the book to its original place. In my haste, it slides noisily under the glass. I pause, breath hitched, as I wait for someone to come running through the door from the hall. After a few beats, the room stays silent, which brings me great relief. I shake my head trying to expel the anxiety wrapping tightly around my muscles. I don't know why I still feel like I'm drowning in worry even when I'm already dead. My crawler is slowly churning in my gut as if sensing the same unsettling atmosphere as I am.

I smack the heel of my hand repetitively onto my forehead, trying to dislodge the feeling. Nothing swims into better focus in my sight or mind as I persevere. There's a heavy, aching blanket of unease sitting on top of my eyes, disorientating everything into a menacing perspective. I still fail at understanding what's real and what's a trickery from the insanity he's embedded deep in my frontal lobe. I can feel it like a bullet poisoning my trains of thought and sound reasoning.

Footsteps sound softly on the floor at an even tempo. I know exactly whose they are and I fumble over myself to curl back into the corner fully before he comes. My movements are thankfully silent as I become one with the house and melt back into the shadows.

He looks somewhat different when he enters. His hands are tense even though they look perfectly normal as they hang by his side. They don't fool me though. I can see the fraught nerves pulse under his golden skin. He looks to have caught more sun than when I saw him last. I can't see his eyes behind the glare of his glasses but the subtle turn of his head indicates him scanning the room for life. Being unable to control how I become visible to others, I shrink further back into the dark. I don't want to be seen yet; I'm enjoying my solace as I adjust to my new beginning on the other side of the line between life and death.

I watch curiously as his thumb caresses his forefingers, as though he's trying to feel something in the air around him. I steal a glance at the book under the glass. The angle of it is ever so slightly off. It looks devastatingly obvious as I stare down at it before me. There's a draught that has always been present in the front room; it leaks in somewhere from the window and chills the air of the entirety of the ground floor in colder months. The draught now cuts through the room, hitting the corner of the book clumsily, throwing off the current so it flows incorrectly. The movement is natural enough for anyone else, but not him. His placement of objects is as illogical as it is perfect. A small corner of a book peeking out from a table means so much more than what an unsuspecting victim could know. A small, minor misplacement in an otherwise seemingly perfect room can offer a discomfort that sits under the skin, just above the collarbone. A dull throb in an irregular place that starts to bite at the parts of your mind still left intact. That's how I know he wanted me here, wanted me to sit here in this room and find it.

Peculiarly, it's more of a sharp kick in the gut when I realise that he won't be angry I've found it. The intense crawling under my skin, in my stomach and chest starts up. My insides plummet downwards. He smiles as I discover myself in one of his traps yet again.

He doesn't stop there. He creeps further into room, places his hand flat on the cover and slides the book out from its place. The page that is bookmarked is dismissed as he thumbs through the pages for another passage. I don't realise I'm also creeping into the room as well. I don't understand the compulsive nature of my steps but I push on anyway. I can feel that I need to see this. There's a strange, peculiar desire to perch on his shoulder and read what he does. He finds his page fairly quickly. He's got an intimate knowledge of this book and his muscles move in a familiar pattern to sift through the pages to locate the correct one.

Upon further inspection, as I lean over to gain a better visual, I realise it's not a page he's found. It's a small, worn piece of paper. It's older than the pages of the book itself and looks as though it's been torn out of another book only to be slotted between the pages of this one. The scrawl is hard to make out from years of wear but I can tell it's a translation from Greek. As I read the words, my crawler clenches round my heart painfully on each syllable I recite in my head.

> *The Lord whose oracle is in Delphi neither indicates clearly nor conceals, but gives a sign.*
> *– Heraclitus Fragment*

CHAPTER TWENTY-ONE

The corner of the room starts to feel uncomfortable in the next few days I stay there. My shoulder blades resting on the wall start to itch aggressively. My obsessive scratching doesn't soothe the pain either. Each time I rock back on my heels to resume my position against the wall, the itching intensifies tenfold. It's most likely the disgusting new decor in the room. If I had the will to, I'd be amused that not only do I dislike the new paint colour, but I'm also allergic to it. Either that or I hate it so intensely that I'm coming out in a rash just being near it. Both are plausible options.

There's an emotion building in me that I can't describe. It feels almost on the cusp of what is real, and what isn't. I can see the shift in the atmosphere around me, enveloping me in solidarity. It's as though I can manipulate my surroundings to spread my mood through the house like an infection. The first time I come to this realisation, it knocks me back into the wall, my breaths deepening. The power I seem to possess if I can do this… it's not right. To flip the dynamic so that I have the power now should be incredible, but it's not. I don't want to be like him.

I'm nothing like him.

I'm a strong believer that the way to become better than your abuser isn't to retaliate with the behaviours they bestowed upon you. For me, the possibility that I could become anything like him and inflict damage on someone, even *him*, feels wrong. I can't stomach it. Knowing that parts of him are burrowed deep in my brain, and then being able to utilise them to provoke fear in anyone, even him, is terrifying. I wouldn't be like him; I'd be him in every aspect. I'd become the very thing I fear in my desperate need to avenge the torture I've endured. Not only that, but I know without even a few seconds to think about it that he'd be proud of me despite being the receiver of my new-found ferocity.

That moment when I'd awoken in my decomposing body and pulled it up to witness him screaming in fear at me had only served me joy for a few short moments. Afterwards, I'd recalled his ashen face and horror-filled eyes as though they were mine when he'd looked down on me for all those years. The resemblance had shot through me and my heart pulsed painfully in my ribcage as my panic set in. Now, my darkness is something I lock up deep inside of me so I don't go down that path. It bangs on the door in my mind a lot, begging to be let out. Begging me to let it consume me.

Despite my feelings of not wanting to be like him, I also don't want to be the version I was of myself when I trembled under his unpredictable temper. I need to be someone different, someone who's *more*. Change is so difficult to understand and navigate now. Despite me not leaving footprints in the living world, I still want to push myself to get where I wanted to be before I knew I was gone.

With that in mind, I crawl out of my not so comfortable 'comfort spot' to try and fight the desire in me to stay there forever. I'm not hiding from him, but I am definitely aware that there is a feeling that I should be hiding from something. There's a change in the air now, a new truth for me to discover. Except I don't want to. I know it will be another burden on my shoulders, another gut-wrenching revelation to rip through my fragile sanity.

I wander out into the hallway, wincing at the decor as I go. I still shudder at the sight of each change as I step through the house. It's never not a constant kick in the face to see how disgustingly chic and cheerful it can be now I've been torn away. There's a vase on a small side table in the hall. It's filled with beautiful flowers. Colourful gladioli are displayed. The sight of them makes me want to scream and throw them against the nearest surface. And that's exactly what I do. The shattered glass and crumpled florals adorning the floor look far more spectacular there than they ever did up on that table. The sight doesn't encourage a smile to grace my face but I feel a small pleasure at my action, nonetheless.

Delicate padding of small feet on the stairs startles me. I whip around, hair flying into my face to look behind me at who could be coming downstairs. It's definitely not him, I'd know his footsteps anywhere.

Small, dainty feet allow a woman to glide down the stairs elegantly, her silk navy-blue skirt fluttering around her pale legs hypnotically. My crawler starts to rage in my stomach, kicking out violently.

Something's wrong.

I swallow, but my throat is so dry. My hands are shaking as I allow my eyes to travel upward. A simple belt hugs a tiny waist and a soft blue blouse that complements the skirt is tucked into it. It's the shock of the glossy red hair that takes the wind out of my lungs. I stop looking upward to prevent seeing exactly what I think is there but her feet carry her down the last two steps and her face drops into my line of sight.

Eleanor.

She's in my home, flouncing around as if it's her own. I back away, crashing my back into the wall behind me as she steps into the hallway and looks down at the mess I've made. Her eyes grow wide and teary, almost frantic. She starts muttering to herself; it sounds almost identical to the way I'd heard her before in her cellar.

"It's okay, you can fix this. It can all still go to plan," she mutters before rushing down the hall searching for...

I don't know.

I watch in disbelief as she steps barefoot through the glass without a flinch. Her mind is too focused on her ramblings to notice the pain as she trails small specks of blood through the hallway.

He won't like that.

It's not long before she's back, falling suddenly to her knees with a brush and dustpan in her unsteady hands, erratically cleaning up the mess. The broken pieces of glass stir under her clumsy movements and she does a poor job of cleaning the mess.

"Did I not put them on the table right?" she wonders to herself as she spares a glance to where her flowers were moments before.

I remain plastered against the wall as I watch on, nausea stirring heavily in my stomach as I try to comprehend what is going on. Why is Eleanor in my home? Why does she know where the cleaning products are? The answer is obvious, but I can't catch it. I don't know if it's because I don't want to or because I can't cope with having to process anything else emotionally. Still, it remains just out of reach for me to pluck out of the multiple thoughts drifting through the breeze in the hallway.

The scene I found myself in days before in the kitchen replays in my mind. I'd thought the changes in the house and her speaking to me were a new way of him tormenting me. Now I can't be sure because back then I also thought I'd survived him. Eleanor was in my house. Was that real? Has she been here long? She was also in the bed on that dreadful day when I tried to fall to my death. My head pounds as though trying to tell me something but it's too much. What this means, what it *could* mean with her being here is a betrayal and a truth so unfathomable, I can't survive it. I know I'm dead but I feel like I'm dying all over again. Death is so human; I still feel as vulnerable and fragile as I did before.

The scrape of glass across the hardwood floor grinds on me viciously. Every scrape is sending a harsh truth straight to my mind, tearing through my resolve to remain clueless. The grinds make me flinch even harder than I would if I heard nails on a chalkboard.

Grind.

She's been here since you saw her here.

Grind.

She's been here, replacing you since you died.

Grind.

She's being the perfect little puppet that you could never be.

Grind.

She's the new you.

The answer suddenly breaks through in all the screeching in my ears. The long menacing grinds fade into the background and the pounding of my heart increases in volume. Each time it knocks on my ribs, my clarity intensifies.

This is what's wrong with Eleanor.

My crawler scrambles around in my stomach, shaking its head at me. I have a part of an answer. I don't have all of it yet. I stare down at Eleanor as she tearfully tried to salvage the flowers I've destroyed. I wince as the petals fall to the ground the more she tries to straighten the stems to make them look new again. She doesn't see them for what they are, though, she mutters to herself constantly that she can save them. However, I can see clearer than her little mind. They're a lost cause. A broken flower can never bloom again. As I look at her flowing red hair falling over her shaking arms, I can't help but feel as though what she holds in her hands is what's to come for her.

I try to feel pity as she tidies away all the broken glass and throws the flowers away in the process, having given up on them after several minutes of fruitless effort. For some reason, it doesn't come naturally to me. I can't seem to find any tears to shed for her as she tries to pull hers from her eyes so he doesn't see when he's home.

Yes, that's right. I've finally understood that she is the new me and I should be feeling as though she's a kindred soul like me and all the others before her. I should feel pangs of sadness deep inside as I watch her step into my shoes so seamlessly. However, I don't; only confusion and something else stirs in me. That emotion I felt building in my hiding spot is back, building within me like a brewing storm. I still can't quite explain it. It does feel otherworldly though.

Her eyes are red-rimmed and there's a sparkle set deep in them that only freshly cried tears can achieve. As stupidly awful as it is to say, she does indeed look pretty even when she cries. Another stunning quality she has managed to possess that I never had. My internal storm thunders in agreement, which only serves to make me more mournful of what I could have been. Had I not met him, would I have been this pretty? Would I have looked after myself like Eleanor and been able to be beautiful in that same commanding way? Her perfection is so precise it unsettles me.

After she's inspected her appearance multiple times in a small mirror I'd never noticed on one of the walls, Eleanor straightens out imaginary creases in her clothes, fluffs her bouncing curls and swerves on her heel to head back towards the stairs. I have to half-walk and half-run just to keep up with her purposeful strides as she manoeuvres through my home. I hesitate for only a second at the top of the stairs before I decided to take off after her to see how this ends. The last time I'd been here was nothing short of unpleasant. The storm inside me ebbs away, letting my anxiety take hold as I push on.

She ends up in the same bedroom where I'd seen her tied to the bed before. Where he'd shown me that there was still jealously coursing through my bones. I'd never felt so exposed than when he'd stripped me to my core and seen the green monster living within my body. I screw up my eyes and beg my decayed mind not to make me relive that memory anymore.

When I finally feel in control again, Eleanor has managed to fuss around the room multiple times as if trying to ensure everything is right. I don't remember having to be this particular when I first met him. She seems to be putting in a lot of effort that I never bothered with. Not at the start anyway. He hid that side of himself from me for a small handful of months. It sends a small thrill of satisfaction through me that, despite her beauty, she has to put in double the effort I made with him to keep him interested. In fact, thinking back now, I'd not really done much at all to keep his eyes on me. He'd seemed to enjoy me as I was. I'd never felt inclined to act the way Eleanor is right now. Not this soon. I can't help but wonder why this situation feels off.

She starts for a moment as heavy boots on the landing sound out through the house. She tip-toe-runs to the mirror to check her appearance once more before he is standing behind me in the doorway. I can feel his breath caress the back of my head. My hair moves slightly and I allow myself a small moment for my eyes to flutter closed, taking in the nostalgia. Then I remember myself.

Stupid girl, how many times do I have to reiterate in my head that I can't allow my warped mind to rule my emotions?

I lunge forwards out from under the warmth his tall frame gave me and decide to watch the scene from afar. I can feel the weight in my body as it's thrown towards him as I push forwards. It takes a horrific amount of strength to pull my head and legs of lead to the head of the bed on the back wall. The closer I am to him, the harder it is to peel away.

"Welcome home." Eleanor's sickly sweet voice filters through the tension. Her eyes shine with admiration as she looks up at him.

He looks as he always does. Strong jaw, seductive lips and a fierce gaze that excites you as much as it encourages caution. His stance is rigid in the doorway. He leans on the frame stiffly, not an ounce of him showing signs of ease. I know from these few, quick observations that he's tensed, ready to strike. My stomach falls to my feet as I anticipate what's to come.

I watch him reply but the pounding in my ears drowns out the words. His arm reaches out and I watch the strength of his intent ripple through his muscles as his hand slips over her cheek. I know as soon as it carries on to bury into her hair that she's done for. His hand curls shut, Eleanor gasps in shock at the change in mood and before she can utter a word, her head is sent hurtling towards the dresser just inside the room to the right of the door frame. I watch her crumple to the floor quietly crying from the pain.

"Don't." He says just one word that conveys so much promise of violence that even I suck in my breath and hold it so as not to upset him. Eleanor's small cries become silent and she tries her best to stop her shoulders from shaking.

He steps back out of the room without another word and leaves her cradling her face in her hands as he continues on to his room. It's only seconds before the blue glow of the television illuminates the dim landing. Once I'm sure he's distracted enough, I pick my way silently through the room to crouch down in front of Eleanor.

She pulls her trembling hands away from her face and her breathing grows increasingly panicked at the blood on them. I sigh as I look at her crumpled face. She's a snivelling mess with blood running from her nose and tears streaming from her eyes. She gets up and goes back to the mirror and I follow. She's still silently crying as she looks at the damage he's done. Even if it heals, she'll still be able to see the evidence of his violence adorned on her flawless face.

"It's begun," I say firmly, eyes dark as I reveal a harsh reality to her reflection.

Eleanor looks directly at me in shock and shrieks in horror. My lips part slightly in shock as I realise I've pushed through and she's actually seen me in the mirror looking at her. Even I'm fearful of the terrifying way my features are turned downward. I look back at her on the floor, not noticing she's fallen down from the shock until she's at my feet looking more terrified of me than she ever did of him.

I inch further so I'm standing towering over her. Now that I'm looking more closely, she's thinner than I remember. The decline of health and nourishment has already begun. It's painfully obvious now that this whole time I've been chasing her down has been for this. I've got to save her. I've got to try my hardest to ensure that there are no others after me. No more deaths and battered women struggling to crawl out from under his thumb. I've got to make sure this blow is his last one for Eleanor. I know I'm here to break his cycle. This is how I win.

That rumbling storm inside me bursts from my soul and floods my mind with clarity. I've finally understood how I move forwards with my morals intact. Vengeance burns hope into my broken heart. I can be whole again; I can feel I've done what's needed to unburden my soul and ease the ache that I hadn't escaped from his talons all those months ago.

Something's wrong with Eleanor, and I'm going to fix it.

CHAPTER TWENTY-TWO

To my displeasure, the moments after seeing Eleanor on the floor with her ruined face encourage a morbid curiosity to build. A desire burns bright to dig deeper into the house and find out every little thing he's done since I passed. It's a daunting task to carry out. To delve into his behaviours and mind once more. I can't hide from him any longer but I also don't trust myself to be that close to him again. Not when I've done so well to stretch the tether between us so far it can almost be broken.

Sadly, I can't be selfish worrying for my sanity when another's depends on me. Eleanor is an entirely different person than me but I saw glimpses of the same terrified expression in her eyes that I'd worn throughout the years being his captive. Her need to please him is what really puts us on opposite sides of the scale. I'd never felt such an obligation or obsession to fuss as much as she does. I was small, timid and quiet. She is frantic, vain and desperate to please. Nonetheless, I don't want to think negatively of her and how our differences should encourage the age-old tradition of pitting women against one another. I can be better than that. I *have* to be better than that, and by default, him.

I prioritise the most important puzzle piece I want to have to hand. The relationship between the two of them. I've never been able to work this out, always assuming her captor would be so different to my own. Now I understand he must be a chameleon, a shape-shifter, to draw in victims of all qualities and hardships. I have to piece together how she became enamoured and how he chose her to be next.

Eleanor is quick to clean up as best she can. Her hair is shaken out as she holds her head high and carries on out to the room he's now occupying. Her face morphs into a beautiful yet seductive smile as she enters the room, hoping to make a desirable entrance. I can't help but follow in fascination as every step she takes, every flick of her hair, is done as a cry for attention from him. This woman is deranged. I can't even fathom how anyone would take his brutality only minutes before then be begging for his admiration in the next moment.

In fact, as I back out of the doorway and turn my head to the left to observe the hallway we've eaten up with our steps, I wonder why she's even sought him out without his request. If I wasn't required to be in his presence, I would stay as far away from him as possible. Maybe even curl up in the empty bed for a tiny, restless nap if he granted me that much. I'd never known what he did when I scampered after him hoping for more time together because I'd never even tried. A small gurgle escapes out of my throat and past my lips. It's a laugh. I just laugh in the empty, echoing hallway at the absurdity of it all.

As cruel as the thought is, I can't help it when my laughter turns to timid delight as I realise I was never that pathetic. The parts of me that I hated for giving into his affection in rare moments paled in comparison to this, and I was grateful for the lesson it was teaching me now in death. I was always the receiver of it, never the instigator. Never an instigator of my moments of weakness or submission to him and happy tears rolls down my cheeks as I take a selfish moment to bask in the minuscule win that makes me feel infinitely better.

"What are you doing?" A sharp, baritone voice I know too well slices through my outburst. My breath catches and I hiccup awkwardly into silence, eyes wide.

A small whimper sounds out in the dark room. The blue glow from the TV is as menacing as always but doesn't allow me to make out where Eleanor has situated herself or what she's doing to upset him so much. That tone is never a good sign and is undoubtedly followed by more violence.

"I... I... thought you'd like to—" She doesn't finish her sentence. A loud thump follows with more whimpers.

"*You* don't think anything. *I* decide what I'd like to do and after how you've behaved today, you don't deserve me," he snarls, his large, muscular figure towering over her as she cowers below.

"I'm sorry, so sorry. I didn't know. If I've done anything to upset you, *please*," she sobs loudly and until now, I hadn't noticed how whiney her voice could be either.

I don't know what he sees in her.

I shudder as the thought takes hold of me as though I should be acting like a jealous ex. I grapple with myself to attain control of my emotions. I can't start to show possessiveness like him, especially not about him either. I'm only here, watching, for Eleanor. She's the one who needs me, even more so than I originally predicted judging by her whines for his approval.

He doesn't like that.

He doesn't like many things about women's behaviour, but that one especially seems to light a fire within him. It's unlike anything I've seen the way his hands clench at his sides as she continues to babble nonsense through her tears.

The curl and uncurl of his fingers are his only tell that his control is faltering. It's still a calculated move. The small action allows him to keep the violence at bay until he needs to assert it on his victim. It has to be at a moment that inspires true terror and drives home the unpredictable nature of his wrath. It was never the same number of seconds after the first finger twitched that the pain started, and he made sure I knew that. Now I watch as the tactic begins for Eleanor.

I can tell by the way she looks around the room constantly during the altercation that this is only her first experience with his brutality. It's almost as though she's trying to decipher if she's in a dream or not. I wish I could reach out to her, reassure her that she might have a shot of getting away. As I watch her reach out and try to caress his arms as they flex with each hit, I realise she might already be too far gone to help. Her need to feel her skin on his is as strange as it is believable. It wouldn't be past him to be able to craft this level of obsession with him even this soon.

Her vivacious red hair starts to lose its usual shine. It dulls more with every punch. It's too soon for the black and blue but soon even her pale skin will darken. He manages to withdraw the light from people like nothing I've ever seen.

She tries to cling to whatever leaves her body as the assault continues, but she eventually lies down motionless and takes the defeat. It's the right thing to do as he slows to a stop. His torso rolls back up to his full height. His shoulders crack back into place. It's been a while since he's attacked someone then.

It begs the question how long it's been since I died and he had the opportunity to move to his next target. He was careful with items that indicated time. I'd have to count seconds, hours, days just to determine how long it had been since the capture. It was the small glances at newspapers when I left the house that helped me figure out if I was ever right about that. Even the number of times he'd hit me would be comforting because I'd be able to count them out as a distraction.

I'd remembered the days since I'd killed him so well, but when that reality fell apart it meant everything else did too. I'd no concept of anything really. Only the sun passing over the house was my indicator a day had gone by. I still didn't know if I could trust that, even. I'd believed I was living a whole other life before I was pulled out of it and put in this one. Who was to say I wasn't in purgatory, my mind being played with?

A warm body pushes through mine, jolting me back to the room. The TV is still running, casting us all in an eery blue glow. My eyes follow the sensation passing through me and fall on the jaw I know so well. It twitches slightly and he pauses just past my shoulder, as though he feels it too. I see his eye wander towards me behind his dark frames. Time slows as eventually his head turns towards me as well. My heart stutters as those captivating eyes meet my own. I try to step back and out from under his gaze but I'm pinned down. My backstabbing heart melts under his electric gaze. My skin breaks out in goosebumps as I stare back at him, mouth agape and mind whirring.

Can he see me?

He looks fiercer than I can recall. His sharp features are still as blindingly gorgeous as I remember. I'd tried not to look at him too much unless it was required of me. Although I never thought myself a shallow creature, I fall for his beauty every time, even with the ugliness I know is underneath.

I can't stop myself when my hand ghosts over his olive skin gently. I wish I knew why I did it, but I feel like a passenger in my body more often than not. This is something that unfortunately hasn't changed for the better in death. I still let the pieces of my mind that have felt his touch rule over me. It only feels unnatural when it's too late. I've already shown him the misled affection I have for him and the only tell I have that he's felt it too is the flash of something in his eyes. He doesn't linger after that. By the time I've pulled my hand back to my side, he's descended down the hall into the bedroom and slammed it shut.

A small cry turns my focus back to a beaten Eleanor on the floor. Sharp pains tear through my heart as I resonate deeply with the anguish and helplessness she's feeling right now. The pain will be excruciating. She won't adapt to it though. In some ways the pain will become a constant companion but in others, his blows will still deliver as much brutality as the last. His violence never lessens in impact and the agony only grows. Then there will be the inner turmoil that surges through her body day and night, torturing her when she's left alone with her thoughts.

She stays curled up on the floor where he left her and I don't blame her for the drastic change in obedience. She doesn't dare to move an inch from where he left her in fear of another reaction. She'll find the balance to it soon enough, if I don't find a way to help her. There will be a delicate chemistry to her movements that she'll have to master. It will take months of being a victim to fists and feet, but then she'll be able to manoeuvre around him more seamlessly.

With one last look to ensure the door is firmly closed, I step softly over to Eleanor's weeping body. Her porcelain skin has a few minor marks. She's lucky this wasn't more damaging, especially with how brazen she was with her assumptions of what he'd want from her. I cringe as I think what might have become of me if I'd ever been that way inclined in my captivity.

Eleanor seems determined to stay curled in a ball for a long while, but I need her to move. There's an urgency for her to pick herself up and wipe off the blood from her nose again before he comes back. Although I want to fix Eleanor, the first thing I need to do is encourage her to learn faster than I did.

But how?

The room we're in is sparse apart from the armchair and sofa facing the TV. This room is simple for a reason and there's nothing I can use to throw or manipulate to get her attention. I look down at my bare feet trying to improvise when the gleam off the wooden floor sparks inspiration. I curl my hand into a fist and knock on the floor in front of her snivelling face. It's a small pattern of four knocks in a rhythm so she hopefully notices it's not the banging of pipes in the house or him in the other room moving things around.

The quiet sobbing stops and her head raises slightly off the floor to look around for the source of the knocking. I knock again and she moves further up so her arms are holding her upper body up off the floor. She looks around the room for anything to explain but finds nothing. I take a deep breath as I slowly move towards the sofa, knocking on the floor as I go.

Come on Eleanor, follow me.

"This can't be happening," she whispers, shaking her head. I'm ready to try something else to get her to move to the sofa when she surprises me and slowly pushes herself up off the floor so she's standing.

I knock again on the floor four times in the same rhythm. She stares at the space in front of the sofa, frowning as she tries to focus on what could be there knocking like that. Eleanor edges closer to the sofa and when she's only a step away, I pat the sofa to the same beat as before, hoping she'll understand she needs to sit. She inhales sharply and the tears in her eyes build up again. I've scared her, even though she knows something is helping her. I withdraw my hand from the sofa and take several small steps backwards to give her space.

I've barely had a chance to consider my next move when he comes back in, his eyes wide and accusing.

"Were you knocking?" he growls. His voice is low and oozing with danger.

"W-what? No, no! I was just sitting here," Eleanor manages to answer him, her voice dripping in apprehension.

"Four times," he spits out. "You knocked *four times*." My and Eleanor's faces both crease up in confusion. Why is he angry about that?

He crouches down, eyes never leaving hers, his nostrils flared. His fist bangs on the floor as he imitates the sound. Her head tilts and her tears fall as she can't seem to understand what he's trying to say. Even I can't and I've had seven years of him. I step forwards but suddenly my crawler slams into my gut in protest. A warning so violent it throws my back on the wall behind me and all the air leaves my lungs.

Knock, knock, knock, knock.

He repeats it again.

"Don't you dare look me in the eyes and feign innocence." His voice is so dark, so thunderous, that even I become acquainted with a new level of rage he possesses.

It all happens so fast after that. My head spins from the force of which I've been thrown back against the wall and I can only catch blurred glimpses of his arms reaching for Eleanor before he's dragging her out of the room and down the hall.

My body sags to the floor after a while. There's a loud noise like gasping almost and it's only when I push my hair from my face and look down at the erratic rise and fall of my stomach that I realise it's me making it. My head is still swimming so I opt to crawl forwards through the haze. I can make out some sort of mark from where his fist was moments before but I'm not close enough.

Dark marks in the hardwood floor start to come into focus as I make it to the sofa and collapse against it, looking down at the marks only an inch from my folded legs. *They're letters*, is my first thought.

Letters that are spelling something but I have to keep squeezing my eyes shut to refocus and ignore the ringing in my ears. When I finally see the words, I throw myself backwards as though they could inflict the same pain on me that he has all these years.

Four knocks. Four letters. Once repeated. Two words. Two names.

LORA.

CROW.

CHAPTER TWENTY-THREE

Night passes and morning is soon here. The evening before is long forgotten if Eleanor's movements are anything to go by but the imperfection on her otherwise perfectly straight nose says different. I watched her rise from the sofa in the morning. It took her a few moments to register past events and remember why she woke in that room rather than theirs. She should start getting used to being discarded in every room on the upper floor. The bed is a rarity for her to sleep in now and she won't know the comfort of a mattress for months. It's vital to the embedding of punishment as the norm and basic necessities as a luxury. It will be a hard pill to swallow for her. She exudes perfection and luxury in every way, as does her home.

She's flippant about her bruised skin as she floats around the house in another stylish outfit. I must give her credit for the commitment to her old life. She doesn't seem deterred by the extra hour it takes for her to get ready in the morning. She pats make-up over the bruises expertly. The concentration weaves through her face viciously and her movements to apply concealer start to become erratic. Then, she will stop, take a breath and she's back to that creepy, calm disposition I hate so much. It doesn't seem right how she seems so normal after last night.

Was I that normal after he beat me for the first time?

I remember vividly that I refused to bow down to him in the beginning. Thinking back, though, that first morning that I suffered, I'd done anything and everything to convince myself I was not in that situation. I couldn't accept it, so I pretended it wasn't what it was for a while. It was fruitless, and I'm not sure it ever really served a purpose. Except a distraction from my busy mind. Maybe I do relate to her after all.

Eleanor takes the new day in her stride. At some point she leaves the house. She returns a short while later with a new vase and the flowers for the hallway. Gladioli again. My heart aches at the sight. I can feel her desperation to worship and please him through the small gesture. It takes her several minutes of prepping and fussing before she's content with the display. It takes her even longer to place them correctly on the table as she scurries back and forth to explore how it looks from every angle. I sit on the steps of the stairs in fascination, watching as she actively goes out of her way for him.

She rushes past me upstairs afterwards, muttering again to herself about everything going to plan. It's a reassurance mantra that she's been using a lot lately. Ever since the basement. There have been no candles or ritual-style qualities of her routine though so I'm still not sure if I saw it right that time. I still get the feeling that I'm in this insanely creepy room whenever I'm with her when she's like this.

There's a dark aura around her, like his darkness is leaking out around her whenever she has to reassure herself.

She scampers into the bedroom. She hasn't ventured in there since last night and I doubt he's cleaned the blood off the furniture for her. Maybe that's what the talking is for. She needs to hype herself up for what's to come. I just follow behind her, trying to dispel the unease even I feel about this. I'm leaning into my narcissistic side, but I'm more concerned about what this is going to do to me.

I try to shake off the feeling, but as I watch her body freeze only a foot past the doorway it becomes more difficult. I mirror the movement. My breath is caught in my throat just as hers is. A scraping sound starts quietly. I frown in confusion. Eleanor's red hair still hangs past her shoulders, her back arrow-straight. Nothing indicates that she's moved. The sound grows louder, echoing out into the landing. I swallow down the bile in my throat. My eyes stay on the back of Eleanor as I step back towards the top of the stairs. I don't think I want to see this.

There's a huge change in the air around my head as my left foot steps down onto the top step. All of a sudden it's as if I'm the one being subjected to the scraping. My eardrums are vibrating in tandem to the scraping. My skin feels hot with pain but I can't see anything on it to explain what's happening. It's almost as if I'm waiting for his nails to start digging into my skin, scraping it back to reveal bone, layer by layer. The vibrations get more insistent and the air around me grows more foul. Once I feel my crawler startle to life deep in my tangled guts, I know I have to end this. My palms slam down hard on the landing, the sound now being the one to echo down the landing and through the house.

My body is hunched over the top of the stairs, heaving as I try to quiet my crawler.

White noise hums in my ears and I welcome the consistency of it. My arms are shaking from holding my body up over the carpets. I wipe my nose with my forearm, a habit from my past. I'm not used to being curled up on the floor without some damage to clean upon my broken face. I'm thankful there's no blood. Not when that's what I was so worried to see in that room in the first place. There are small mercies in death, I suppose.

I grip the wall as I pull myself to my feet again and lean heavily on it once I've stumbled back onto the landing. My position now allows me a better view of the doorway that Eleanor is still standing in. There's no indication that she's moved during my moment of panic. It's when my breathing slows as I stare at her that I notice the scraping is still there. I can feel it grinding on my brain with each drag. My right eye twitches.

Before I can decide a next course of action, my body propels forwards to stand behind Eleanor and peer into the bedroom. I barely feel my feet pad on the floor as I move. The doorway just comes closer and closer until I'm only inches away from her. The left side of her profile starts to reveal itself bit by bit as I get closer to her. I manage to clock a small shift in the material of her top as I do. Her left arm is moving.

I hurry forwards now understanding it's Eleanor doing something, nothing worse. The green silk of her blouse shifts around her arm as it moves back and forth directly on top of the dresser. It's the piece of furniture he slammed her head against to bludgeon her nose. My first thought is that she's scrubbing the blood off it. What it actually is, when my gaze falls upon it, is far more terrifying.

Her burgundy nail polish has broken off her thumbnail from the scraping. Small splinters of wood are scattered around her hand on the dresser. I watch as her nail digs into the wood and scrapes along the grain unnaturally. The depth at which it dives into the top of the dresser is alarming and I flinch as I watch the movement. My own thumbs fold into my palm, fingers curling protectively around them. The scraping grinds more ferociously now that I know what's causing it. I have to resist the urge to heave as I watch splinter after splinter of wood bury itself under her nail. The blood pours, sullying the varnished wood further, but she doesn't stop.

When I finally manage to pull my eyes away from it, I look at her face. There are tears streaming down her cheeks but from her expression I know they're not from the pain she's inflicting on herself. She stares at the wall in front of her, salt pouring over the rims of her sorrowful eyes. She looks desperate and lost at the same time. Her bottom lip quivers but she doesn't utter a word. It's the same trance-like state I've seen her in before.

"This won't erase what he's done," I state softly, trying to offer wisdom. She can clean, pick or scrape the blood off the furniture but it won't change what happened there. I've disproved that theory too many times to count.

The scratching sounds stop, her thumb unhooks from under the wood and settles back by her side as she turns her head to look over her left shoulder slightly. Towards me. Her eyes remain downcast. I understand her fear of seeing the ghost of the woman before. Not only that, but a woman she knew and never saw the signs. I've yet to determine if she recognised me in the mirror this past evening, but I feel in my bones deep down that she knows it's me.

"Eleanor, get out before it's too late," I urge. Her lashes flutter, trying to keep more tears from falling.

"Everything will be perfect. Everything will go to plan," she whispers distractedly as she focuses back on the wall before her.

A cough startles me but I don't move from my place just inside the doorway by the dresser. I stare at her hunched shoulder as she half coughs, half laughs into the empty space. Her untarnished hand lifts and disappears in front of her face. I don't see her expression but I can hear more tears fall. They fall from under her chin and drip steadily to the floor. I can hear the tiny splashes on the hardwood floor so clearly.

As she steps further into the room and faces the dresser resting up against the wall, I can see the back of her hand is resting on her lips to muffle her laughter. If I heard the sound without a visual, I'd think someone was whimpering in terror. Her whole demeanour perplexes me. She's an oxymoron personified.

The first claw at the already disfigured dresser is somewhat expected but manages to push me backwards into the wall in shock. My hands grip the door frame for emotional support as I watch her once soft and supple arms lash out in anger over and over. Her muscles ripple savagely under her porcelain skin. Her snarling face as she tries to pull the wood apart is so *imperfect* that I wonder if it's definitely Eleanor in front of me.

Is it really her?

Did he really capture my only acquaintance in this remote town to spite me in my death?

When the jagged pieces of wood are scattered over the bed and over the floor, the same practised smile carves itself into her face. I press my feet into the debris on the floor over and over until I'm standing inches away from her. I stare hard at her vacant eyes, tight forehead and strained smile. It occurs to me there's a facade there that she wears as though it's her normality, that she uses throughout all her interactions. It's faultless if you've never seen what's underneath.

I'm overcome with a huge wave of empathy. She must have been through something terrible to be so practised at pretending to be someone else. All I see now, as she paints a perfect picture of happiness with her features, is her true self, her skin still littered with the unhinged emotions I witnessed only minutes ago.

I can't seem to let go of the revelation over the hours that follow. Even when night falls and the inevitability of his return looms over us both. She's not cleaned up the mess she made either. Eleanor remains as still as a statue in the room. I haven't seen her leave since I stumbled out into the hall, eager to get away from the unsettling atmosphere building in the room. Admittedly I can't swear to the fact I've been watching for her next move with bated breath, but I would know if she'd left. The scene has been playing on repeat in my head since it occurred. He'll be back any minute and I should be worrying or wondering what he'll do when he sees the mess, but that seems a million miles away.

I should be glad for the peace that befalls me. For once my thoughts aren't dedicated to anything regarding him.

Somehow the nervous energy from today boils the acid in my stomach with increased intensity. The bile that burns up my throat in response to the nausea is scalding hot. Even in my death I worry for the burning of a hole in my neck from how extreme the changes in my body are. My crawler just stays heavy in my stomach, encouraging my discomfort to build until I can't bear it anymore.

By the time any development occurs, I've sunk to the floor on the landing just a few feet from the doorway to the bedroom. I'm sitting facing it for the viewpoint. I can see about an inch of her body from this position and I much prefer it that way. My curiosity can be sated whilst I watch what's to come without having to see everything. I'll see enough and that's all I really need.

The clatter is what rouses me from a half slumber propped up against the wall. Even with her kicking up the mess she's made, there's a certain grace to it. Her stumble looks as precise as her strut. Her hands are still bloody but the red stains have dried now. Her clothing isn't creased and falls over her body as seamlessly as it always does. It seems impossible. It feels inhumane even watching her as she just casually approaches the stairs and descends to the ground floor. I shake my head in disbelief.

Something is wrong with Eleanor, and she's scaring me.

CHAPTER TWENTY-FOUR

The debris is still scattered on the floor carelessly when the front door shuts. Eleanor didn't return upstairs to try to cover her tracks like she's done before. She's been born young into this game though, his desired pattern of behaviour has yet to be carved into her very soul. Still, I would imagine this second beating so soon after the first will be more painful to endure. Whether experiencing that applies to me yet is unknown. I've not moved from the landing in the hope of avoiding being the spectator again.

He thuds up the stairs causally, unaware of the untidiness that awaits him. My heart involuntarily pounds as he creeps closer with every step. Logically, I know I'm not to blame and no longer a living victim in the house, but my crawler claws its way up to my throat to mute me as it used to.

Two brown boots come into view, stopping just before the first splinter of wood on the edge of her mess. I daren't look up at his face. It's not anger directed at me but the thought of watching the flicker of his fury build into searing hot rage in his eyes frightens me. I've never made a mess like this before. I'm in brand-new territory. The air grows thicker and warmer the longer he remains standing still just a few feet away from my body curled up against the wall. His body burns beautifully bright when he's feeling destructive but the sight of it is deceiving as to how deadly it is. I've been burned before but never scorched.

As the seconds pass by at an agonising pace, I realise the longer this goes on, the worse the outcome will be. I have to find her before he does. Maybe there's a way to warn her or usher her out of the house.

I push up from the floor and fly past his rigid body. My feet barely touch the ground as I hurry down to the first floor and start checking the rooms. She's not in the kitchen or the fake front room though. I try to look out through the windows to see if she's in the garden but she's not. Has she run away without my help?

I laugh in cautious belief that she may have seen straight since her breakdown in the bedroom. My crawler shakes its head at me, now burrowed deep in my gut. It's right. I don't feel any lighter or at ease in this house. The misery that emanates from the walls starts to unravel another plot I've yet to become part of. After so many years of everything being wrong, I mistake small glimmers of useless hope as something they're not. The house laughs at me. I know it does by the way my chest tightens as the room spins.

It hits me then, as the spinning starts a churning in my stomach and a bulb to light behind my eyes. It occurs to me that this house has been at the pinnacle of my journey since I had that blissful memory of killing him in cold blood on awful beige carpet.

What if these walls are lying to me?

My pupils are blown as they flit left and right to try to follow the rotating walls in front of them. My blood thrums in my ears, deafening my thoughts. I reach behind me for something to ground me but I only grasp onto air. It's thick, sticky and only amplifies the discomfort I feel.

Is this even real?

I eventually manage to pluck my feet off the floor enough to turn and pelt back upstairs. I have to see if I'm right. I know there's something telling me that I need to go back to the dresser for my answers.

I slow as I realise I'm running over the aftermath of the destruction that Eleanor kicked onto the landing earlier. I look down as I try to come to a halt but the shock of seeing a crisp clean floor knocks me down to the floor hard. My whole body breaks out in goosebumps and my crawler starts to pulse deep in my abdomen.

The house doesn't slow its spinning and I wonder if I'm the one spinning, not the other way around. I scrunch my eyes up to try and ease the debilitating sickness turning in my stomach. My knees slam onto the floor hard. My right arm flies out in all directions, frantically trying to feel for anything sharp or foreign on the carpet. But it's just a smooth, clean surface. I bang my fists on the rug repeatedly in frustration as the tears I've been fighting slither out from under my eyelids. Even they paint an irregular sour streak down my face. I shake in overstimulation; my head lolls dangerously as though I'm about to pass out.

You can't.

But I want to.

I don't understand why I would do this to myself. I've done nothing but try to save my mind from him. I've encouraged it to stay strong and remain unbeaten. Had it convinced me so easily that I had been all this time? Had I ever really had transparency with myself? My principles, my morals, my pride in being more than just a victim? Were they all built on lies?

I don't understand how I'm here, mourning my sanity and having such an intense reaction to who I am if I've already become someone else? There's a version of me that I have and then there's his as well, battling for land just under my skull. My head throbs painfully as I try to slow my thoughts before they get carried away. When my head gets this tangled and messy, I feel something trying to fight its way through. A climax building in the most unpleasant way.

I somehow propel myself back onto my feet and half fall through the doorway of the bedroom I was aiming for. My hand rests on a smooth surface and my head turns to inspect it. I slam back into the half-open door. It ricochets loudly off the wall and me a few times. It's then I realise I've been stumbling a little. There's a small worry in the back of my mind that they might hear all the noise I'm making and come running, but I'm too preoccupied to really acknowledge and invest in that currently. The wood on the dresser is smooth, flat and it's the cleanest it's ever looked. I bend down in front to further inspect the patch I watched Eleanor's head slam into and, even up close, my eyes a mere inch from the edge, I find nothing. Not even a tiny speck that might have been missed in an obsessive cleaning spell.

I drop to my knees to inspect the carpet for any signs of her blood as well but nothing. The room is immaculate and also barren. Only a few small ornaments and decorations but there's no sign of life in this room. It's too immaculate, as though no one's been in here for days. Even when I was with him, there would be certain things I could leave alone. His need for things to be in order would only stretch so far. Most of the time, the odd coffee cup on the side could be left till morning or the blood on the carpet he'd like to leave for a few days so it would remind him of how it got there. Some were motivated by a sinister side of his persona, but others were just simply because they weren't important to him.

It was a baffling trait of his to watch over the first few months where all I had was him and four walls around me. He could step into a room and instantly know a book or a vase was the tiniest bit off centre. Yet, there were other things that just didn't faze him. Granted, I found that out only when I was too distraught to remember to tidy up some nights. The trial-and-error process I had gone through was horrific. The fact there was always half a chance he'd blow up at me for each instance was enough for me to tirelessly make sure everything was always in the right place.

I pull myself back into the room and the carpet that was starting to blur in front of me comes back into full focus. There's still no blood before me of course. I sigh in frustration. I was half hoping that after falling out of my flashback I'd find myself back in a room with a destroyed dresser. The dresser is in immaculate condition, though, laughing at me. The smooth oak surface is only wearing a light scattering of dust. There's not a single indication of Eleanor's violence in these four walls. I've never been so breathtakingly scared of a room before. It looks so normal, so barren. I can't take it.

I run into the rest of the rooms in the house after that, forcing myself to face the harsh reality that I find every single one empty with no signs of being lived in. The spinning comes back but I bear it better the second time around. Even with my sight compromised I can see enough to know that there's no one home. Not even a lingering smell of a previously cooked meal in the kitchen. I can feel deep in my bones the cold hard truth. There's not been anyone home for days.

So what happened today?

I end up in the front room looking out onto the street. Dusk has fallen outside but the street lights haven't yet turned on. As I step close to the window, I notice small little strands of grass tickling the ledge outside. I frown; we've never had a particularly overgrown garden out front, mainly so as not to draw attention. The contrast between the setting of the front room that the typical village busybodies can peek at and the messy garden would definitely raise eyebrows. Maybe even encourage a complaint or two about the disregard to the 'ideal look' for one of the most beautiful corners of the world. I wouldn't put it past a few people I've seen around these parts. I'm also familiar with how some small villages can be, not that I know too much about this one even after living here just over six years.

Now I'm dead, it's not up to me to manage these things. It would be him. The long weeds swaying in the breeze suggest that he's not bothered with this small detail either. Millions of possible explanations swarm my head. It's so hard to pick out which ones are credible and which ones are just riddled with all the impossible scenarios my anxiety stirs up. There's one that my crawler plucks from behind my eyes and drags down into my gut to cling onto.

What if no one's kept the garden up because no one's been here to do it?

If that is the right question to ask, then where the hell does that leave me? Where am I? What am I? Why doesn't anything make sense when there's no reason for me to be victim to more warped thoughts and confusion?

Deep down, as my crawler still clings aggressively to that thought, I wonder if managing to find true clarity will be the saving grace I want it to be or if it just gets infinitely worse the further I dive in head first.

CHAPTER TWENTY-FIVE

'm starting to think that nothing is wrong with anything or anyone except me. It's almost like there's something still living in me that sends me spiralling into delusion. A parasite eating away at my last few rational thoughts I have left. I can feel the parts of me that I want to keep slip away from me with each day that passes by. The cracks in my heart widen a little each time. It should deter me from remaining haunting the house but it doesn't.

Like I'd know how to stop haunting this awful house.

There hasn't been a whisper of movement in the rooms since that night. The walls are still coated in the bold blues but they seem darker somehow and iridescent in some lights as the passing sun streams in through the windows. The same patterns dance over my empty eyes as I wander aimlessly through door frames. The darker the walls become, the happier I am. The depth of blue resembles the bruises I bore on my body months ago. Every time the glint of the blue catches my eyes it reminds me of the beauty I had beneath them. Not physical, maybe, but definitely the beauty of my strength, will and most of all intelligence. I lasted seven years and he's young still. I must be his longest conquest and I owe that to what fragments of my mind I held dear and utilised in the most terrifying moments. I still have that beauty despite my death.

My insides are still being gnawed away bit by bit. I feel emptier every time one day ends and another begins. The world carries on but I'm pulling myself apart looking for answers that never come. The bones of this place are the same ones they've always been, but the flesh I knew best on them never returns. This new bold skin that I can't escape remains. Even after all this time alone to finally think and I can't remember ever once having the urge to change the decor. The only time I ever paid attention to my hatred for those awful beige surfaces was when I scrubbed them clean to try and remove him from my life once and for all.

It makes me wonder, though, in my distorted reality in which I'd managed to strike down my enemy and start building a life of my own from the ashes of what was left of me, what else I could've conjured up in my head. What if the scrubbing was my scraping off the paint or painting the walls a different colour? It's entirely possible but I don't want it. The denial is stupid but precious to me so I cling to it and hope if I keep it up long enough I can just avoid it forever. Seems like I have a lot of time now, anyway.

It's still doesn't fit though. When I came to in my dead body, the reality I knew was ripped apart entirely. Every little detail I'd fallen for laughed at me as it morphed into something I didn't recognise. I'd cowered on the ground floor for so long with a hole in my heart. All these little things I'd done. I'd woken up in the mornings with an ease in my shoulders. I'd made a coffee my way. I'd *remembered* how I used to take my coffee before he changed that. I'd thrown my anxiety to the back of my mind and ventured outdoors.

The so called 'hauntings' that I'd experienced, looking back, they were still as awful as they were in the moment, but they'd also offered me the opportunity to push on. I'd still shaken myself off and carried on. Sometimes I'd run home and that was okay because I could try again. I'd discovered so much inner strength that I'd never dared to use before and it was beautiful. It was a terrifying and exhausting experience but it paid off in millions. Getting that kind of perseverance back was priceless.

I don't think I'd ever mourned that. I don't even think I'd had a breath that meant I could even think of what I'd lost. Not truly. As much of a trembling mess as I was, I feel like I'd give anything to be back there. My life was a rollercoaster of dozens of emotions. The excitement of coming back up from a plummet downward gave me motivation to keep going. It's always amazing to have confirmation that what goes down must come up. And it did. Time and time again, I'd feel this intense awe as I woke up to a silent house and a healing body. Now I only seem to go deeper into the pit and if my rollercoaster was a lie, that means I'll never come back up to sunlight. I'm destined for darkness.

Tears do me no good and they're so worthless now. So common that they've lost any value they once held for me and certainly for him. I feel them on my cheeks or catch the glisten of their trail on my skin in mirrors. The only thing I feel for them is indifference. Of course, I'm frustrated that they're still a regular occurrence in my life or undead life now but they're unstoppable. I cry for so many things and what's worse is I don't think a sane person could invalidate any of them. I cry for what I lost, for what I dreamed for myself that I can no longer have and I cry for the pain I suffer now when I thought death would be a peaceful departure from him. I hate it all.

In these moments as I roam the empty house, my skin crawls in discomfort. My eyes stream out of the frustration of not understanding why I'm still here. I know deep down there's a purpose to what I've seen and experienced but I can't quite reach that far within me to find it. I've observed something that tells me what's next, but I don't know it yet. I knew way back with Eleanor that she was the key to everything. Now I'm wondering where to start with finding her again. She's a constant in the background of my life and has been since before I died. I need to unlock what's happened in that time frame and how he knew to target her.

Looking back, I'd never paid much mind to her. I'd listened half-heartedly to her stories and attempts at small talk. I was far too concerned about trying to aim a small smile at her so she thought I was listening rather than anything else. I was on edge all the time about how I portrayed myself in public and my lack of understanding around what normal socialising looked like was a worry I leaned into heavily. Maybe I'd have been more observant if I'd known I'd needed to watch for his toxicity invading others but I'd underestimated his cunning nature. I'd never once questioned what he did when he left the house during my confinement. No, on the contrary, I'd been grateful to be allowed those small bursts of freedom where I could relax my shoulders a little and try to find ways to heal faster. The tears would fall then in total shock and awe that his reality had granted me such a privilege as being alone in the house without him.

It was stupid, but so innocently done by my past self. I'd just been so overwhelmed all the time no matter the situation and Eleanor had slipped through the cracks with ease. I try to think back to the supermarket where she'd been following me as I did my shopping but my mind easily evades showing me anything more. I strain myself to try to push through the walls around those memories. My fingernails claw at my face as my eyes scrunch shut trying to focus. No matter how many times I visit a memory, Eleanor looks happy, calm and anything but a victim. I'd known from my early days I'd scrambled for attention but no one had offered me anything more than an odd look before running off. She didn't. There were no desperate pleas in her eyes as I imagined mine looked like in those early stages. I worry now as my mind fights me if I did see those eyes as hers, though. What if I'd overlooked it? Had he managed to make me blind to others?

My mind is racing but it halts when I hear the catch on the front door. My breath hitches as I'm standing on the upper floor and I stay as quiet as possible to listen for what's happening below. There's an unsteady rhythm of footsteps. They're heavy in nature, which means I know they belong to him. There's also a muffled, lighter pattern of footsteps that don't have any order whatsoever. I frown as I try to picture in my head what those sounds look like. I step back softly on the carpet and lean back so I can take a peek at the front door just at the bottom of the stairs.

I have to steady myself from the shock of seeing him and Eleanor wrestle through the door. Once I've found my footing and pressed myself back behind that corner to peek at the scene downstairs, I notice something odd. It's not wrestling. He's fighting with her unconscious body through the entry. She's well covered in her clothes. The same ones I saw her wearing days ago. The sheer material of her sleeves mean I can see the darkened blotches underneath. I want to know where they've been, why there's a secondary location where he's taken her to subject her to his conditioning methods. I've never known him to do that. However, I've never really known him before me, so I suppose there's still much to learn.

I creep down a few steps as he drags her body under the stairs. It dawns on me then.

The basement.

I haven't given it much thought or even ventured down there to see if he did manage to dispose of my dead body. He must have though because he flings the door open and just lets her go. Her limp figure rocks unsteadily as he detaches himself from her before it falls. Her legs crumple under her, bones cracking as they slam on the stone steps. I feel every uneven surface as the sound of her tumbling down the stairs echoes out into the hallway and travels up to me overlooking the door from the staircase. The chipped stone of the fifth step that crumbled away before we moved in, its rough surface scraping her already abused skin. Then there's a small screw sticking out on the seventh that will snag her clothes and even pierce her skin. Only slightly, though; it doesn't protrude out far enough to cause any major harm. Then there's the misleading smoothness of the last three steps. They've eroded away over time but are smoother than the other steps. They look more forgiving but the fact they've lost half their coverage means they provide a quicker and more brutal descent down onto the floor.

The loud crunch as she finally crashes to the floor still startles me even though I'm expecting it. I experience everything I went through as a spectator and the noises hit differently from this perspective. I suffer all over again. The sound of the pain being inflicted feels worse than the injury of it in real time. Almost as though hearing the violence hurts more than being the receiver of it.

Watching his lack of reaction to what he's done also hurts. It makes my insides burn in rage that he's incapable of empathy or self-reflection. This journey he goes through time after time with woman after woman, never learning that it doesn't fill a void. He repeats the cycle with the same outcome that doesn't provide satisfaction. I wonder if there would be any woman or any outcome that would be enough for him. In my time as a ghost haunting him, I haven't unlocked anything new. He's the same with a witness as he is without. There's no indication there's a goal he's aiming for, but there has to be. There's a reason for his insatiable desire to do what he does to women, and I want to know what it is.

His hand reaches out and just with his fingertips, he slams the door shut. A rush of air sends my hair flying out of my face. He rounds the staircase then and heads up towards me. I press myself against the bannister so we don't collide but he must sense something is amiss as he slows to a stop. His boots settle only inches away from my toes on the same step. There should be a siren sounding behind my eyes when he turns and his hand reaches out towards my face. I should be running from it as it advances towards me. However, I remain half dreading, half anticipating what will happen.

The moment his fingers gently brush over my cheek, I experience that same sense of losing myself. His touch is so gentle, so tender that my eyes start to water. He would become the man I wanted him to be on the odd occasion in the past. I'd fall for him and give him everything in those moments. I could never describe how he manipulated me into such affections back then and I certainly can't now. I'm dead. I'm meant to be stronger against his charms, especially when I know he's not trying to use them. I doubt he even knows I'm here. But here I am, leaning into his hand, my own settling over his in desperation for the love his gesture might offer.

He frowns at his hand but keeps it where it is, his thumb absently caressing the air as he sees it. He leans forwards in curiosity, his lips parted and inviting. I don't know why I do it. It's as if something behind me shoves me forwards and up the one step between us on the stairs. I stop just a centimetre from his face. I've never seen it so smooth and free of tension this close before. My gut leaves me to my own reckless instincts and I end up slowly closing the gap between us and kissing him on the lips. He inhales sharply through his nose but doesn't pull away.

In the end, it's me that ends the kiss after a few seconds of the lapse in my better judgement. I watch his face for a reaction. His brow is furrowed and he rubs his lips in confusion. I wonder if there's a tingle of my presence that's lingering on them. It's concerning that I want there to be.

I want you to feel me.

He shakes his head as though dispelling the moment as a trick of the mind before carrying on upstairs. He stops at the top of them and turns back, looking directly at where

I'm standing. The pause is only three seconds or so but it's long enough for me to wonder.

"You can't see me," I whisper in false confidence. I even look behind me to check.

Then he turns away and disappears round the corner, leaving me to process what the *fuck* I was thinking. I lean back heavily on the bannister, panting. There are no words for the thoughts rattling around in my head. I can't even begin to fathom the state of mind I find myself in. My fingers lift to my sore lips. They tingle in longing as they feel his wander further away from them. I wonder if they feel sore because of that, like they feel physical pain being away from him.

Physical pain with or without him.

I haven't even had the time to rejoice at the discovery that I wasn't going mad these last few days but now I'm alone I can. Although I still don't understand how I missed them both leaving the house, I know now that they were definitely here. There were moments I wondered if I was back in some alternate reality conjured up in my head.

Unfortunately, it's not all good news. What's just happened now on the staircase has changed my outlook on this situation entirely. I might not have been crazy about him and Eleanor being in the house, but I'm undeniably crazy when it comes to him. And that's not good for anyone involved in this messed-up little corner of the world we're inhabiting.

CHAPTER TWENTY-SIX

There's blood on the door under the stairs. It wasn't there the night he let her fall into that awful room below the house. I would be a liar if I didn't say that I'd dedicated my time more to my own issues with that night than Eleanor's. My selfish nature rears its ugly head again but I don't find myself riddled with as much guilt this time. I feel like I'm entitled to analyse my feelings with what I've gone through. I've got nothing to prove and no hero complex to live up to.

The blood bothers me though. What have I missed? She wasn't bleeding when I saw her and she never touched the door. His hands were clean, so it's not something that happened in that moment. It's a dark, sticky mark on the wood, so it's old. I know all the consistencies of blood by now so I can assume it must've happened overnight. Most likely whilst I sat curled up in the front room downstairs to distance myself from him. It seems I'd also detached myself from Eleanor by consequence. Not that my presence has done much to deter the horrors she's faced.

I hesitate to venture down there for a multitude of reasons but I have to. I manage to slip through the door easily when I put my mind to it. My uncertainty of this move was a factor I thought would make this hard, but it becomes second nature. The door opens silently much to my delight and I'm able to slip down the stairs easily. My hands rest on the wall, feeling their way through the gloom. Déjà vu floods through me as I recall walking down into her own basement weeks ago and what I came to find there.

I curse as I forget the worn-away bottom steps. I've never actually walked down the steps like this before. He'd be with me, pushing, shoving or dragging if I were even granted permission to make my own way downstairs. Most times it was a similar journey to the one Eleanor took. There's an eye-watering stench that has been building the deeper I venture under the house. Between that and the darkness, my senses are overloaded and become unreliable at best.

The same hum of her talking to herself filters through the stagnant air. So, she's here and she's conscious. It's coming from behind the table. The one I woke up on. I swallow thickly before pushing forwards. I don't want my fear to rule me and I'll learn and see nothing I don't already know. I know I died, I know my dead body was in this room and I need to be able to push it aside to understand what purpose I serve haunting this house rather than finding peace with my death.

I make it to just halfway past the table when I stop. The murmurs are louder and I can also hear that awful rocking sound. I can imagine exactly what she's doing almost instantly. The cement floor shouldn't creak as she rocks, though, but I can hear that creaking anyway. I dispel the thought of it quickly, not wanting to latch onto something that I know will terrify me if I explore it. Instead, I just listen to the grind of her bones against the surface as she pushes forwards and backwards. It's takes me a second but my hand rests on the cold metal table to support me as I crouch below to see her.

Her clothes are torn and her bruises look black in the dim lighting. The only light he's allowed her is a small lamp on the far wall with a dying bulb. The warm glow is a sharp contrast on her blue skin. I can't help but think back to the night I followed her in the car park and how different I looked under the glow of the streetlight to her. We're not so different now.

Her beauty has diminished into a tired, ragged version of the woman she once was. It's so drastic that it makes me question how long I've been alone here whilst they were elsewhere. It took me weeks, even months to look as fragile as she does now.

"It's okay. You're okay. It's okay. You're okay." She stutters the words out as she rocks back and forth. She has to force the words out every now and then as she repeats herself. The short pauses and fumbling of her words give away the fact she doesn't believe what she's saying but she wants the mantra to plant a seed of belief. I wish it would work for her.

Her eyes flicker back and forth as she picks new parts of the floor to look at with each swing of her irises to the left or right. Her lips are scabbed over and rough as though she's chewed away at them in worry over and over. Her lower jaw wobbles around her words, adding a tremor to her pronunciations. It's so far from the person I know that I just stare. I'm not sure what I look for but I just stay there watching her face struggle to fit the new emotions she's experiencing. The creases in her brow stand out like a sore thumb from the smooth pale skin I'd seen there not too long ago.

The room floods back to me the more I stare at her expression and find nothing further to analyse. The stench of the basement is still as prominent but there's a bitter tang to it now. I can taste it like cold metal in my mouth. Blood. Someone is bleeding and I know it's not me.

She's shrouded in shadows underneath the table. I grip it and drag it away from the wall. My nails dig under the edge to ease the strain of the movement. I don't dwell on what an injustice is that I'm still so weak even dead. The table pulls away and groans loudly. I pray that the sound doesn't vibrate through the walls and up to him if he's still here. Suddenly I'm cursing my ignorance of his presence that I adopted after that awful lapse of self-control. Maybe if I'd have taken more notice, I'd know if he was in the house still. Or even if he's distracted enough to pay no mind to me down here with Eleanor.

Now, from being able to observe her from above, I see it. A thumbnail grinding deep into the palm of her right hand. Mottled skin peeled away and scattered around a red pool of blood. The revealed flesh is uneven and being worked and scraped away to allow the thumbnail deeper into the hand.

"No!" I scream. I feel my jaw unlock and drop lower than I've ever experienced before. The scream gurgles in the back of the throat and pushes out with force. The pitch climbs and if I could I'd even flinch from the sound. It's blood-curdling.

Eleanor slows to a stop as her eyes lock on mine. Her eyes widen in horror. I can see the silent scream float out of her frozen lips. She looks like she's frozen out of fear. My jaw clicks back into place as the hurt that I'm causing that look on her face sets deep in my bones. I want to apologise; it's clear I've pushed through again and she can actually see me. The words don't come, though, and the fear she feels still floods out of her eyes like a beacon. It shines bright, as though it's the morning sun as it rises over the cliffs, filling up the room and blinding me. It tingles as it hits my eyes, coaxing the tears back again. I'm so tired of crying.

She raises her arm, her bloody palm on display as she muffles her terrified whimpers with the back of her hand. I try to flinch as I see more of the extensive damage she's done with her nervous yet disgusting tick, but I can't. The other thing I can't do is understand how such a destructive habit would offer her reassurance down here. What I'd craved in the cold basement was warmth and comfort to ease the aches and scrapes of my body. She was worsening her condition instead. The complete opposite of what I did. I'm no psychologist, though, so I'm unsure if her methods are ones that can be explained. At least she's got something unplugged up there, the same as me. I may be mad, but so is she. We're just on opposite ends of the word.

"Please," she whispers, her left hand still hovering over her mouth. I remain standing there looking down at her tiny body curled up on itself. "It's all going to be okay. All to the plan."

"No. It's not," I snap. She squeals as my voice cuts through her pleas. The whimpers become more erratic.

How can she be so detached from her reality?

Nothing is going to plan here. There shouldn't be anything here that she wants or needs. She needs to understand she's not going to be okay. There's no future in which she walks out of this for the better. Not with the mindset she has and the desperation to please him that I've seen nestled deep in her core. Who she is, is changing. She's losing control. The restraint any normal person would have in their obsession with pleasing someone else isn't something she possesses.

I can't be the nurturing figure I want to be with her. She needs the iron fist swinging down on her. A firmness I'm worried I might not have. Though here in this room she looks at me as though I'm the most terrifying thing she's ever seen. As much as it disgusts me that I can encourage that reaction from someone I want more than anything to see me as an ally, I can use this for my cause.

Eleanor is scared of me, and it's the only thing that can make her listen to someone other than him. She lives to please him. I've seen for myself that she isn't deterred from her adoration of him even after falling victim to his violence. I can't compete with the devotion by being an empathetic spectator. I have to be something that does inspire that kind of all-consuming fear that keeps you awake into the early hours of the morning. The kind that has you looking over your shoulder, avoiding mirrors so you don't see shadows following you. The fear that small children have when they turn the lights off downstairs and go full pelt up the stairs towards the light to feel safe. She needs that kind of uncertainty of what ill fate could befall her if she doesn't comply.

It's perfect, I realise. Mainly because he won't provide a safe haven for her. She'll go running to him and he won't have any urge to protect or soothe her worries. He'll just corrupt her anxious mind further and aid me unknowingly.

I know now that it's not about trying to fix Eleanor anymore. I have to haunt her. Properly.

CHAPTER TWENTY-SEVEN

leanor doesn't come out of the basement for a few more days. Her palm is still a bloody mess when she ventures up into the light of the hallway. It's still dark up here but not as dark as the basement. Her eyes need time to adjust to the natural light. The abuse she's put her skin through looks worse in natural light. The skin is bright and puffy and it gleams as her hand shields her eyes.

He notices immediately. Any handiwork on her body that's not his, of course he notices. She's not aware that his shoulders are curling as he leans to further inspect. I don't like the tension that radiates off his body. His right arm swipes out quickly and grabs her forearm. I can see his fingers dig into her arm mercilessly.

"What this?" His voice is cold, his jaw tight.

It's a cruel question. We both know he knows what it is. He just wants her to admit it. If she says she doesn't know, she's a liar. If she admits the truth, she's condemning herself to his temper. Stepping into her shoes right now, she'll be weighing up which option is the least damaging for her.

Deep down, though, she knows it's a useless debate and the more time she spends mulling over her answer, the more her silence will aggravate him.

He releases her arm but not before shoving at it so she stumbles back. I can see his hand shake with anger as he does it. He's still trying to hold his wrath back for now. Drawing this out is part of his game. Eleanor's hand lowers to her side but she carefully keeps the wound in his view. I can see her hand twitch as she fights the impulse to hide it.

Good, I think, *she's learning.*

The internal struggle she's showing through her small movements will be logged by his keen eyes. The physical appearance of her hesitance to obey will irritate him. I can imagine his jaw clenching as he watches those little tells.

Her lips tremble. "It's just..." She slams her lips shut. She doesn't know what to say. Her head tilts down feebly to avoid eye contact but he pinches her chin in between his fingers and pulls it back up.

"It's just what?" he urges her for more.

God, how I hated this when I was his victim. I had my need to please him to avoid torture pushing the words up my throat, but my fear of knowing that no answer would be right would push them back down. It would end up as this huge clump lodged in my throat. At least Eleanor has the grace to clamp her mouth shut. I would gargle and choke on the words in her place. It's irritating how well she wears it compared to me and I have to struggle with my emotions to stamp the envy back out. I shouldn't be feeling this way towards someone who needs my help.

"It's just something I did to punish myself," she scrambles to get the words out and it's clear she's making

238

it up on the spot. Her eyes are wide, framed by watery fluttering eyelashes. She's trying to portray innocence but it's done poorly. I really need to work on her. "For you. I had to do it for you."

Her repetition of that last part puts the final nail in her coffin. That last sentence was said an octave higher with so much force and confidence. It's clear she's figured it was the perfect excuse. It's unfortunate the delivery was lacking. It's a flimsy reason. A blatant lie. More importantly, it's pouring gasoline on his fire.

"For me? When did I ever suggest that you could do anything for me?" He's furious, I can feel the heat of it radiate onto my skin as I stand behind him peering over his shoulder at the scene.

"N-never. I just—"

"You don't *just* anything!" his voice booms. I step back startled and Eleanor does the exact same thing. It's a peculiar mirror image where for once we both align in our actions. I'm not sure if that moment is interesting or unsettling to me.

"I-I know and I'm sorry." She forgets her hand and holds both of hers up in a small sign of surrender.

I've seen that gesture from people when trying to calm someone down. It will only escalate the situation here but I can't stop the train wreck happening before me. I can only watch to see what happens.

He doesn't say much. He doesn't need to. I can hear what he's saying by his silence. It's a quality he possesses that is enviable. He understands silence and when not to fill it with mindless chatter. In so few words he does so much. It was an admirable thing that I'd found attractive in my younger days and in some ways, I can't deny him my appreciation of the skill even now.

"Please," she whispers as the waterworks begin. Her eyes leak and even I have to admit the way she acts in this situation feels fake.

I shouldn't say that at all. I don't know why I seem to make such harsh statements about her when I want to help. She just doesn't hold herself well with him. First there was the desperation to please him despite his character, then there was the breakdown in the bedroom, which I do think was real now. Now, she's standing in front of him with half-hearted attempts to smooth over the confrontation. The tears are forced and despite her efforts to appear something else she ends up looking odd. So far from what I did in my time with him. I can't seem to validate it the same way I could for my behaviour. I'd have handled it so differently. More importantly, I'd have handled it the right way. It's an insult to me what she's doing instead.

He shares the same sentiment, it seems, as he takes a step forward menacingly. I hate that I have something in common with him but I blame it on my years with him and all the manipulation I endured. The knots he tied in my head are still untangling so I'm not free of him yet.

The crack of his elbow into the side of her head echoes through the hallway. I cover my ears instinctively. The noise was so much louder than I expected. I lean left around his body, hands still covering my head to see his face. From my angle, his lips are curled upward in a smirk. He's proud of that.

Eleanor's upper body stays leant back from the impact. Her injured hand stays by her side, which is a plus. She's understood what's caused this outburst in the first place and she keeps it as far away from his outburst as possible. I'm glad she understands where not to escalate now. I can't fathom how she's learnt a few things in one area and yet nothing at all in another. There's so much she's not considering in her interactions with him that she needs to learn from.

I see his dark figure surge forwards as his hand grabs her throat viciously. She's pushed backwards, stumbling through the doorway behind her into the kitchen. His hand doesn't stop though and he shoves downwards hard on her neck so she's bent backwards over the counter. The loud cry that reaches my ears pierces right through me. I can tell by the awkward way her body is being pinned against the island that it must be excruciating. That's not even considering how difficult it will be to breathe in that position.

"You disgust me," he grits out, his hand squeezing impossibly tighter around her throat. It will be a pleasing shade of purple for him to admire tomorrow.

I don't watch much more. I hear the groans and gasps for breath as he expresses his disgust several times on her. The noises are so much harder to stomach when they come from her mouth than the ones his fists make.

He eventually strolls past me, wiping the blood off his hands with a dark towel. He flings it on the ground when he's done with it for her to clean up. I stand at the foot of the stairs, watching him disappear up them before I rush to see Eleanor. She's wiping her tears away and awkwardly trying to manoeuvre her screaming body around the kitchen.

When I've finally ventured around the island to where she's hobbled over to, I can hear her talking to herself again.

"It's okay. It's just the plan. You're going to be okay," she mutters.

I'm dumbfounded. How can she possibly be so naive after what she's just experienced? Anger floods through my body with force. This isn't right; she's not right. She's been using the same few sentences to convince herself that she's okay and I can't stand her for it. She's too far gone with her devotion to him. My blood boils as that thought.

No. You're not going to do this, Eleanor.

I try to smack her, too, maybe knock some sense into her. It's exactly the same thing he does but seeing as she responds so well to it and I'm looking for an outlet for my frustrations, I go with it. My hand sails through her face as though she's not there. I frown in confusion. I'm not sure how I'm controlling my actions. I'd willed my hand to make impact against her cheek and it hadn't.

"It's all going to plan," she's still chanting, nodding to herself.

"No it isn't," I growl out. I've never heard myself sound so firm as I'm staring down at her pale face.

She howls in anguish, then tries to scramble away from me clumsily. I can't lie that I don't feel any satisfaction at being the one to make her break her normally flawless composure. I feel a lot of it. I shouldn't, but it's nice to see that she can suffer through what I did with the same lack of precision. She doesn't make it far into the corner of the kitchen.

Am I cornering her? When did I start doing that?

"Please, just let me be," she sobs at me.

No, Eleanor. I won't leave you be until you're fixed. I can't allow you to suffer the same fate whilst I have the ability to help.

"You know I can't do that," I reply, voice still firm. My meekness won't do her any good.

"I know," she nods defeatedly, her lip trembling as more tears cascade down her swollen cheeks.

It occurs to me, once I've watched her flee the room back upstairs, what she said. I peer around the door frame as she studies herself in the bathroom mirror, exactly as I used to. She's not got any flight in her response to him; she's not ready to run at any moment. I definitely was at this stage. It's only been a few weeks; she should still be able to remember the taste of what freedom is and yearn for it. But she doesn't. If anything, as she exits and strides back into the living room to keep him company, she wants to be near him. She couldn't make it more obvious that she wants nothing to do with me, and I'm the one with good intentions. She's blissfully happier with him and she fears me. I couldn't be more confused than I am when I'm around her.

The way she leans so heavily into his conditioning, the devotion he's inspired in her is so far from what I know. She is me in the moments when he subjects her to his brutality but she so quickly flits back to wanting to be someone worthy of his approval. I need to understand why she does this. I feel like it's important but I don't know why. My crawler nods deep in my gut. It doesn't come up as much but every now and then it encourages me in the right direction.

I leave them alone in the living room. I don't want to witness her attempts to please him. Watching that, even thinking about it, makes me feel sick. My stomach sinks at the thought of her catering to his every need in the perfect way that he wants. I don't ask myself why, and my crawler shakes its head in agreement as well. If I explored why, it would break me.

CHAPTER TWENTY-EIGHT

It's somewhat quiet over the next few days. I stick to Eleanor's side as much as I can bear. She still has this buzzing energy under her skin constantly whenever he's not in the house. The window sill has a speck of dust on it. The flowers need replacing. The remote for his TV isn't pointing directly at it from where it rests on the arm of his chair. I watch her straighten it, checking back and forth between the chair and TV to ensure it's right.

I go to follow her back out of the room to observe her other obsessive tidying habits but my feet stay rooted to the floor. The armchair. The days I used to sink into it for comfort and reassurance seem so far away now. The indentation in the cushions are undeniably his, though. But I wonder…

The leather envelopes me lovingly, welcoming me back. It's the first time I've sat in it since I discovered he was alive. It feels nice to be doing something so bold whilst he's away. I can't help but melt into the embrace of it. A low hum of energy pulses under my fingers. I can't place what it reminds me of. Most likely the sense of power I convinced myself I had back then. A reminiscent time of when I felt in control of my fate and that fighting my way out of his clutches had meant something.

Not anymore.

In my exploration of the chair, my fingers stumble on the remote Eleanor has just straightened. I hesitate at a simple thought. It's merely curiosity, but I always did wonder what exactly he watched on the screen. There was only so much I could catch from the slight reflections on his glasses. Back then, by his side, I'd never paid attention to it. I'd immersed myself in my internal downward spiral. I'd locked myself in my mind whenever I could to try to figure out what was wrong with me. Why I was always nearby for him, silently obeying his every wish.

Now, with extensive knowledge of his routines, I knew I could give into my desire to know everything. Fortunately for me, the remote is old, as is the TV, so I know how to work it. It's been years since I've held a control for anything electrical and the weight of it in my hand is a brand-new experience all over again. I'm living in an age of technology that I've never laid my fingers upon until now.

Lucky for me, I'm still intellectual enough to easily work out what buttons do what. A small thing to be grateful for that I kept as my own all these years. As soon as the screen comes to life and my face is bathed in the blue glow, it's done.

The music is what startles me. I watch the fingers I know intimately in the worst ways pluck at strings. I frown at the instrument. I was never able to play an instrument myself, but I know a few. This one, it's almost a harp but different. A stringed instrument that's played similarly but not. I struggle to understand it. The tune it plays is hauntingly beautiful though. The notes are full and blend seamlessly into one another. The man who plays it, he narrates his sinful mind through the music he plays. It's captivating in a sinister way. The sounds don't float peacefully through the air, they trigger a slow churn of uncertainty in my guts. Each note twangs noisily through the room, scraping painfully on my nerves. I can feel the vibrations on my skin and the carve of each message on my skin.

As much as I try to fathom what the messages are, the next note will ring out eerily through the air and I lose my train of thought. The wobble of each sound throws me off balance. My body feels too heavy for the chair to hold and I struggle to stop myself being swallowed into the upholstery whole. It's like quicksand as my limbs sink deeper into the leather.

I look up as I dig my fingers into the arms of his chair. He's staring straight at me. I can feel the leather hot against my skin as it bubbles around me, gaining more coverage over my body. He smiles in a smug manner. The only time I'd see such a smile was moments before I'd give in to his demands. I think I'll always remember this moment and how loud I screamed in protest as I experience everything like an out-of-body experience. I start to panic. I can't keep going through this time after time.

Please.

My fingernails claw at the leather frantically. There's no thought or precision in my movements as my anxiety seeps deeper into my core. The churn in my stomach starts to move quicker. The nausea grips me, one hand wrapped around my stomach and the other reaching out to form an alliance with the anxiety pounding fiercely in my heart. The music keeps playing. I hear it getting louder.

Is it getting louder?

The more his fingers pluck expertly at the strings, the more the darkness inside me builds. I'm so far back in the sofa now that his scent encircles my head, suffocating me. It's not a bad smell, it never has been. It's been a weakness of mine because, no matter how hard I try not to, I always find his scent so attractive. Even the whiffs I'd manage to catch from him when he was inflicting pain provided comfort. It was something nice in an environment that offered me nothing bout misery. As sad as that sounds. It still physically hurts me that I have to admit that something he provided to me had a positive effect. He certainly liked being a source of pleasure and pain for me. I think the unpredictability of that excited him.

Where is my crawler?

Normally by now I'd have the reliable movement around my insides of a creature that felt like me and not a foreign entity formed from years of manipulation. The chair seems to be blocking anything that is truly me. The turmoil inside me seeps further into my veins, poisoning more and more of me as it goes. That prompts a sickening surge in my anxiety. I feel it rise from my stomach up into my chest. It's trying to choke me with fear.

The leather is burning now. I feel like my skin is boiling under it. I finally rip my eyes away from the TV and look down. The chair isn't cream anymore, it's just black sludge oozing all over my body. I try to scream but my voice is gone. I try to move but I'm in too deep, my limbs are rendered useless. I'm completely trapped.

"I think that's enough for now, don't you, little crow?" A tinny voice echoes out into the room. The music is still playing but only faintly now.

God, please no.

I look up and my fear is confirmed. He's not only able to see me, but he's live in this moment the same as me. He's sitting, plucking the instrument on the screen as if this is a completely normal occurrence. He studies me carefully. I don't know why. This is the most open my expression has been in a long time. I always thought he'd stare at me for so long because he was trying to see past the facade. As I watch his expression, though, it's not what he's doing today. He's cataloguing my face, committing to memory how I look right now.

I can't break eye contact. I can feel his curiosity poking and prodding at me ruthlessly but I can't look away. I'm as entranced by him as he is by me. It's a strange encounter between us and we both know it. I've never been so sure he won't be able to hurt me but so terrified of him in the same breath.

My skin feels raw. I don't even know what to say or do to make it stop.

"Hmm. I didn't think you'd be silent now. Interesting." His sharp gaze sweeps me up and down. I shrink under his judgemental gaze.

"What the fuck do you expect me to say?" I breathe out through the nausea exasperatedly.

"And you're angrier now. More assertive." He smirks at that. I get the unsettling notion that he's proud of that.

I flash back to all those times I defied him at the very start and he'd jump me so quickly. I'd come to expect a blow to the chest or head if I even raised my voice. I don't understand why he seems so amused by me now.

And how is this even happening?

"Little crow, still so small and naive. Even in death," he chuckles darkly.

This has got to be in my head. There's no way this is really what's happening. I've been roaming as a ghost in this house for weeks and I'm confident he doesn't know I'm here. In the basement when I first saw him after discovering my death, he was terrified of me. This can't be the same reality as that.

It just can't.

"Fuck off," I gasp as the sludge starts to slowly release me.

"Audacious too. It seems you've ended up so far from the nest I built for you," he tuts mockingly.

"I bet that kills you doesn't it?" I heave as the agony of my body eases. "I'm nothing like what you made me."

"You're different to the others, yes. It seems that makes you entertaining to me for now." The octave of his voice drops as his finished that sentence. I shudder at the implication of it. I'm only safe for now.

I pluck my arms from the chair and peel myself off it completely. I feel sore and tender all over. My legs are jelly but I navigate well on them. I swipe the remote as I step forwards to the screen, crouching low to face him eye to eye.

"I'm not your little crow," I hiss at his pixelated face. "And I'm definitely not your *fucking entertainment*, you bastard."

I stab the off button on the remote viciously and he smiles as he disappears from the screen. I release a huge sigh of relief and rest my heavy head in my shaking hands. It took so much strength to do that. With the exhaustion of the chair incident as well, I'm dead on my feet.

I ensure I place the remote back on the chair exactly as I left it before stepping out of the room. It's like nothing's happened. I flee down the hallway with a renewed sense of urgency. I need to get far away from that room for a while. I'm not sure if it's just my mind playing tricks on me, but as I descend down the stairs, I'm sure I've heard that song before.

CHAPTER TWENTY-NINE

There's been a steady build in the atmosphere here. I can feel the change in the air as I wander aimlessly, still avoiding the living room upstairs. There's a deep vibration in my bones that intensifies as the days bleed into each other. I've been unable to put my finger on what I seem to know deep down is coming. I haven't even been able to figure out if the outcome will be good or bad for the situation I'm still in. It's too difficult to separate my hopes it will be positive from the validity of the feeling of what it will actually be.

Eleanor seems to be more… Eleanor? I can't describe it but it's not enough to say she's more erratic. She's difficult, jumpy and obsessed as ever with the order of everything around the house. The likeness to him is uncanny sometimes and it's a struggle to comprehend that he treats her with so much volatility. I can't seem to justify it, not that it ever should be. It's a puzzle that becomes increasingly complicated the more time stretches out in the house.

He seems fine. It's clear he's in control of the atmosphere even if that is an inhumane quality to possess. He moves effortlessly through the thick tension in each room. It definitely feels more like him in the house. He monopolises the space with ease and his musk is choking me and Eleanor. I can see that lump in her throat that she struggles with just like me. It swells more each time I see it. She doesn't have much time.

Time until what though?

There are no clues surrounding him or her. The beatings have settled down somewhat; I figure it's because she's learning but I don't stick around much to watch them. Witnessing something so cruel is hard, but controlling what emotions it conjures up inside me is harder. I don't like the way I feel around those two. It takes me back to traitorous thoughts and feelings that I shouldn't have. I can't risk going down that road. It opens up barely healed wounds, especially those directly linked to my pride. So, I don't watch. I don't observe. I only listen if I can't avoid it and even that is enough to start the downward spiral.

She holds herself better after each instance. She's wearing it worryingly well, not only physically but emotionally. Her shine has become duller, but she is still wandering the house with an unbelievable amount of energy. Her features have sunken so she looks worse for wear, if not a little tired. Although her hair doesn't have the same level of shine and her clothes hang awkwardly with her injuries affecting posture, it's not what concerns me. It's that awful, delusional smile on her face. It's one I'm unfamiliar with. The muscles in my face don't know that shape and even my warped mind doesn't know that level of happiness in the midst of bruises and pain.

I can see the twitch in her eye grow more severe and I know I'm running out of time. There's so much wrong with her adaptation to her relationship with him. If that's what you can call it. She's not learning how to get through this until she can escape, she's conditioning herself to accept her fate. She's pushing herself to find happiness in her abuse. It's astounding. It crushes me how disappointed I am in her. I really thought she'd do better.

Nevertheless, I need to push through that. There's an irritating little feeling on the back of my neck as I watch Eleanor clatter around the ground floor with little grace. She's just as on edge as me, but she's bearing the weight of it better. As she grabs several pans and throws them on the hob, I realise that she hasn't cooked since she's been here. It's not an unexpected fact. I never cooked much either, even though it had given me a sense of control and zen when my life got tough. This was before him and it was a gradual phasing out of that. One day I was running to the kitchen to throw together a hot dinner, the next I barely looked at the kitchen. It was like that with a lot of my behaviours, though. I felt so weak and clueless when it hit me I had changed so much without protest. Unfortunately, I had no one there to reassure me and tell me it wasn't my fault. Some people are too skilled for what they do. I was done from the moment he orchestrated our first meeting.

Another clang rings out through the kitchen. She has no idea what's she doing and the noise is enraging me. I like quiet; I don't like the loud noises that rattle around in my head. There's already too much up there.

"What are you doing?" He's home early, and clearly not expecting her to cook him a meal.

She whirls around with that creepy smile on her face. She looks like a devoted housewife going through a psychotic episode. I can't look away even though it's freaking me out.

"I thought it would be better for us to have a proper meal instead of scraps of food every now and then," she declares happily.

There are so many things wrong with that sentence. So many things she shouldn't have said. 'I think', for example: she doesn't get to think and she should know this. He's in control and her battling for it will be her downfall. She's getting too excitable and eager to please again and it's clouding her judgement on how to dance with her captor. Then to outright say she has a better plan for how they both eat is beyond foolish. To even insinuate she has a superior thought or idea to his is a death sentence. I'd received punishments too severe to revisit for something smaller than that. I've never seen what this kind of cluelessness gets you though. I have a feeling I'm about to find out.

He stands there in the kitchen and his fingers curl into his palms slowly. His tell is speaking volumes of what's to come. She's blissfully unaware as she turns back to her reckless attempts at deciphering how to cook. His eyes are burning as he watches her. I can hear the rumble of his wrath ooze out into the room. The thick air in the kitchen welcomes the addition and the gloom of it adds to the sinister feel.

I should run, I think. I should get as far away from this as I can. I'm not willing to give up my selective ignorance to what happens between them. I know it well. I have seven years of this to look back on should I need the light to be held on what she suffers for her insane lack of awareness and survival instinct. But I'm pinned to the spot on the floor. I can taste the metal tinge in my blood as the nails sink through my feet and into the floor below.

He wants me to see this.

I don't know why the thought breaks through into my consciousness. I know it's not true, that he has no power over me now, but I feel the sickening tug of my flesh on my feet when I try to move. Knowing I could cause myself pain even though I should be free from it is terrifying, so I remain where I stand and just hope I can get through this.

Eleanor's back is still to him. She's not seen his temper rise slowly as he grapples with how to inflict punishment on her. I'm expecting to see a level of brutality that would be unlike anything I could imagine. I can feel the promise of it radiate off his body and ripple through the air.

"You thought?" he questions, his voice low. I can hear the strain in his jaw as he keeps his anger just under the surface.

The two words say so much. A million things are conveyed as her shoulders stiffen. She's hearing all the underlying insinuations in them. How dare she think? Where did she get the audacity to try to control his routine? Where did he go wrong for her to think she can act this way? I could search for more, but she's swivelled around carefully to face him.

"Please forgive me," she whispers, her arms gripping the counter behind her for emotional support.

He stares her down harshly, his jaw clenched. It's a bold statement. The longer he stays coiled, ready to pounce, the more her fear will take over. The torture of expecting what happens next is just as delicious as the art of conditioning her behaviour once more. She shivers under his gaze; her eyes dart around his face looking for the indication of when he'll make his next move. She's already so worked up in mere seconds. It will feed his ego with how easily he can unravel her composure.

"It's not forgiveness you should be asking for," he snaps. *It should be mercy.*

I hiccup through a small sob. I don't want to be here for this. I can feel my agreement to his behaviour seep through my body. I don't have control over my thoughts and feelings as I watch their exchange.

Eleanor is too reckless, too obsessive. It's irritating to watch her scurry around the house, making far-fetched assumptions around what she can control now she's trapped here under his heavy thumb. The fact she wants to walk that tightrope between being agreeable and going too far with her desires to be perfect for him is what bothers me so. She's so disrespectful to the ones before her. It's a kick to the stomach every move she makes. She's not focusing on surviving; she wants to thrive with him. It's an insult to my memory, my trauma. That's why I jerk my head so it's nodding in solidarity with his disdain for her. I feel just as betrayed.

As he stalks towards her, I notice the hob is lit. The blue flames lick at the pan above. The heels of her hands aren't far from them. If they just flickered a little longer, they'd be lapping at her porcelain skin. The screech of the pan jolts me out of my trance. He's upon her now, reaching around her body as he removes the pan from its spot. She leans back and for a moment I think her long copper waves will catch fire. They don't. Her eyelashes do though.

It happens slowly first. His arm extends, his knuckles brushing over her skin. It's false affection, a common deceit he uses before he pulls it out from under her. His fingers fist into her hair, his other hand digs into her hip as he turns her so she's facing the flames. Next thing, she's folded neatly over in a sharp manoeuvre, her head planted down directly on the burner that's alight. I jump, trying to create distance between us, but I feel the bite of the nails in my feet. I remain there watching from only two metres away from them.

Before now, he's only ever been the personification of fire. A living, breathing ball of burning hatred and scorching desire for control. He's never once turned to fire like this. He knew he could burn people from the inside out without any need to light a match. To physically set her face on fire, there must be something deep rooted in his distaste for her to be this ruthless.

She's back to full height after only a moment or two. He's not prolonged the attack for any extensive damage to adorn her face. It needs to be done physically by his strength alone. He won't leave it to the elements to tarnish her skin the way he wants. It's not been inflicted organically by his own design.

He watches her as she stumbles away from him whimpering and heaving in shock at what's just happened. She spirals around the small space in the corner clutching her face. There's a small cloth on the side and she presses it to her tender, burning skin. I have no idea the pain she must be feeling, having survived my journey with him without this level of torture. Her hands shake aggressively. She's reeling from not only the sickness of what he's just done, but from how quickly it happened. If I'd have blinked it would have almost been over. The shock value must be the reason for the upward curl of his mouth. He's admiring his handiwork.

"W-why?" she stutters out. I'm amazed she doesn't understand. I can't figure her out.

He doesn't answer. Why would he? Part of the fun is watching her little mind wrestle with trying to understand what's occurred. She'll revisit the short conversation with him for days wondering what triggered him. I know why, but there's something about her ignorance and her arrogance that makes me wonder if she ever will. She doesn't seem to process her time with him like any normal victim would. I'm trying really hard to justify her behaviours but I fall short.

She breaks through her cries and throws to the side the cloth she was holding against her poor skin. I look at the angry red skin and singed eyebrow. The fury in her eyes matches it so well. She looks devastating in her own wrath. The emotions running through her features and tensing her muscles look nothing like the intimidating image she wants. She looks heartbroken and tumultuous.

"All I've done is worship the ground you walked on," she spits, "yet even *my* efforts leave you unsatisfied."

My eyebrows raise in shock; she's really going there with him. Personally, I wouldn't poke the beast after I'd seen what heights he's willing to go to in order to send his message. Again, she's recklessly brave in all the wrong places in time. There's something behind her eyes that make them bulge with a restless, manic energy. She stirs up something awful in my guts.

"You're implying you have expectations of me," he growls, approaching her again. He stands toe to toe with her and flicks the seared skin on her face. "You should know better."

The tone of his voice drops and there's a long, deep rumble through the room. I can feel the bass of it vibrate all over my body like before. I'm hit with this uncontrollable desire to please him. I look around the room, trying to understand why it feels like the walls are closing in as those four words start swirling around me. I stand rooted to the spot watching the tension-filled air swarm around me. I'm the eye of this storm.

As my eyes search the room left to right, I find Eleanor's. She's leaning back away from him as he looms over her threateningly. However, she's not paying him mind. Her mouth is agape as she stares directly at me.

I will never know why I do this as I'm staring at her helpless expression, but I summon everything I have inside of me. My crawler comes to life, squeezing my heart so it has no say as my mind takes over. Later, I'll wonder how my crawler went from my comfort to my traitor. A deep bubble of power surges up through my chest and up my throat. I don't recognise the voice that leaves my mouth, but I do know that I mean every word I speak as she looks to me for advice. These are the only words I can give her.

"You should know better, Eleanor."

She screams and drops to the floor. The nails in my feet are gone so I walk over to stand beside him looking down at her unconscious body. I can feel his thoughts push through into my mind.

She'll never learn.

CHAPTER THIRTY

Something's wrong with Eleanor.

I can feel it deep down in my core as I watch her crawl upstairs to the bedroom presumably. He left not long after the events of earlier this evening. Waking up in isolation was a gift to me so he hardly let me, but with her it's a punishment. I know it is by how she moans in anguish that he's not there to give her attention.

She makes me ill. I feel this insane urge to vomit all over her whenever I observe her now. Every single thing she does makes my skin crawl. There's something dark and ugly festering in me when I watch over her. It's not jealousy. Although I know have some unresolved feelings for my captor, I don't feel jealousy when I watch her pine for him. The more effort she makes to try and trigger affection from him shows me how desperate she's becoming. I didn't need to be desperate for that. I had all of that without lifting so much as a finger trying to impress him.

Eleanor is borderline psychotic now. She's smashing things that she's placed around the house for him. Her rage is taking her over in the most unflattering way. The vase that always held fresh gladioli for him is gone. It's funny how that came back full circle. Once upon a time it was me breaking her things, now she does it herself. Little ornaments here and there are thrown as well. As quickly as she makes a mess, though, she berates herself and fumbles around haphazardly to clean it up.

It's not particularly interesting for me to watch but I still follow her up the stairs. There's something about this that I need to see. My crawler scrambles back up to my chest, sitting there heavily as I glide through the doorway into the bedroom. The chest of drawers to my left are being ransacked with a vengeance.

"Where is it?" she mumbles to herself.

She's clawing at several items of clothing, flinging them behind her. They scatter around the room randomly. It's a mess and it perfectly depicts Eleanor's state of mind.

She gasps as her fingers land with a thud on something more solid. I stand over her left side, leaning down over her head so I can see what it is. I'm painfully invested in what belonging she wants to destroy next.

She plucks it from the back of the drawer and runs her hand over the worn leather cover. It's a notebook. Or a journal is more likely, with how thick it is, stuffed with lots of photos and bits of paper. I wonder where she found the time to document her life when she was here.

"Some fucking use this was," she snaps harshly as she pushes up onto her feet.

She takes a moment to look at the black leather cover once more before throwing it with all her strength at the wall. All I can hear is her heaving as she stares at the spot on

261

the wall it clattered against. Her shoulders rise and fall with anger. I don't have time to move out of her way as she spins on her heels and storms through my body and out of the room. I watch her go. That itch on the back of my neck starts to nag again. It's like something or someone is behind me.

As I turn to look at the remnants of the journal scattered all over the floor, my first thought is that it's *me*.

The photo on the floor is old. I haven't looked into a lens in years and my features are full, healthy and most importantly, happy. It's from my brief stint on social media. The last photo I posted. My legs are crossed as I sit outside a small cafe back in the city. His tanned hand rests on my thigh as I smile shyly at the camera. I never did like having my photo taken.

What's it doing in her journal?

I pick through the loose bits of paper in the room and snatch the book up. A few rogue pieces of paper flutter out but I pay them no mind. The book is what I need to read. It's a lot of handwritten clumps of notes spanning over a few hundred pages. I read a few and bile starts to crawl up my throat.

Routine Lora.
Shop visits are sporadic. Normally 8pm–9pm.
She likes the cover of darkness.
Summer – her visits are less frequent.

It's a messy scrawl a few pages deep. My head is spinning. Why is there a notebook with my routine inside? Why is that important? Deep down, I know, but I want to be sure. I sift back through to the first page. I have to know how this starts.

The first page isn't notes. It's a little mood board almost. A collage of aesthetically pleasing images. The gladioli that she loves so much are there; there are several candles pictured as well. The dark blues and golds jump out on the page. It's exactly what the house has become. A bold, glamorous representation of the colours that best suit him. It's as though he's thrown up on the page and she's sealed it in. I huff at the sheer absurdity of it until I stop.

My fingers are covering two small photos in the far-left corner. I shift my stance and hold the book in my right hand. My fingertips peel off of the pictures and my breath catches. The only two photos I've ever put out publicly with him are stuck neatly down in the corner. One overlaps the other and there's intent with that. The corner of one covers a portion of my face on the other. He's a bold statement in both. A well-groomed, golden arm that stakes claim on me but portrays loving affection at the same time. It's a lie.

It was all lies.

I'm starting to stitch together some pieces of the puzzle. My feelings of something being wrong with Eleanor. I wasn't looking at her from the right perspective. That much is clear. I flip back through the journal waiting for something else of me to jump out from the pages. Something that will make everything swimming around behind my eyes make sense.

Timid. Jumpy. Recluse. Pathetic. Scared. Quiet.

My lips tremble in anger. I don't need to read on to know she's describing me word by word. The title of the page says it all.

Everything I'm NOT.

I sink my nails into the leather, clutching it with as much strength as my rage feeds me. This woman, who I have been hell bent on trying to save from him all this time, had taken the time to sit down and remark on how pathetic and timid I was. Not only that but she'd be vehement in making sure she asserted that she was nothing like me and by default would never want to be.

Why is she doing this?

I can only describe her as delusional and cruel from the way she's articulated herself on paper. All that concern and empathy that I invested in her dissipates so fast. Then hurt starts to pang painfully in my chest. My crawler envelopes my heart but despite its efforts, I can still feel the excruciating pain of her betrayal.

I thumb through the pages unable to stop myself. The words blur a lot, but a few spring out. She likes the word 'pathetic' a lot. Her narcissism jumps out of the page. She's overly complimentary of herself. Each observation of me is then countered with how unlike me she is. How much better she can hold herself. That she's prettier than me. Cares for her appearance more than me. It goes on.

I cough a little, trying to wrestle down the hurt that threatens to turn on the waterworks. I will not cry about this. I will not allow her to be another reason my tears fall. Every interaction is now tainted. No longer is she the companion I need her to be. It's laughable that I thought us kindred spirits at the start. Hoping she'd be saved by my efforts. Now I don't owe her anything. Her diary paints a true picture of her feelings about me. I wonder if she kept me around for a pick-me-up.

Poor old Lora, but at least I look better than her.

I scoff and flip a rather heavy page over. I almost drop the book when I see his face staring straight at me. He's a timeless, handsome sight to behold. He looks as perfect here as he always does. It's only his eyes that convey the depths of his ferocity. I don't pay any mind to the way my fingers caress his face before I look to the next page. The familiar scrawl is there, although the handwriting is neater, prettier. I can see the change in approach to observations of him compared to me. She took her time with him.

Seems uninterested in other people. Holds attention from others well. Works out? Strong arms.

I snap the book shut. Strong arms? I bet she knows how strong they can be now. Why was she observing us both? We were rarely seen together. There are only small pieces of her thoughts from these simple notes. I notice that I've taken up only a small section of her journal and he's the rest. Way to make a girl feel special, Eleanor.

You crazy stalker bitch.

It gets more interesting towards the end. I can't stomach much of what she says about him so I skip through those deranged little notes until I'm reaching towards the end. The pages aren't dated but I have a certainty as I read through them that these were made days before my death.

She's withdrawn and unappreciative when with him.
They don't venture out much together.
He seems as indifferent to her as he does to everyone else.

She has more bruises—

I stutter as my heart sends searing pain through my chest. I blink steadily at the ceiling trying to keep my tears at bay. My lips wobble, making my jaw ache with how hard I fight to not give into my emotions.

She knew.

I wore my bruises over my body so carelessly after learning how awful people were. It didn't matter much nowadays if you had a couple of marks on your skin or if you looked malnourished. No one cares and no one wants to get involved in a problem. The fact that Eleanor did, though, and she's ended up here is a knife to the heart. She's wilfully committed to her ignorance. Not only that but she called me pathetic. She saw me suffer and instead of sympathising, she tore my character to shreds.

When the ceiling starts to blur, I look back at the book I'm still clutching in my right hand. I've just got to finish it.

It's no surprise she's been hurt. She doesn't present well. She doesn't act like she's lucky to have him. He needs someone who knows that.

Questions start to slice through my reeling mind. Did she follow us just to pursue a relationship with him in my place? Did she really hate me so much? Did she build a fake friendship with me to get to him?

The room feels claustrophobic as I recall my time following Eleanor for weeks. I was convinced she was a victim, but she's not. She's a villain. A conniving, horrible person who admired him in all his glory. I remember now:

that night outside the shops. She wanted someone gone. I always assumed it was work. What if it wasn't? What if that was me? It had to be, the way she acted on the call. I should've known there was only one person to make her act the way she did back then.

I keep a firm grip on the book and pick up all the scattered pieces from the floor as well. I don't know what I'm doing but I know I'm not done with this book yet. It will prove its use soon enough. I shove all the photos and notes clumsily into the awful thing and rush out of the room. I don't take notice of where that awful woman is. I just run away and sag into the corner of the front room downstairs.

I have to have a plan moving forwards.

What do I even do now?

Is it still the right thing to save her from him?

I don't know if I can anymore.

CHAPTER THIRTY-ONE

The sun has gone down by the time I move. The pieces of the journal are laid out precisely on the coffee table. The worst ones about me and the most intrusive about him. I ensure all the ones with intent to create the situation she's in now are there as well. She's laid bare for him to see if he ventures in this room.

I've done it deliberately in a room he doesn't venture into a lot. I don't feel like it's right to force it upon him that way. I may be heartbroken by the revelation of her scheming, but I still falter at exposing her with such malice. If he sees my layout in the front room, then he does; if he doesn't, then that's fine. It's not meant to be.

To be honest, I'm at war with myself. I've no clear motive here. I want to expose Eleanor, but I worry about why I need to. I'm dead. It doesn't benefit me anymore to enlighten anyone on what she is. Secondly, I can only expose her to him. Some part of me doesn't want him to benefit from knowing. He's never been so unaware of what's under his nose and although it's her that's bested him, I have to respect it. I haven't got one over on him like that in all my years with him. Even if it hurts, I'm glad someone finally managed to accomplish what I couldn't.

Waiting for what happens next is somewhat boring but I appreciate the quiet. I sit and watch the moonlight reflect off the glass before me. There's not much of the table's surface showing with all the torn pages from Eleanor's journal spread out all over it. It's so dark in this house when night falls. That dark blue that covers all the walls soaks up the moonlight so there's barely any visibility come late evening. She's made it easier for him to melt into the shadows.

He sneaks in and sits on the sofa behind me with little noise. I don't hear him as much as I feel him. His calf presses against my left side as he sits. I've been sitting cross-legged on the floor, back pressed against the sofa since I started placing all my evidence in order on the table. Thankfully, being dead means my back isn't screaming in discomfort in this position.

He hums in thought as he looks down at what I've made. *For him.*

His glasses glint every now and then. That's how I know he's actually looking through it all. His hands clench into fists in my peripheral every now and then. He silently simmers behind me as each revelation sinks in. I wonder, as he sits there soaking it all up, if he ever had any idea. I don't know if I wish he had or hadn't. It doesn't seem right for me to be so happy that she may have bested him. She's no better than him with her ill intentions.

His hand slams down on a photo amongst all the torn pieces of paper. I look up startled but his face is darkness. I can almost see the thunderclouds circling round his head as his mood worsens. His ability to manipulate the light around him is impressive and confusing. I'm glad I'm a ghost to him in this room. His rage is suffocating. He'll be wanting to lay hands on the first person in his sight. I'm glad it's not going to be me.

He drags the photo through the clutter of scraps from Eleanor's journal, his palm covering the entirety of it. I can't remember which one it was and looking back at what he's left behind on the table doesn't enlighten me further. He cradles it delicately in his palm, which stirs up more confusion in me. I frown at the contrast in his actions.

I end up kneeling by his side on the sofa, leaning over his broad shoulders to peer at the photo he seems to be so enamoured with. It's one I don't remember putting on the table. It looks so striking, though, I'm sure I'd recognise it. I can't seem to look away from the iridescent midnight-blue tones. It's a photo of him facing the camera but the shadows hang from his sharp features. He's nothing but a silhouette. My gaze lifts to the pale fingers I can see perched on his left shoulder. The almost translucent skin showing the blue veins underneath is hard not to recognise. As I explore more, I see the sunken face that used to be mine and the grey eyes glaring straight at the camera. My hair is that awful black colour, but it shines blue and green as I grapple with my balance looming over him.

The most disturbing part about the photo is how perfectly we fit together. A master of pain and suffering with his spectator watching from behind. It's turning my guts over and over. The nausea is creeping up on me again. The photo is as striking as it is absolutely terrifying. I never took a photo with him once I was completely trapped under his thumb. I never even looked that scary. I was too busy being the one living in constant fear and torment to look like I do in the photo.

It's been several long minutes that he's been captivated by the photo, but eventually he slides it into his pocket. I've never seen him have an attachment to anything except himself. I've never even seen him carry a bag. Not even when we moved to the middle of nowhere. It's a move that makes me watch him carefully as he rests his elbows on his knees, looking at what's left of my layout. I sit back on my heels with bated breath. His back ripples with tension. I can see the way his muscles move, readying to strike. I don't linger too much on them. My lapses in the feelings I have for him are becoming more frequent, and the information about Eleanor has pushed me further to him.

"Seems like she was as fascinated with you as I am, little crow," he muses quietly.

I fall back into the sofa, in hopes it swallows me whole.

Can he see me? Does he know I'm here?

I watch wide-eyed as he reaches out towards the journal pieces and starts shuffling them around. My crawler starts to dance around under my skin all over my body. It clenches on my ribcage painfully.

I can't breathe.

I can feel each piece click in my chest as it finds its place with guidance of his fingertips. I can feel the bones encased around my heart crack painfully each time the puzzle pieces slot seamlessly together. My crawler clenches tightly onto my ribs, grinding painfully on them as it scrambles for grip. I can feel my body go hot and my skin ice cold as the unbearable foreboding feeling consumes me.

Something's happening.

I peel myself off the sofa, stepping forwards through the pain of my overwhelmed body and mind. My balance is still off and I wobble uncertainly towards the picture he's painting. I know what he's doing; I can see the narrative present itself concisely before him as he slots it into place. My hands shake, then my arms and eventually my chest tremors.

"Please," I whisper. To him. To fate.

Don't let this be.

With one final roll of his shoulder, his arm returns to rest on his knee. There's a lump in my throat that I can't work around. I can't sob or scream or cry. I just choke on my despair as I look down. The words may as well be written in blood and splattered all over the walls for the fear they awaken in me. I haven't been this scared or inconsolable. Not even as his little crow.

I want to be Lora.

I can be better than Lora.

He deserves more than Lora.

Lora is pathetic.

Lora deserves it.

I'm nothing like Lora.

I can be what Lora can't be for him.

He won't need to keep me in line.

Lora needs to go.

Lora needs to die.

I'm going to make him kill her, and then he's mine.

The embarrassment hits me hardest. I think of all the cautious smiles and slivers of trust I gave her since we met. I think of the way I clung to her attention after so long of not knowing another's companionship. The way I'd fought my trauma to fight for her. To try and save her from abuse and yet she'd wished it on me. She'd wished for my downfall, my despair and pain.

She was strategically placed into my life. I still don't understand why she needed to forge a relationship with me. Although I was naive and thought nothing of her will to strong-arm me into walking with her round the shops in comfortable silence, I never gave anything away about my situation. I'd been broken in years before her, and I knew better than to spill my darkest secrets. I'd lost trust in people's ability to help long ago as well, so she was always fighting a losing battle with me.

It still hurts that I didn't see this though. Looking back, it's crystal clear. The worst part is, she didn't hide it well. I was so invested in myself and my inner turmoil, I was blind in the end. I'd prided myself on intelligence only days ago and this is what I have to show for it. I gargle out a wet laugh. If I don't laugh at how much I've overestimated myself, I'll cry.

I'm so over crying.

I stand over the table until dusk. I try to comprehend what I see before me. Try to make the burden of it all easier to bear. I still feel heavy, bare feet sunken into the floor. If I carry any more weight on my shoulders, I'll be neck deep in the earth underneath the house.

How can I feel even more plagued by abusers than when I was alive?

One clear fact I'll carry with me as the days pass is obvious.

Something is wrong with Eleanor and she doesn't deserve me or my help.

CHAPTER THIRTY-TWO

My mind is still reeling from mere hours ago when my whole motivation to be here comes crashing down. I can't stop it though. My crawler isn't relenting on its torture on my ribs, my chest is painful and my body is hot and cold. It's not over yet. The signs are all here and I have to follow them.

When I turn on my heel, I jump back at his body still sitting exactly where I last saw him all those hours ago. He's not moved either. I hate myself for finding comfort in that fact. My chest eases slightly as I realise he's been by my side throughout, even unintentionally. I struggle with how a simple act has such an effect. The hold he has over me is always just under the surface of my fragile armour. I can't seem to shut him out. He's within me as much as I try to deny it. I'd call for an exorcism if I were still alive.

He's attuned to my movements as he rises from the sofa, ready to move. His hands start to clench by his sides and his jaw is locked in determination. There's a plan in his cold eyes and it's all for Eleanor. I don't dare do anything in case it deters him. I want to see this. I want to know what she thinks justifies her actions.

"I'll take care of it, little crow," he speaks, low and soft. I close my eyes for a second as the words encase me in the warmth of his affection.

Why am I so grateful to him for this?

He takes off like a man starting a war to defend my honour. I smile at the sight. It takes me a moment to remember myself and fight down the feelings rooted deep inside. I'm still in denial, even in death. I have to hurry after him to keep up.

I don't want to miss this.

I see his dark figure climb the stairs. I've never seen anyone do it with so much malice, but he manages it. Not only that, but he wears it so well that he looks almost glorious. His golden skin looks like honey under the light. It's as I follow him that I notice he is the epitome of dark blues and golds as he moves. He blends so well into the colours and somehow they match his energy perfectly. Even his shadow dances beautifully in the golden glow of the house. I feel like I've stepped into another world with how differently I now look at the house. It wasn't even hours ago that I still loathed the decor as I wandered aimlessly around the rooms.

Of course, the room he glides into is the living room. The blue glow of the TV is flooding it with an ominous feel. Only this time, he's on the screen again and looking right at me. I stop short two footsteps into the room. His eyes bore holes into my chest, adding to the pain there. I watch his hand as it nears his instrument, his fingers plucking the string. The first note vibrates around the room and my crawler scrambles around my ribcage, awakened. I'm frozen, mouth agape, goosebumps popping up all over my trembling arms.

Why is it so familiar?

My crawler dances to the beat, trying to tell me something. It's just out of reach at the back of my mind. Every time I run towards it, it evaporates before I can reach it. The notes float around me harmlessly but the damage my crawler causes encourages my fear of them. My arm lifts of its own accord and reaches for the disruption in the air. It flutters around my hand, similar to how a bird's wing would. The touch is as welcome as it isn't. My crawler shudders as the wings flap over my knuckles. There's an agitation there that I can't shake off.

Why do I know this so well?

A more powerful note rings out, one that ricochets down my ears, echoing loudly. I hear the gutting sound of my chest starting to crack. The feeling starts at my collarbone and jaggedly cuts across my chest down to the ends of my ribcage. My beating heart is bare and beating in my chest. It's ripped open and my crawler leaps out. It's a terrifying little thing, with long dark legs and a feathered black body.

I can't help but stare as it scuttles all over the floor, scratching at anything it can find before it halts right in front of my toes. I can feel the air lap at them as my crawler rises and falls, panting heavily above them. Then the air stills as it does. I feel like I'm in a vacuum.

The cracking starts again, only this time it's my crawler. I watch its legs snap one crack at a time. Each crunch of the transformation pounds in my skull. It's then that I figure it out. The way it moves, the way it's *always* moved, even when inside me. I look up slowly, trying to delay what I know is right. Grey eyes meet blue and it takes a moment to start from them to notice the ominous smile. He begins to play his song with more vigour, emphasising every single note. The crawler at my feet greets every note with a sharp movement as it dances around my feet tauntingly. That song has been within me since that night. My crawler has been playing the same tune in my guts, ribs, chest and head for months. The rhythm of my madness carefully composed by the hands of him.

I never had my mind. I was always his – body, mind and soul.

The music builds as my crawler breaks its bones over and over as it morphs into something else. The feathers on its body have expanded. The two back legs almost look like wings. Two other legs snap backwards into them and feathers sprout as they morph into the wings in a tragically flawless manner. The other legs start to thicken and pulse as they snap and suddenly I'm looking at small black feet. Claws curve from them in several directions. They glint a stunning blue before the glow from the television screen.

I swallow down the bitter, burning bile in my throat, clogging my airways.

I know that bird.

It looks up at me, a devious yet affectionate glint in its eyes as it observes me. I don't move an inch. I barely acknowledge the failed attempts to calm my trembling fingers. It's a stunning bird and one I know all too well. It stands back at my feet, claws just barely grazing my toes. I'm toe to toe with it like a reflection in a mirror. I can hear it in my head; its voice sounds like mine as it sings to me.

"I am you, as you are me."

It's a crow.

It tilts its head at me silently. The movements are jerky, not smooth, and for some reason that unnerves me more than I expect. The eyes hold as much curiosity as they do judgement. It's insane that the one ally I thought I had turns out to be this. Every single person or thing I had in my life that I clung to for support has betrayed me in the end. I have to respect that he's never been something he's not with me. I always knew what he was; even in those first few days of meeting him, he didn't hide it. I was too lonely to push him away when I saw more flaws in him, and that's on me.

I look over at him; he's sitting in his chair, fingers sunk deep into the leather as he waits for Eleanor to return. I try to recall a moment when he ever tried to manipulate me into thinking he was something he wasn't. There are some small moments from when we met when his charm was heavy, but even in the moments when he was intimate and gentle with me, it was unequivocally him. That's what terrified me so much. To see someone adore you one moment and then feel enough hatred to torture you the next is a different level of fear to experience. The fear bleeds into everything you do, think or feel. You can't trust anything anymore as your whole headspace runs wild. The number of times I'd feel I couldn't trust myself in my own body. The way it melted into his warm embraces after an episode of brutality. I was so afraid to feel that way with him but also not to. It was a constant war raging inside me.

The crow at my feet loses interest in me, and even though my crawler is in bird form, it still crawls over to him on the couch. I watch its winged arms and clawed feet climb up the sofa. It pauses as it reaches the top of the armchair, just next to his head resting there. Its beady eye watches me and even though there's only a beak there, I swear I see a smile. I can hear it laughing at me in my head.

I hate that it sounds like me.

I'm at the point of being certain I'll pass out from the overwhelming turn of events in the room. My eyes roll back as my head spins trying to understand what this means.

Have I been dancing to his song all this time then?

I don't get much further in my thoughts. The moment the room comes back into focus, I wrestle my inner turmoil to the back of my mind. The crow is still staring at me as I turn my attention back to it. This time, I *know* it smiles as me before it starts to melt. I don't think I'll ever forget the creepy, sinister way it looks as its expression remains the same as it turns to sludge. It's black tar bubbling over the top of the armchair, oozing backwards towards the neck that's resting there, unassuming.

I want to call out, but there's no way he'll hear me. All I manage is a hitch in my breath and a hand flying to my mouth. My eyes widen as the disfigured crow slowly seeps into his neck. I watch until it's all gone. His golden skin replaces the black. His neck rolls as though he's just cracking it after a long day, or in anticipation of what's to come.

The front door slamming shut downstairs sends a jolt of shock through my body. I've completely disregarded the entire reason we're up here. Even though my senses are running wild, I'm absolutely positive of what is to come next.

Eleanor's going to die.

CHAPTER THIRTY-THREE

Eleanor walks into the room with a level of confidence I find laughable. Everything I observe about her now is tainted with loathing and distrust. Now when she smiles I see how fake it is. Her eyes have nothing in them. She looks sociopathic as her features morph into a perfect picture of willingness to please. I can't stand it now. All I can wonder when I watch her like this is if she planned to look that way to be better than me.

Is she trying not look as pathetic as me?

My thoughts are so bitter.

She doesn't notice his grip tighten on the arms of his chair as she floats through the room is one of her elegant outfits. I hate how good she looks even when she's deep into his cruelty. His eyes don't leave the screen. The music drifting through the air towards me gives me a sense of calm. I try to fight it, but at this point I don't trust any of my thoughts or feelings to know what I should or shouldn't allow myself. I'm tired of fighting an uphill battle at this point and just allow the tranquillity to wash over me and smooth over my sharp edges.

He flicks his wrist sharply and she obeys his command silently. Her feet are clad in ridiculously high heels. She toes them off before she situates herself kneeling before him. I wonder how it feels sinking to her knees before him, knowing now that she suffers the same way I did with him. I wonder if she knows she was never better than me. I'd try to find a silver lining and say that maybe she's learnt something valuable, but I know better than to dream.

Her doe eyes look comical as she flutters her lashes, peering up at him. There's a small tick in his jaw. His irritation is evident as his muscles grind with tension.

How was he so easily fooled?

As loath as I am to speculate on his taste, I can't help but ask *why*. Why the hell is Eleanor his next victim? She's loud, confident and inserts herself into the centre of attention whenever she can. She has no will of her own, a follower. I never considered myself a leader, but I knew my own mind and I fought against his manipulations as long as I could. I was a challenge and he enjoyed the unpredictability of my behaviour. Eleanor isn't and what he struggles to control with her lights a fire underneath me, let alone him. He doesn't have to work or manipulate for her affection; she gives it freely. He can't flex his skills with her and I can see it eating away at him.

The shadows wrap around him and his darkness deepens. His skin turns from gold to black. It glistens in the blue glow just like the crow's feathers did. The veins running up and down his forearms pulse to his music. He looks bigger in the chair. His shoulders are broader and almost crammed into the chair now whereas before he was more of a slim, quietly strong sort of man.

I belatedly realise as his fingers twitch, ready to strike, that he doesn't have a weapon. It's a startling reminder of my own death that he's going to kill her with his bare hands like he did me. It's disappointing she has the same ending as me. I was hoping for something more given the circumstances.

"Confess," he states simply. There's no mistaking how close to the edge he is.

"To what?" Eleanor whispers, starting to realise the trap she's walking into.

He shifts in his seat. It conveys the message that he's not willing to wait for her to play games with him. Her doe eyes are now filled with uncertainty. I'd bet money that she has multiple things to confess. I can see her flounder as she tries to establish which confession he's referring to.

Tick tock, Eleanor.

If there's one thing he's not, it's patient.

After only a few seconds, he rises to his full height. She shuffles back on her knees only slightly but it's doesn't change how he stands over her. His shadow engulfs her small body easily. When she's plunged into darkness, her mask is compromised. She looks every bit the scheming bitch I know she is. I never even realised that I'd only seen her in light whilst haunting her. The candles, the lamps and the glow of the TV. She's never been submerged in grey like this and her true face without light is petrifying.

"I-I'm sorry." I'm not convinced that she knows what she's apologising for.

"*Confess*," he hisses in her face.

"Is this about being friends with Lora?" she asks; I can hear the bitterness in her voice. Maybe even a little jealousy.

It must kill her that the reason for her impending punishment has me at the root of it. I stifle the smile trying to break through my serious facade. I don't know why I try to pretend to be someone I'm not when no one can see me anyway.

"No," he replies. He gestures for her to elaborate though.

"I didn't know she was here before me, I only found out recently. I didn't think it would matter," she scrambles. "Your relationship didn't seem that g—" She's struck with a blow to her face before she finishes that sentence.

"Stop lying," he grits out. "And never make assumptions about things you don't know." He sounds unbelievably defensive of our relationship.

It's nice. Almost gratifying.

What Eleanor does next takes me by surprise. She sighs. She rocks back onto her feet and stands up at her full height, only inches away from him.

"Yes. I knew," she smiles. "I knew everything about her, about you. I created our first meeting. I got here exactly the way I wanted to and I *deserve* this." Her voice rises as her secrets spill out from her lips.

He just watches her, deadly still as she rips off all her facades and shows him exactly who she is. It's an ugly show. She looks nothing like the poster girl I'd held her as in my head for so many months. Now she looks like what she truly is and I have to laugh at how careless she's being.

"You can't see it, but I'm like you. I'm your true match. I can meet your ferocity and cunning nature with my own." She's hysterical at this point after only eight sentences. "You need me as much as I need you. Can't you see how easily I please you? How I never wander round the coastline, mourning the life I had before you? I'm not hard work and I know what I have with you is precious," she pleads.

She's transferring her weight from one foot to another to stall her energy. I can see her body rock forwards towards him, yearning for contact but fortunately, in this scenario, she knows better.

"That's the problem." His voice is cold, but the warmth of his amusement at her empty excuses for what she's done floods through me as I stand watching from behind.

Eleanor stops short at his answer. I can see the darkness in her swirl round in her eyes.

"I'm not a problem." She glares at him indignantly.

"But you are." He smiles.

"How the *fuck* am I a problem?" she growls.

He doesn't answer. It's an open question that she'll never get the answers to. She's being subjected to the most effective form of torture. She'll never know why, or what she did wrong. She'll never have the chance to, either, and I hope she can live with that as I have to live with the uncertainty of what made her use and discard me without thought.

Her mouth opens and closes a few times as she looks up at his face. I can only imagine how he must look. Those handsome defined features morphing into sharp jagged edges that can cut you down effortlessly. His teeth stay white, his skin still golden, but a deep-rooted evil spills out of his eyes and mouth when he becomes the predator.

His neck tilts and the crack of it rings out through the dimly lit room.

It's happening.

The creak in the floorboards as he steps towards her spurs her into mindless action. Her arms fling out over her body and face, trying to shield her from him. The terror he's long since embedded in her soul keeps her rooted to the spot. When the salt pours from her eyes and her skin turns red from the heat of his malice, I start to panic.

This isn't right, despite who she is.

My moral compass is spinning endlessly and I have to leap into the fray without its guidance. I run into the space between them, trying with all my might to block his swings. It proves to be a failure on my part. The blows keep coming and I can only feel the rush of his arms slice through my ghost as he continues the assault.

There's one swing that I instinctively lean back from, placing my face just in front of his. I stare at his face as time slows down. His shoulder rolls powerfully with his punch and his face curves into a smile. It's one of pure euphoria and pleasure. This is him in his element. His eyes glint with delight. He looks so defined. Everything about him slots into place. This is his home, where he feels the most joy. It shouldn't hurt me to learn that, but it does. I hate to think this look was staring down at me as he beat me the night of my death.

I wish I knew why I can't pin down my feelings about him.

Eleanor sobs and stumbles around the room trying to get away. It's a pointless endeavour but I suppose it's better than her remaining stuck to the spot in front of him and just taking it. I'm glad she's managed to pull her feet from the floor and move. She coughs heavily with her full chest. It must be some kind of fluid in her lungs. It occurs to me she might have a crawler, but it's easily pushed aside. She has no need for one seeing as she never saw anything wrong with her situation. The disturbance in her lungs renders her still for a moment and that's all it takes for one powerful hit to her face to send her falling to the floor.

He grabs her bruised leg peeking out from under her torn flowing skirt and drags her back to him. I bite my lips as I hear the sound of her nails scraping at the floorboards, trying to stop the inevitable. She's flipped over onto her back so she's staring up at the figure stood over her. Her nails are torn and split but she still painfully claws at the floor. The splinters plunge further into her nail beds but she doesn't relent. I'd find it odd if I hadn't seen her relationship with pain before. She doesn't feel it the same way normal people do.

His knee lands heavy on her chest. All the air in her lungs rushes out her mouth, her eyes bulging. She tries to throw off his weight, her arms and legs flailing. His knee pushes further into her chest. The panic in her eyes spreads down her body, and rather than flailing, she starts to almost vibrate in fear. The tremors in her limbs are a stark comparison to his still body.

"You did this to yourself. You forged your own fate." Those are his last words.

Eleanor can't respond; she looks almost half dead with the pressure on her chest. It must be difficult to breathe. Then his knee starts to push into her chest once more. There are only a few seconds of this before a muffled crack echoes. Her ribs are broken and her black heart is crushed under his strength.

I belatedly realise I didn't do anything to stop him. The heaviness of the guilt adds to the weight already on my frail shoulders. Another burden to carry with me now I'm stuck here haunting the house.

I walk over to her body and crouch down at her head. She almost looks innocent in death. All of the unstable energy she possessed has seeped out into the air. It's a sour stench that hangs over her face. My eyes water. I still feel like I have to award her some dignity, despite her intentions. She suffered just as I did, and I know I wasn't perfect when he found me. It calls for some decency at least.

I lean over, placing my thumb and fingers on each of her eyelids, and start to drag them down. I'm only about halfway through taking the moral high ground when I'm sucked out of the room. I grunt at the sheer force of being thrown backwards.

My lungs scream when I land heavily on my back. My fingers sink into the ground. It's not solid. It's sand.

Oh god, why am I here again?

I sit up instantly, black sand flying around me. I don't think I can take another revelation in this place. It's just as dark as before. My head whips around looking for a way out.

There's a figure, a dark silhouette standing a few metres ahead of me. Their hair billows in the wind as they stare out into the black that surrounds us both. I kick at the sand as I scramble to my feet and push forwards. I don't want to be cautious with this one. I just need to rip the bandage off and get it done. I'll have to face the mysterious figure at some point and I'm too exhausted for the strain it would put on me to drag it out.

I reach them in record time, panting at how hard it was to run through the sand to get this close. My hand lands on their shoulder, more firmly than I want it to. I can't control it though. It's almost as if I needed to be firm.

"Hey," I breathe out.

The figure freezes and starts to shake as it turns to face me. As it turns, the side profile looks vaguely familiar but I can't seem to get the cogs turning in my head. The figure stays engulfed in shadows until they are facing me.

My hand slips, my jaw drops and my heart stutters in my chest. There's no crawler this time, but I can feel the motion of it in my body, dancing to his song. Eleanor's sore, leaking eyes plead with me. Her chest is still caved in from her death. Her long arm reaches out to me for comfort and I slap it away in disbelief.

"Please," she sobs. "Help me."

Fuck.

CHAPTER THIRTY-FOUR

"What are you doing here, Eleanor?" I grit out.

There are so many questions rattling around in my head but I go with the most obvious one first. I thought this was my space, my 'pre-limbo', as I've decided to call it. I'm unapologetically selfish about this place. It's the one place where he's not. It helped me through my delusions and the lie I was living at the start. Although none of that meant my life moved on for the better, I was happy to have a place that was reliable and told me the truth. I saw it as a piece of my sane mind manifested on this beach.

"I-I don't know. I just woke up here, you have to help me get back." I screech out a laugh at that last part.

"Get back to what?" I laugh. "Him?"

Her tears stop and she turns defensive but in a timid way. She seems more reserved with me than with him. An interesting way to be when you've looked a monster in the eye and spewed off enough hateful words for him to kill you.

"Maybe," she admits softly. I'm not buying her little innocent act.

"He killed you, Eleanor. You're of no value to him and

he should not be someone you want to go back to." I shake my head at her, pacing to try and keep up with my mind working overtime.

"But—"

"But *nothing!*" My hand cuts her off, ordering her silence.

I'd be lying if I said I didn't enjoy how much power I possess now. She's listening to me. She's giving me the floor. No one's done that for me in all the years I've been alive. Not since my parents died, anyway. I have so much I want to say but I want my words to mean something. I want to be able to convey so much in so little, just like he does. I want to have that ability to say nothing and something all at once. I need my message to be clear here.

"Tell me." My voice is low and dangerous. I don't know where this is coming from.

"What do you mean?" she asks. If I didn't know how good an actress she was, I'd buy that confused look painted on her face.

"How many?" I shout. "How many women have you pitted yourself against? How many others have you called pathetic or thought yourself better than?"

I can't control the words that spring out of my mouth. I'm so thirsty for answers and so angry at her. All the sorrow I felt as I stared at her dead body has subsided considerably. I'm not stupid. I know there must have been other women. It pulls me back to that second meeting with her when she confessed she had no women around her to call friends. It's an inevitable fact that there are others out there who thought of her as a friend or a confidante until she weaponised their flaws against them. I know I was lucky as well. I know I hadn't endured half of what I should have, had it not been for my untimely demise.

"Lora, don't," she warns hesitantly.

"I already have." My eyes are blazing with fury. She has the mind to look as intimidated as I want her to be.

"I'm in therapy, I think mentally—" the excuses start.

"No."

"I… I had a bad childhoo—"

"No."

"I was taken advantage of just like—"

"Don't you dare," I warn. I will not let her finish that sentence and paint herself as the victim.

"They just wanted me instead, that's not—"

"Just stop." I laugh in disbelief. "Do you truly think I'd believe that? I've seen so much, Eleanor. I know what you are. I know what you've done. I just want you to say it."

The same tantrum takes over her as it did him back in the living room. Her arms fly up in exasperation as if I'm the inconvenience to her. I don't think she's ever been held accountable or, at the very least, been backed into a corner like she has right now. I'm the lucky one who gets to do it.

"I don't know why it matters so much to you," she exclaims, stomping her feet like a child. She really is awful.

"You don't need to know."

"Fine! I like it, okay? I like feeling like I'm better. Prettier. Smarter. Skinnier, although well done for having won that one, Lora. I could never get to your level." She shakes her head bitterly.

Why would she ever want to?

"Not the question." I already know why she does it. I need to know *how many* she's done this to. I feel so protective

292

over the people she's wronged before me. She owes them this confession as much as she does me.

"I don't know," she mutters lowly.

I tap my foot. Even in the sand, the thud of it is loud and clean. I'm not wasting anymore words on her stalling. This interaction is happening. She's laying out her dark soul on the sand before me. I'm dead; I've got all the time in the world to waste on her now.

Her shredded nails are picking at her arms as she hugs herself. I don't acknowledge the action. She'll be drawing blood in a short matter of time. I wince at the glimpse of her frayed nails tugging away from her fingers. The splinters scratch at her skin but at the same time they dig further under her nails. Fresh blood pours out from her fingers and leaves streaks down her arms. The soft skin on her slender arms is slowly being torn away. For someone so vain, she has a unique obsession with destroying her body at any given moment.

She's been staring at the floor, spaced out as she scratches. I wonder if she's sifting through all the lies she keeps in her head to find the right one. The thought fills me with rage and I kick the sand at my feet up into her vacant face. She coughs and splutters as she tries to fall back out of the way. The sand swarms around her though as it falls back to the ground. She's plummeted back into its cloud and her disturbance of its descent leaves her spluttering on the ground, clawing at her throat.

She ends up rolling over, pushing her upper body up onto her elbows as she splutters. Black liquid drops out of her mouth as though she's expelling poison. I wouldn't do that though. I'm not the person who goes low. No physical harm will come to her. Well, no more than what she's experienced just now. I just want her to understand what she's done. To appreciate the mercy that I will show her because, in comparison to what she's done, it's a drop in the ocean.

"Tick tock, Eleanor," I sing.

I can hear his voice marry with mine, singing the same words. I shudder at that. He's said similar words to me before and for me to use them now feels as much empowering as concerning. It only takes me a short moment to comfort myself with the fact that Eleanor has earned this. She's put in the work to hurt others and she can suffer the consequences of her actions.

Repercussions are a bitch, aren't they?

"Drudging all of this up isn't going to undo what I've done, Lora." Her fist slams down onto the sand.

"I agree." I shrug.

She peers up at me, still hunched over on the ground. She spits out more black sand swimming in her saliva. She sighs, still trying to catch her breath.

"Okay. Let's do this." She shifts onto her side and eventually finds comfort kneeling in the sand. She wipes her mouth before looking me dead in the eyes. "There were a few. I learned from a young age how desirable I was and after several unsuccessful attempts at monogamy myself, I decided to branch out into relationships that allowed me to be free with my sexuality."

There's so much arrogance in one sentence it almost flattens me out on the sand with how much her ego inflates. Even admitting it to me, to a woman she wronged so brutally, she's unapologetic. I wish I could draw remorse out of her but that's a lost dream before it's even begun.

"All that time rehearsing what you were going to say in your head and that's the best you could do?" I mock.

The reason she's given is pointless and doesn't even make sense. She's tried so hard to make herself sound intelligent that she's ended up speaking nonsense. She's not even alluded to the women. That's all I want. I just want the women she's wronged. I want to know who felt the same heartbreak I did when a friend wished them the worst. When a woman who you felt vulnerable with reached out and ripped it from you, offering it up to further her own cause. I want that pain.

"Look, I've hurt people to get what I want. I know that. But they all *let me*," she huffs. Then she stops and smiles. "Even you did, Lora. You were just like the others, so desperate to escape your relationship that it didn't take much to slip in and offer a considerable upgrade. One that knew how to behave and keep their man satisfied," she smirks.

I shift on my feet uneasily. I have a horrible, awful feeling that there's something deeper here.

"Are you…" I swallow before starting again. "Are you saying that these other women were also being abused?" I question.

Please don't let this be true.

"Clearly." She laughs in disbelief, as though I'm asking a stupid question. "Why do you think they were being beaten?"

"Unlike you, I don't like to lie to myself about why men are violent, Eleanor." I struggle to get the words out.

There's a pause as I wait for her to react. Maybe show some remorse or guilt. Eleanor shows no signs of those emotions though and continues to look at me with pity.

"How could you?" I whisper.

"Yours, though, he's a different kind of man. I've never known one like him," she continues. "So infatuated with his 'little crow'. From what you look like now," she gestures to my pale blonde hair and my healthier looking body, "he was definitely hard on you. I figured he must be so sick of you to let you walk around looking like a corpse. Only he really did love you, didn't he?"

"He doesn't love anyone." He couldn't be capable of real love with how he treated me all those years.

"You were everywhere in that house. The look he'd get in his eyes when he'd look down and see me instead of you. I had to move myself in and redecorate to try and erase you, but you were part of him. Every little thing I did to get him to cherish me was wasted by comparison to you." Her mouth screws up in bitterness.

"Does it hurt to know you weren't better than me in the end?" I ask.

She glares up at me, breathing heavily through her nose.

"I'd say I paid for it with my life. I hope that's enough for you," she spits out bitterly.

Looking at her on the ground, even with the venom she spits, she looks so small. She had to do so much wrong in her life to make herself bigger. It's always the people who feel insignificant that build the most convincing delusions around themselves. Eleanor is no exception to that. If she has to say she's better or write it down in a journal then she knows deep down she isn't. All the words she used to describe me now belong to her. Her own insecurities lie bare before us.

"Lora, why are we here? I'm scared and I just want to go back home." She starts to cry. I almost get whiplash from how quickly her mood changes.

"You're not going home." *You idiot.* "You're dead." I'm completely unemotional as I deliver the devastating news.

"I-I thought that was a dream. Or maybe you were haunting me again like you have been doing for weeks." Her hands start to shake as the reality sinks in.

"No. You died. Your sins finally caught up to you," I snap.

The ground beneath us starts to vibrate, a loud rumbling sounding out. Eleanor screams and it's then I realise her legs are completely submerged in the sand. She claws at the sand to pull herself out but nothing works. Her panic builds as sand starts to slip under her nails. I clench my fists to ease it as I watch her sink.

"Lora! Help!" She thrusts her gnarled hand towards me but I just stand there.

She starts to cry but instead of salt, black sand pours out of her eyes. The whites of her eyes turn red as the sand scratches its way out and over the rims. Pure, unfiltered horror floods through her face and it blooms beautifully the further she sinks. I look at the blood and bruises all over her body and familiarity pangs through my chest. Has she not been through enough, despite everything? I step forward, my arm pulls away from my side but then flops back down after barely moving a few inches. I can't bring myself to stop it.

"Why?" she wails loudly as he body starts to disappear into the sand. I just know that sand is taking her somewhere befitting of her personality.

I've thought about this moment since I found the journal. I never thought I'd get the chance to say anything to her before he killed her but now I'm here I've got an opportunity for closure. Even more than that, these next few words will be the last she ever hears.

I step up to the edge of the pit that's appeared around her, toes digging into the sand as it shifts beneath me. I hope I look as certain as the words I'm about to say.

"You had deliberate intentions to cause misery and pain to others to feed your own cause. I can only imagine the damage that your disloyalty and blackened heart has done to your victims. You're a criminal, Eleanor, of the sickest kind," I proclaim as she struggles against sinking further into the depths. It's up to her shoulders now. "You have no grounds to convince *anyone* to exonerate you now."

Her body jerks as the sand surges around her neck. She opens her mouth to say something but I'm done listening to her. I wait a few moments until she's almost gone, her face looking up at me from the surface.

"I am your judgement now, Eleanor, and I only have four words for you."

Her hands pause in their struggle. Teary eyes find mine as I stare down at her. She's whimpering pathetically trying to play victim. Ironically she looks as pathetic as I'm sure she thought the women she broke were. How she saw me, her last victim. The one she couldn't have. The one who has the upper hand now. I've never felt power like it. I can almost hear all those women's ill wishes on Eleanor ringing in my ears as I speak for all of us in her last moments.

"I hope it hurts."

Then she's gone, dragged under as sand fills her eyes and mouth. I smile slightly. It feels good to finally say what I needed to. I haven't felt that free to speak in a long time.

I kneel on the sand and run my fingers through where

she just disappeared. There's no trace of her here anymore. It seems I've been successful in removing at least one toxic person from my life.

When I pull my hand back, it's translucent and bony. My eyes trail up my arm and I find blue veins running up and down my arms that are barely anything more than skin and bone. Blue bruises litter all over my skin. Bruises I haven't had since him. I pull at my hair and it's black again.

"No, no, no, no, no, no, no, no," I repeat over and over as I pull the slip dress off over my head.

My harrowing, malnourished body is back. The more I pull and tug at my body, the more I can't deny that I've lost my past self. The last thing I had that was mine before him has gone, just seconds after I felt more myself than I had in a while.

Please, just stop.

I want to be over the pain and the torment. I want to be flung so far away from all of this. I wish so badly that I was actually dead and there was no part after that I had to live. I'm so tired. I just want to rest now. It goes black after that last thought rattles though my screaming mind.

When I finally awaken, I'm lying on the floor of the living room just a few paces from where Eleanor's dead body was. I look over but there's not a trace of her anymore. In fact, the room looks different. It's cleaner and lighter. It's such a far stretch from what it was to what it is now but also the same. I can't seem to put my finger on it.

"Welcome to the final act, little crow."

CHAPTER THIRTY-FIVE

My head is spinning. I'm not used to so much light and it spears through my eyes, causing searing hot pain behind them. I can't focus on anything as my eyes roll backwards to try to ease it. My body starts to lose control of itself, my neck bulging and my limbs jittering. I'm seizing on the floor.

That's new.

"Shh," his voice soothes right by my ears. I barely hear it over the ringing. "Apologies, little crow. Sometimes I forget how powerful I am."

The swelling in my neck recedes and my head instantly turns to look at him. He has the nerve to look sheepish as his hands smooth over my body and my muscles relax. His touch offers a gentle warmth to my cold skin at a level that it's never done before. I pull my arm away, even though it feels amazing. I don't trust this situation or him.

"Never mind, I was done anyway." His eyes are tighter but his smile remains.

Done with what?

It's then that I notice the gentle hum of his warmth settling deep into my bones. The burdens I carry float off my body and my cement-filled veins ease up on their heaviness. I sit up, inspecting my body slowly. I'm still just as frail but I don't look or feel it. My hair is still black and my skin is no longer bruised but it shines an eery blue when the light passes over it.

"What is that?" I ask as I finally look back at him. His eyes are already on me, watching me intently.

"Seven years of punishment and conditioning. How did you think you survived?" He folds his arms across his broad chest. He looks taller. Stronger.

This is a test. The need to be as smart as he needs me to be floods my mind. I grit my teeth to fight it, but my morphed mind is already scouring through memories to understand what he's alluding to. Some of my most painful memories flash before my eyes. The nights when I thought the abuse would finally kill me resurface, making me live through all the trauma. I frown as, moments after those memories end, I see him carry my limp form to our bed.

When he lays me down, his hands handle me with care and he seduces me into believing for a few moments that he loves me. I always wondered why he always made me feel so good when he did that. My aches and pains were forgotten. I remember in the earlier days that I even felt as though his hands had never touched me. Most of the time back then, I'd find it difficult to believe he'd even laid hands on me afterwards. The realisation hits then and I rise up, coming to stand before him.

"You were healing me?" I'm answering him but I'm staring at his hands in fascination.

The hands I'm boring holes into with my gaze lifts and nudges my chin so I look up at him.

"I never let you die on me, little crow." I scoff at that and remove his hand. "Contrary to what you believe, you are standing in this room with me, are you not?"

My jaw drops, trying to conjure up a retort, but I have nothing. He's not wrong.

How am I here, alive?

"I tried to avoid it, but in the end you had to be given a different perspective," he goes on, pacing around the room casually as he speaks. "There was so much riding on this, on *you*. I needed it to be perfect. I knew the moment I first saw you that you were the one I needed."

I shake my head as he carries on. I'm still stuck on the fact he can heal me. I know the name he used for me is from the myth about the messenger of the god Apollo. He'd vaguely reference it from time to time, especially when he started referring to me as 'little crow', but this is something else.

My eyes squeeze shut as I try to remember what Apollo was the god of. I know he was strongly associated with the plague, and that's the one I thought rang true for him. The extreme weight loss, the aching body and the mess he put in my mind. I'd definitely call that a plague on me. Even my mentality could be described as me being overcome with a deadly sickness. I do remember thinking how ironic it was that he could also then be associated with healing.

But he can't be.

"But you did so beautifully, I did wonder at one point if you'd turn on Eleanor like I planned, but you did. It was entertaining to say the least." He chuckles at the memory.

"You were there? And you knew about me and Eleanor?"
My head's going to fall off.

"Of course I knew. She played a huge part in your transformation, like I knew she would." He smiles proudly at me.

"Wait, *you* chose Eleanor? She was stalking us!" My head throbs painfully, trying to reach for the answers that are swimming around in my head. I can't explain, but I know deep down why she was picked.

"Yes, I did," he chuckles. "Certainly, a different breed to the usual suspects, bar you, my little crow, of course." He tilts his head affectionately at me.

Despite everything within me telling me that I can't take it, I gesture for him to go on. It's not an obvious action, more of a glint in my eyes that allows him to see my curiosity grow.

"I knew what she was. A typical target but with something extra. And that's what you needed."

"Extra?" I stutter, bemused.

"Well, usually the women are from the same pool of infidelity. I've felt the keen sting of that in the years when I believed that no one could ever want more if they had me." I bite down on my lip so I don't react to that. "You laugh, little crow, but isn't it supposed to be that you never need more than the person who loves you? Wasn't that what you wanted your mother to be for your father? She certainly did some damage to you growing up, didn't she?"

"You don't speak about my mother," I spit out, but the words are softer than I intended. I don't sound as intimidating as I want to be.

"But I do, because I see everything. I watched you as you were raised by a broken man and an unfaithful woman.

I saw the betrayal you felt by her as well. I knew then you had such a strong hatred for people like her and you'd grow into the mindset I needed you to have over time. Then, when you were ripe, I plucked you and brought you here."

I can't seem to grasp onto his words the way I need to. The horrifying truth that I've been watched since I was a *child* rings in my ears. All those nights listening to my father cry himself to sleep over my mother until he'd had enough. He's pulling me back to the night I found their bodies in the bedroom. My father's, my mother's and one of my mother's several affair partners. My father had been so hurt, so lost and helpless because he couldn't fix his family that he'd taken a shotgun up to the bedroom and ended it once and for all. I remember thinking she'd deserved it back then but it was a thought I'd buried deep inside me. I never forgave her for what she turned my father into in the end but I tried to reason that I shouldn't wish ill on anyone, especially the dead. Thinking back, that was the first time I'd really allowed my resentment towards her to take over. After that I'd isolated myself... then I'd jumped on the first man who showed me affection.

God, how could I not see that?

"After that, wouldn't you agree with my standing on women like that? Is fidelity not the most important trait to look for in a lover? Loyalty is a needle in a haystack now. It's a terrible fate I've watched over the years as more people destroy others' lives and trust in each other. It's what I intend to... *purify* the earth of in what I do."

"But *I've* never been—" I start.

"I know," he replies sharply, cutting me off. "You were entirely different, a light illuminating everyone's darkness, but you saw too much good in the world. You had to be broken down and built back up to understand how cruel it can be. I needed you to be protected."

His hands cup my face and he bends slightly to stare into my wide eyes. His face is so soft, so full of devotion and *love*. I've never seen him so open with his emotions. I can't even remember the last time I could drink him in like I am now. The shadows that usually shroud his face in darkness are done. Instead, there's a warm glow cast over his skin, softening his striking features. My stomach flutters with nervous energy as I feel myself falling for his beauty. I almost feel self-conscious of how I look as he studies me so intently.

"For me?" I whisper, I can hear the tremor of hope in my voice and I hate it. My heart betrays me and so do my eyes as they fall for him all over again.

"Yes, all for you, little crow." My heart swells, his voice enveloping me in warmth.

He gently coaxes my face towards him and my heart leaps as his mouth descends. I go to meet his lips with mine, but he holds me in place and instead places a kiss on my forehead. Somehow, it's better than what I was aiming for as he lingers there for a few moments and I can bask in his scent. I don't know how he's managed to do it, but every time I catch a glimpse of him or recognise his scent, it never reminds me of the bad times. I can only recall the comfort he brings me and the promise of never being apart. Later, when he's gone, everything else will come flooding back and I'll remember why I can't be this weak around him, how much pain and suffering he's caused. I'll shed tears for the moment I yearned for a kiss and mourn the time in my life where he wasn't inserted so firmly into it.

He pulls away from me slowly. As he does, his hands retreat from my cheeks and the reality of the situation hits me hard again. I scramble around in my head to find where we left off and what more I need to know.

"Why Eleanor?" I ask.

He hums, amused at my question. I don't know why it's funny.

"There's a multitude of reasons. The jealousy was first. I wanted you to appreciate what you had with me and acknowledge that you loved me deep down underneath everything else."

"I didn't—" I protest.

A swift raise of his hand cuts me off. It's good he did; the lie was already starting to taste bitter on my tongue.

"Don't lie," he snaps.

My lips press together and he takes that as obedience. Unfortunately for the screaming girl inside of me, he's right. I am obedient and it's an out-of-body experience that I'm present for. It doesn't make sense to me either.

"Second," he continues, "it's enough for me for a woman to be disloyal and selfish, but for you I knew they had to be more. She fitted the bill. I appeared in her peripheral a few times and that's all it took for her to turn her attentions to me. She was a simple creature. It was easy to manipulate her with a new target she could chase with little decorum. You took to your opinion of her so well, little crow. It was poetic watching you turn on her slowly as time went on."

"You've seen me all this time? Even in death?" I can barely get the words out.

"Of course." He offers me a small smile.

It explains the interactions I had with him before I

realised I was dead. How he'd appear in front of me taunting me.

"Although you weren't really dead, so to say. I needed you to think you were. I needed a way to give you the push you needed." He shrugs.

"Push? What do you mean?" This horrible sinking feeling erupts in my stomach. Sweat breaks out on my forehead.

"What motivated you in the beginning when you thought you'd killed me?" he prods.

I can't keep up with all the memories and thoughts he's coaxing out of my head. They catch on my lashes and scrape on my teeth as they leave me and fly through the air to him. I'm balancing on a scale that he could tip at any moment and send me spiralling down a black hole of despair.

"I-I don't..." He clicks his tongue sharply at me as I try to play dumb. This is a conversation I'm underprepared for and I'm certain I won't win. I sigh defeatedly. "I thought there was something wrong with Eleanor."

"And there was." He gives me that at least. "What did you do wrong?"

He's enjoying this game way too much. Especially because I'm trapped here, forced to play with him. I've got no aces up my sleeve and he has the winning hand. It's a cruel way to enlighten me on how optimistic I've been. Seeing the good in people has caused me nothing but agony in a thousand different forms.

"I assumed." My eyes are cast downward as I sit in shame at my thoughtlessness.

I regret it and throw myself a few steps back from him as I realise my mistake. I should know better than to lose myself in front of him. I refuse to reform back to that timid

307

girl I was all those months ago. When I look up at his face from across the room, he looks amused more than anything.

"Correct. You haven't appreciated the gifts I've given you, little crow. It's… disappointing." He rubs his chin in thought.

"My gifts?"

I have gifts?

"How do you think you know what's going to happen before it does? What about your 'crawler' as you like to call it?" His hands are closed behind his back as he strolls towards me.

I think back to the crawler and how I watched him absorb it into his skin once it broke free from my chest. The way it danced to his song.

The way it turned into a crow.

"What did you do to me?" I whisper.

I'm not sure I want the answer.

"I think that's obvious." He looks at me like I'm stupid.

I hate it when he does that. He knows I'm not.

"You are as much me as I am you, little crow. I needed you to find your own way there. You needed to believe in my way of thinking."

"I'm nothing like you." I'm adamant as I push off the floor with anger and stand toe to toe with him.

A stray piece of hair hangs over my face and he tucks it behind my ear gently. I can't help the way my gaze drinks in his face once again. It triggers another memory. I haven't seen this face so clearly since the first few months of us dating. The shadows had a way of turning his face into something gruesome in those first few blissful weeks after meeting him. After that, he never really lifted them enough to give me that warm open face I'd fallen for all those years ago. Now, however, he does constantly throughout our conversation.

"You are now. You've grown, little crow. So much so that it's time you fulfilled your purpose." He steps back, arms out gesturing to the room.

The walls start to melt into scenes of my life playing out. Every wall shows me or the ghost of me watching Eleanor. One by one, they all start to come together. My eyes widen in shock as I watch myself haunt her, stalk her and scare her for days on end. Every time I pushed through and she saw me, I was ensuring she lived in fear of me. I cringe at how terrible I was to her, even though all I was doing was trying to help. Each word spoken, every sentence we'd shared all came across wrong. In those moments, I was punishing her for something I hadn't known she'd done yet. I can see it now so clearly that it was all by design. He'd taken everything I did or said to her out of context and crafted it into something it wasn't, to fuel his own ambitions.

My insides shatter as my reality is ripped apart and stitched together again right in front of my eyes. My mind rewinds back to the night I replayed my death. I was there. The woman I used to be was right before me warning me of this very ending. I'd ignored her, though, hadn't I? Eleanor had been my fixation from the start and whilst I was watching her, no one was watching him. I'd cry for the betrayal to myself if I hadn't cried oceans in this house already. I'd accept this with dry eyes and a steady hand. After all, it's already done.

"That's not even the best part," he whispers in my ear from behind me. "Not only did you unknowingly terrorise her for what she did to you, but you delivered my message perfectly."

"Tick tock," he sings from behind me, in time with the scene playing out on every single wall of moments ago with Eleanor.

"I am as much you as you are me," I whisper.

Again, I feel as though I could cry but I don't. The shock overpowers the undeniable heartbreak that I came full circle back to him. All this time feeling as though I was moving forwards, embracing who I wanted to be, and it was all an illusion he'd carefully built around me. I was his vessel whenever he needed me to be.

"You should be intelligent enough to figure the rest out," he smirks.

As he backs away, I notice a small halo of leaves adorns his head. I frown, recognising them vaguely.

Is that laurel?

My heart plummets deep into the pit of my stomach. My name. Lora. It means 'crowned with laurel'. My lungs give out and I start to heave.

Even my name is him. Like I was born into this.

I only hear his footsteps fade before I lose myself in a maze of memories. All of their strands are twirling around and knotting themselves up before I can grasp onto them. There would be no pulling them apart to separate the fact from his fiction.

I have no idea how I'm meant to figure the rest out.

CHAPTER THIRTY-SIX

What more does he want from me?

The question's been thrown from left to right around my head for what seems like forever. Everything that's been chucked at me in the last twenty-four hours is too much to fit into my tiny head. I can feel all the thoughts and revelations pulsing together, scratching at my skull. It's so chaotic everywhere inside me that I exert more pressure on myself to figure it all out before I become totally engulfed in the mayhem.

Logically, the best course of action in unravelling all the knots is to break down everything I can into simple little parts. I can't handle tackling the full thing at once. However, there's an itch at the top of my head like there's something I'm missing.

Maybe it's not about looking at me.

I hesitate as the thought occurs to me that I need to stop looking at myself. If this is all about moulding me into what he needs for his pleasure, I don't know if that's the right move. It feels final, though. I can't budge from it as I sit on the floor with my back against the sofa. If I had focused more on him and what he was doing maybe I'd have known more. Maybe I'd have seen it all coming from miles away but I was too busy surviving by making myself as small as possible whenever he was around. I mean, God forbid if I looked at him funnily back then so I'd make sure I only caught glimpses when he was distracted.

The only thing I can think of is the TV he was always watching, but I've seen what's on there. I know now that it was actually him using it as a tool to embed himself into my very being. I was so deaf when I was kneeling beside him all those years. I still don't know if that was by design. I just remember all the blue illuminating the room. Looking back, the room was so dark that I couldn't see too much. I had thought that with one sense dulled, the others would heighten. I've been wrong about so much, now, it doesn't surprise me that I am again.

The music still plays on repeat in my head, even when I'm not thinking about it. It's a permanent fixture up there now, tangled up in every corner of my mind with everything else. I can feel the phantom movements of my lost crawler moving in time with it on occasion. It all seems so painfully clever the way he's done it and I hate that it's admirable. I know I've sent a message since the beginning that I'm strong, but I don't think I am. I was manipulated with such ease. Even now, the tune in my head, which he plays so well, pulls on my heart as much as it turns my stomach.

I rush down the stairs back to my corner in the front room. There's a small voice in the back of my mind that wonders if, now he's told me I was never dead, people passing by can see me as I skid into the corner and curl up there. This room has been a source of quiet and comfort whenever I needed it. Maybe it can quiet the hurt and pain for a little while so I can focus.

I push my black hair back out of my face. It was unbelievably cruel of him to give me back my blonde locks and untouched body only to rip it away from me again. I still haven't found the time to process how devastating it was to go through the turmoil of having my identity torn away from me after just getting it back. I'd built a home in that body, confident I was free from his wickedness. I hate myself for ever feeling that I was safe in death.

I sigh as I look around the room. Surprisingly, it's clean. Eleanor's journal has long since disappeared from the table. I know just from the feel of the house now that it's long gone. The decor she had a hand in is still there but it all seems brighter now. The blue doesn't seem as dark anymore and the light seems to bounce around the room more easily. I should feel better with the new development but honestly I felt safer in the shadows. Now everything is too exposed and the light makes me feel cold. A shiver runs down my back in agreement.

I shriek as his book flies out from under the glass of the coffee table and lands at my feet. I'd forgotten about it long ago. Now it begs to be seen. I flip through the pages I've already seen, trying to find something I may have missed. It's a boring and uneventful read. I'm nearing the end when I stumble upon a page of handwritten scribbles. I frown as it reminds me of Eleanor. It's frightening how similar she is to him and how unobservant I was to it. I throw the book away from me as my anger at myself takes over for a split second.

It's a few seconds after glaring at it before I manage to pick it back up and relocate the page. His handwriting is difficult to read to say the least but my heart starts to pound with urgency.

I have to read this.

I look up and around the room, the light makes me have to squint. I don't know what I'm checking for, but the room remains the same silent one it's always been. I get my head back down and focus on making out the words. It looks like a messy, disorganised checklist. Some words have been checked off and scribbled out multiple times. When I make out the words 'music' and 'crow', I just know this is about me.

There's one word that I feel inexplicably drawn to. It's smudged and difficult to make out. My fingertips run over the scrawl and the ink follows them. I snatch my hand back quickly. There's something I've checked off what must be minutes ago and I need to know what it is. There's something in my gut telling me I already know but I ignore it. For a second, I almost thought my crawler had come back.

Prophecy.

It strikes straight through to my beating heart. I can feel it shudder in my ribcage. The word continues its attack and I feel it in my guts, my stomach, my throat, my head and my eyes. It rains down on me in quick succession, knives slicing through the fog in my mind until I'm left in blinding clarity.

I rewind back to the start of my story, and how adamant I was that mine intertwined with that of the crow to Apollo. I hadn't understood how deep that ran or that I was sitting on the truth the whole time. I wasn't the crow, then, I was a woman lost in his orbit that knew no mercy, but I'd begun the inevitable journey to now. I blink rapidly trying to keep up as my thoughts untangle and snap back into their rightful place.

There's no recollection of how I even found that story. I remember he'd feed me small portions of it but he'd never said the exact words that foretold that small tale. I'd known that *before*. I'd known that as if it were part of me. I'd known it from the moment I was gifted the crawler and listened to its every word as though it was my gut feeling. My insides sink as I recall the moment my crawler sprang free from my body and seeped back into his. He'd been with me all along. Every little thought I'd had led me to this. I'd listened to him, used him, consulted him for comfort and, most devastatingly, I'd come to rely on him in moments of confusion or despair. He'd been my protector all this time and my traitorous mind loved him irrevocably for it.

My heart hammers in my chest, its rhythm so familiar. My heart beats for him and follows his song to each note like it's never done anything different. I place my hand over my heart to try and muffle the sound. It's almost deafening as my heartbeat floods out into the room, bouncing off the walls melodically. I can't deny that it isn't a beautiful sound. If only it didn't narrate a catastrophic blow to my soul.

I love him.

I slam the book shut in between my damp palms. I can feel the sweat running down my face as the room blurs. My palm on the cover suddenly burns and I snatch it back. The hiss of pain whistles through my teeth. The sound I make sets me on edge.

I turn my hand over to inspect the damage. Five words have been burned into my palm. The writing is mirrored. I instinctively know it's the title of the book seared into my skin. The words laugh at me loudly, their cackles increasing in volume at the same rate as the music does. I can feel his song pounding on my eardrums violently.

It all screeches to a halting silence as my gaze drops to the cover of the book. My eyes already sting.

The Composition of a Crow.

I can feel my insides swirling; the room tilts and my eyes roll back. My cheek hits the floor with a thud loud along with the book. The walls are blurry but the light isn't as hard to adjust to as before. Even with the knock to my face I still feel clearer and lighter than ever. I can feel my reluctance at what's happening being pushed to the back of my body. I'm helpless as the parts of me that once wanted to be free are buried deep in the back of my mind. I can't scream as I feel my body soften and my head clear from all the trauma and betrayal he inspired from me. I just lay there on the floor, cheek bruised, mouth agape as the last of me slips away and my traitorous mind takes over.

I love him. I serve him.

EPILOGUE

My God is light.
My God is healing.
My God is to whom I am kneeling.

A black-winged messenger is what you see.
A service I love because he loves me.

I was once pure and white,
A perfect reflection of his light.
All was changed when evil was seen.
Unfaithful women can be so mean.

Their intent is to cause irreversible harm.
This kind of wrong disrupted his calm.
So a sickness he sends to fester in their heads.
A God of plague makes them suffer until dead.

He locked me in his beautiful mind.
Now I cannot be anything, especially kind.

I am an extension of his emotions.
My tears for his hurt could fill oceans.

I bore his hurt and I took his anger.
In his stormy seas I will be his anchor.
His fire burns me to black and blue.
My feathers now have a gorgeous hue.

I did not tremble when I was changed.
For everything occurred just as arranged.
He took me away from hurt and grief.
I know now he was anything but a thief.

His music I hear even in deep slumber.
I was not on his list as just another number.
He made me what I am today.
With all the little games we'd play.

I am forever indebted and eternally grateful.
That our encounter all those years ago was fateful.
He is one with me and I am with him.
There isn't a more beautiful ending that could've been.

ACKNOWLEDGEMENTS

As much hard work as this book has been for me to write some days, I fear the acknowledgements is going to be where I make the most mistakes. That being said, I'd like to start off by saying that everyone who has helped me through this journey knows exactly who they are. If I've missed you please feel free to visit and give me a good telling off.

Firstly, I'd like to thank my second home, Newcastle and the tiny little Indian restaurant that served me one of the best curries I've ever had. Sat there surrounded by loved ones was where I first pitched a very dark story about a woman suffering unimaginable abuse, with twists and turns that (hopefully) no one sees coming. I don't think any of us knew at the time it would end up here and I'm eternally grateful that it has.

My uncle Geoff, who lives in Newcastle and introduced me to why Northerners are the best people, thank you for being a huge support! I remember it was in your home I first read *Gone Girl*, which was the book that ignited my passion for unpredictable plot twists and the thriller genre. Everything really did start in Newcastle!

After the long, gruelling road of submissions and rejections, I'd like to thank the incredible team at The Book Guild for believing in my book when I was starting to think no one would. Everyone there has been nothing short of amazing and kind. A special mention to my editor, who had me and my husband crying with laughter one evening when flagging up sentences that we didn't even understand what I was trying to say in the end! Let this be a lesson learnt, everyone needs an editor.

Speaking of the long, gruelling road of rejections and the process of trying to publish *The Composition of a Crow,* I wanted to personally thank Alison who was the beacon of hope during the rather brutal endeavour of becoming a published author. Having experienced the process of publishing a book yourself, your guidance and experience helped me push on and keep believing in myself to get me to where I am today. I'm not sure I would've kept pursuing this with a vengeance if not for you.

I'd like to take the time to thank my family who have supported me throughout the entire process. My mum, for being my harshest critic and for saying those words that will stay with me forever '*I think you might actually have something here, Emma.*' Coming from someone who reads an enormous amount of incredible books by amazing authors, that comment really did change the game. My dad and brother, thank you for showing an interest and enthusiasm when the last thing you two like to do is pick up a book! My dad especially, sending my book to literally everyone you know – I love it! Graham and Isabel, you showing your unwavering support is humbling.

My friends, there are too many to name and mention

individually but thank you all for being there and urging me to keep writing the book. There have been times when your belief in me has got me through some tough spots.

My hairdresser Rob, who I've known for years now, thank you for being my go to for anything Greek Mythology. The hours we've talked about myths and horror is going to be viewed as unhealthy by most, but we love what we love! With you being a fellow creative and crazy talented artist, going to see you inspires me and lifts my creative block every time without fail.

Saving the best 'til second to last, my husband. I'm very lucky to have someone who supports me the way you do. How you managed to read the entire book as one of my beta readers when you don't enjoy reading is beyond me. You've been my biggest fan since day one and your excitement and investment in the plot and twists is more than I could've asked for. You are the kindest, most caring partner a woman could ask for and I hope you know I consider myself lucky everyday that I have with you. I love you.

Finally, a special mention to all the people I've met in my life who have suffered some form of abuse from their loved ones. The number of people this applies to will always be too many and I admire your resilience and bravery. Even when you stayed, I saw the courage that took and the complexity of your situations. I knew getting out wasn't as easy as outsiders sometimes believe. Without you, this book wouldn't exist. I hope this book finds you well. I wish nothing but happiness and prosperity for your futures.